Trouble Comes to Hornville

Trouble Comes to Hornville

Fred Wrazel

Copyright © 2015 by Fred Wrazel.

Library of Congress Control Number: 2015920137
ISBN: Hardcover   978-1-5144-3233-4
          Softcover   978-1-5144-3232-7
          eBook   978-1-5144-3231-0

All rights reserved. No part of this book may be reproduced or transmitted in any form or by any means, electronic or mechanical, including photocopying, recording, or by any information storage and retrieval system, without permission in writing from the copyright owner.

This is a work of fiction. Names, characters, places and incidents either are the product of the author's imagination or are used fictitiously, and any resemblance to any actual persons, living or dead, events, or locales is entirely coincidental.

Any people depicted in stock imagery provided by Thinkstock are models, and such images are being used for illustrative purposes only. Certain stock imagery © Thinkstock.

Print information available on the last page.

Rev. date: 12/17/2015

To order additional copies of this book, contact:
Xlibris
1-888-795-4274
www.Xlibris.com
Orders@Xlibris.com
729075

CONTENTS

Chapter 1 School Days… and Murder! 1

Chapter 2 New Girl in Town 7

Chapter 3 Newsy vs. Nosy 13

Chapter 4 The Accidental Hero 21

Chapter 5 Halloween High-Jinks 38

Chapter 6 Tall Stranger, Short Thief 59

Chapter 7 Mrs. McClatchy's Boarder 81

Chapter 8 Sneakin' Out 91

Chapter 9 Midnight Rendezvous 99

Chapter 10 "Sharkey" Bait 114

Chapter 11 Miss Hecker Has a Heart 130

Chapter 12 Gruesome Discovery 134

Chapter 13 Cheaters! Finks! Crooks! 148

Chapter 14 Another Gangland Slaying 173

Chapter 15 Smoking Out the Bad Guys 179

Chapter 16 Agent Markham, Girl Spy 188

Chapter 17 Butchie Seeks Revenge 198

Chapter 18 Homer Brings Big News........................ 216

Chapter 19 Vanished! 225

Chapter 20 Doughnuts, Detectives, and… Danger!.... 234

Chapter 21 Pow Wow at Peckley's Boatyard 241

Chapter 22 Snug Harbor Hooligans 253

Chapter 23 Kid-Snatched! 274

Chapter 24 Trapped on the Wausupee 280

Chapter 25 Brave Boys and Bullets 292

Chapter 26 Captain Homer at the Helm 316

Chapter 27 Serendipitous Refuge 330

Chapter 28 Showdown with Sharkey 343

Chapter 29 Rewards… and Repercussions............ 356

Biography 373

Foreword

Dear Reader:

    I penned this literally gem back in 60's (in truth, I pecked it out on an aging Smith Carona manual typewriter), not long after my wife Janet an I had been blessed with the fourth and last of our exceptional daughters. Since then, said daughters have extended our family with four tolerable sons-in-law, eight reasonably acceptable grandchildren, and thus far eight delightful great-grandchildren.

    Our youngest child, Donna Marie Schantz, is responsible for resurrecting my dusty original manuscript and causing it to be published. So, but for Donna, a/k/a RLK (Rotten Little Kid), you and the rest of the reading world would have never known about the trouble that came to Hornville!

Fred Wrazel
November 2015

CHAPTER 1

School Days… and Murder!

"Get up, Danny! It's after eight already! If I have to come up there to get you, so help me, there'll be another murder to talk about this morning!" Mrs. Van Kuyper's impatient voice echoed up the stairwell and penetrated her son's room.

Heaving a long sigh, Danny peeled off his quilt and slowly swung his feet to the floor. He picked up his shoe and dropped it beyond the edge of the throw rug, thereby signaling defeat to his mother below. He knew if she felt compelled to come upstairs to drag him out of bed he'd be in real trouble. Murder – isn't that how she had put it?

Unfortunately it was a beautiful day, brimming with the green and gold typical of early September in Wisconsin, and capped by a bright blue sky. Danny stood at his open window scratching idly under his undershirt as he watched his sister, Doris, looking smart in her new back-to-school outfit, hurry down the sidewalk toward Hornville High.

"Hi, Millie! Wait for me!" she cried out cheerily as she waved to her girlfriend down the street. Danny shook his head in sad wonderment. All things female were beyond his understanding. Why, the girls were actually glad summer vacation was over; the other day he had heard them say so, with his own two ears!

Another murder. Is that what his mother had said? The confused lad shook his sleepy head.

Danny fished yesterday's socks from under his bed and slipped them on. He selected a clean shirt and cotton slacks from his closet, dressed quickly, and deposited his dirty blue jeans and torn T-shirt in the bathroom hamper, but only after using the soiled T-shirt to wipe the dust off his shoes. Then, using a lot of water on the comb, he made a part of sorts on the left side, and ambled downstairs to breakfast.

"I declare," his mother greeted him with mild reproach. "All summer you're up with the birds, but when school begins, so does the sleeping sickness."

Danny nodded dumbly as he hunched over his cornflakes, and warily shot a warning glance at his little brother Herbie, who shared his room. Too late.

"Danny wasn't sleepin' when you an' Dad got up, Mom," blabbed the Innocent Little Squealer as he munched his toast. Loudest little bigmouth in the first grade, Danny was sure, looking toward his mother for her predictable reaction to Herbie's revelation. But apparently none would be forthcoming; she seemed much too interested in the kitchen radio. At last the little squealer slid off his chair and skipped off, headed toward the upstairs bathroom.

"Brush your teeth, dear," Mrs. Van Kuyper called after him absentmindedly, her attention still centered on the radio news broadcast. Whatever the nature of it, Danny was grateful it had kept his mother too preoccupied to have heard Herbie's incriminating remarks.

Such a darling little brother! Soon he'd be back downstairs to kiss mama bye-bye and then skip out the door for the first day of first grade. Even Herbie was glad to have school open again, which made Danny wonder about him. It was not unforgiveable to have a sister who liked school, but a brother! A thing like that could be detrimental to Danny's social status, which wasn't too high anyhow.

Expecting further rebuke over his tardiness, Danny dug busily into his cereal as his mother turned away from the radio and back to him. But her expected attack still caught him by surprise.

"Look at that filthy undershirt!" Elsie Van Kuyper wailed in despair.

Danny looked down, and hated himself. If only he had buttoned the top button of his shirt, she would never have noticed.

"Did you change your underwear this morning?"

No answer.

"Did you *sleep* in that underwear last night?"

Still no answer.

"What do you think we buy pajamas for? To clutter up drawer space?"

"They're no good for sleeping!" the boy defended himself.

"Why not?"

"'Cause when I turn over, they don't."

"Don't be silly! If the rest of this family can be civilized enough to wear pajamas, you can too!

"I'll wear 'em, Mom. I promise." Danny was anxious to depart. Even school was better than this barrage.

"Change your underwear before you leave the house, young man," the agitated woman ordered sternly.

Danny took this as his signal to leave.

"And change your socks, too," his mother added as he bounded up the stairs. "Good gravy, they're even different colors," he heard her say to herself as he rounded the landing. "Whatever will become of that boy?"

Danny had no answer for his mother's question, not that she seemed to expect one. His brain, finally awake, was busily sifting the bits and pieces which had filtered through to him from the radio news broadcast which had so monopolized his mother's attention.

The reason the scolding he'd received had been so uncharacteristically mild, he realized, rummaging through his bureau for a clean undershirt and a pair of socks that actually matched, was because of the radio's spellbinding effect on his mother. What was it the announcer had said?

"Unidentified body found… shot six times… weighted with concrete blocks… right below Center Street Bridge in downtown Hornville…"

"Wow!" Danny exclaimed to himself as he re-buckled his belt. Never in his entire lifespan of 13 years had he ever heard the word "murder" connected with the name of his home town. No doubt he'd hear further details in school – much of it of dubious accuracy, to be sure – but it would be something to ease the sting of starting a new school year.

Silently he padded down the carpeted stairs. Seeing his mother hovering near the front door, he slipped past the swinging door into the kitchen and out the back door. After all, a guy could get to school by way of the alley as well as the street.

CHAPTER 2

New Girl in Town

Lincoln School housed all of north-side Hornville's eligible students from kindergarten through eighth grade, after which they merged with the district's other grade school for a four-year stint at Hornville High.

Daniel Van Kuyper had spent his entire scholastic career to date at Lincoln School, each year returning with less enthusiasm than the year before. And now as he began his final year in the long-familiar place, even the slightest trace of any such enthusiasm was totally lacking.

Danny still had half a block to cover when the final buzzer sounded, but was unconcerned as he dog-trotted through the open doorway and loped up the stairs to the second floor. He was sure that in the confusion of opening day his brief tardiness would go unnoticed.

Alas, not so. Flanking the doorway of the eighth grade room stood old Miss Hecker, looking as tall and frosty as ever. She had been at Lincoln School longer than Danny could remember – 30 years, someone had said – and he had taken hope in summertime rumors that she might retire. But there she was; it appeared any retirement plans she might have had were postponed until tomorrow, at least.

"Good morning, Miss Hecker," Danny tried to smile. She had never taught him before, but they were far from strangers to one another. He wished they were.

The matriarch of Lincoln School pointedly studied her watch, then followed Danny into the chatter-filled classroom - his ears picked up words like "gruesome", "bullet holes", "bloody" and "icky" out of the excited buzz - and closed the door.

Danny slipped into the seat of an unoccupied rear desk and watched Miss Hecker's march to the front of the room. There she turned and stared wordlessly at the class. It took a second or two before she was generally noticed, but then the silence was almost instant. And complete. Miss Hecker was strictly no-nonsense, and it was obvious that every eighth grader in the room knew it.

"I have prepared a seating chart, which we will employ this afternoon after we've had our turn at the school bookstore," the grand dame announced crisply, "So this morning I shall read the roll call alphabetically. Please answer to your name promptly and clearly. Elmer Adams," she began.

"Here!"

"Jessica Barnes."

"Here!"

Same old gang as last year, Danny mused. He had started kindergarten with most of these kids. There was little coming and going as far as Hornville was concerned.

"Jennifer Markham."

Danny's head bobbed up. A new name! He hadn't even heard her reply.

Curiously, his eyes darted from girl to girl. Same old silly bunch, just a little better dressed and brushed than usual. Finally he spotted the stranger, seated in the front row, directly in front of Miss Hecker. She was small, with too much hair more brown than red, and had her hands folded primly in front of her on the desk.

Roger Zaborski, seated next to Danny, was the last name called, and the first order of business was complete. Miss Hecker busied herself at her desk.

"Hey, Rog," Danny whispered across the aisle. "Who's the new girl?"

"I dunno much," Roger shrugged. "Moved in last week with the Millers."

"Just her?"

"Her'n her little brother."

A sharp glance down the aisle from Miss Hecker terminated their conversation. Danny rubbed his chin thoughtfully. The Millers operated the only bakery store on the north side. Too bad his new classmate wasn't a boy.

Miss Hecker was on her feet again. "I presume you were all prudent enough to bring a pencil, pen, and loose-leaf paper with you this morning," she said.

A general nodding of heads made Danny feel singly imprudent.

"If not, borrow pencil and paper from your neighbor."

Danny hastily sponged the necessaries from Roger.

"We'll have several review tests of seventh grade work this morning, principally arithmetic and grammar. The grades will count. You've had all summer to stay in practice." Several groans of protest arose. A sharp rap of the ever-present ruler on her desk brought them to an immediate halt.

"I will not tolerate that sort of reaction in here," Miss Hecker said, her voice firm with authority. "If you have any objections to what I teach, or how I teach it, I suggest you have your parents take it up with the school board.

"And while we're on the general subject of classroom behavior," she continued, "I have posted a list of rules for this class on the back bulletin board. I advise you to read them soon – carefully – and on your own time.

"No excuses, no exceptions. Most of you know me, perhaps better than I know you. Therefore, you know I mean what I say."

All twenty-three students appeared to nod in unison. Possibly only twenty-two.

"One of my pet peeves is tardiness. None of you live that far from school; if you can make it here at all, you can make it on time. Punishment for tardiness is ten minutes detention for every minute late. Maximum one hour. Daniel Van Kuyper, please stand."

Slowly, with a strong sense of foreboding, Danny obliged.

"You were three minutes late this morning, Daniel. A half hour detention should be ample time to complete one hundred sentences of 'I must not be tardy again'."

Danny nodded glumly. He felt like debating the accuracy of Miss Hecker's watch, but thought better of it. Apparently it was going to be another long, hard year.

As he sat down, he was aware that all faces were turned toward him, but he took note of only one, the newcomer's, Jennifer Markham. He could think of only one word to describe it.

Troubled.

CHAPTER 3

Newsy vs. Nosy

Dinner at the Van Kuypers was always a time for talk. Elsie Van Kuyper loved to talk. Her husband, Ray, nearly always had plenty to say. Yet their daughter, Doris, had the talent to make them both look tongue-tied. Herbie was still young enough to be cute just by opening his mouth, and smart enough to make the most of it.

In this steady flood of words Danny's lack of participation was seldom noticed, which suited him fine. Not that he was particularly fascinated by what the others had to say. It was just that whenever he stumbled or was dragged into the conversation, he usually wound up on the receiving end of some lecture or lesson, or having one of his alleged faults aired.

Further, his food would get cold while he made the effort to pay attention to the uninvited discourse directed at him. He tried to avoid these involvements on the grounds that they were a waste of time.

At dinner following the first day of school, the chief topic of conversation – the matter of the grisly corpse found weighted down in the Wausupee River

– was quickly run through. The dead man, apparently slain only hours before the discovery of his body beneath the Center Street Bridge, had been tentatively identified as one Douglas "Doggie" Blodgett, a small-time Chicago hoodlum. He was one of several such types who had recently dropped out of sight as rumors of a gang war circulated in that city.

For the past week, using an assumed name and a forged license, the victim had lived and worked in Hornville as a bartender at the Snug Harbor, an aging but well-preserved river front tavern set on a squat pier thrust out over the clear waters of the Wausupee. It was apparently the last place the late Mr. Blodgett was seen alive. He had "stepped outside for a moment" the previous midnight, and never returned.

The proprietor of the Snug Harbor, an also aging but equally well-preserved long-time local character by the name of Alfred "Sharkey" Bates, disclaimed any connection with the incident, and the Hornville police were apparently willing to accept Bates' explanation. Further, the old tavern keeper's excellent business reputation, extending back some 20 years, stood him in good stead.

"Yeah, looks like some big-city mobsters tracked down this Blodgett and did him in," Ray Van Kuyper expounded knowledgeably, twirling up a forkful of spaghetti. "They're used to dumping corpses into rivers the color of old coffee, and never having them found again. But our unpolluted creek crossed 'em up."

Danny was disappointed to hear that the murderers were probably foreigners. He was in no position to do much out-of-town sleuthing.

"Brrrr!" Doris shivered. "To think that sort of thing could happen right in downtown Hornville."

Her father laughed. "That's a small town for you, Doris," he said. "Let's face it; most nights after twelve, you could fire off a cannon down Central Avenue and not hit anybody."

"Well, I prefer it that way," Elsie Van Kuyper munched righteously. "I'm sorry that man departed the way he did, but he won't be missed. He didn't belong here in the first place."

"Well, he won't complete his departure before Thursday," her husband informed her. "That's when Henry Rydzik is holding a funeral service for him."

"What?" Mrs. Van Kuyper was indignant. "Rydzik's Funeral Parlor?" The same people who buried my dear departed mother?"

"Well, don't blame Henry," her spouse replied. "The county coroner assigned him the job, and if nobody comes forward to claim the body, he's stuck with it."

"That poor, lost soul," Doris commented, sipping her milk. "Mourned by nobody. What a lonely thing his funeral will be, his last appearance on earth."

"Don't bet on it," her father smiled wryly. "There'll be plenty of morbid curiosity seekers there, if nobody else." His gaze shifted unnoticed toward his wife and he said no more.

"Humpf!" Mrs. Van Kuyper snorted, still fuming as she shook her fork at nobody in particular. "You'd think Henry Rydzik would know better." She stabbed at her plate indignantly.

The matter of the murder having been disposed of, Danny's sister took over the conversation. This was Doris' junior year at Hornville High. She was a member of the pom-pom girls, and the Hornville Hornets seemed destined for a good year in football and basketball – much more fun to cheer a winner. Student council elections just a month away and the Good News Party were considering her as their candidate for Secretary... lots of dreamy athletic types managing the Good News Party this year... the every-other Friday dances started next week, etc. etc. Danny marveled at his sister's volubility. And her remarks eased a trifle his misgivings about high school; with all that going on, he reasoned, there couldn't be much time left for books.

Then it happened. While Doris was temporarily muted by a bite of meatball, Mr. Van Kuyper tossed the conversational ball to Danny. "What's new in the eighth grade, son?" he asked.

"Oh, nuthin' much."

"Well, what's the nothing much?"

"O-o-o-o," Danny's memory groped back over a dull day, spiced only by a number of totally implausible tales concerning the murder. He finally came up with an item which seemed fairly harmless and non-controversial. "We gotta new kid in class, is all."

"Oh?" chimed in a suddenly interested Elsie Van Kuyper. "Who?" There weren't that many newcomers to Hornville.

"Her name's Jennifer Markham."

"Markham?" Mrs. Van K. hastily riffled through her mental street index. "That's a new name around here. Do you know where she lives?"

"I heard she lives upstairs over the bakery."

"With the Millers? Is she related to them?"

"I dunno." Danny emptied his laden fork into his mouth. He wanted to eat, not talk.

"Her folks there, too?" his mother persisted. "In that small apartment?"

The boy had to swallow prematurely, aided by a saving sip of water. "I dunno," he finally managed. "I don't think so. I heard she's just got a little brother, is all."

"Now isn't that curious?" Danny's mother mused aloud. "What is an old pair like the Millers doing with two little children? Why, they're both past sixty, if they're a day."

The head of the household eyed his wife, looking slightly annoyed. "Elsie Van Kuyper, you're much too young to be such a nosey old lady," he said gently.

"Come now, Ray. You know you're as curious as I am."

"Curious maybe, but not nosey. I'm sure if we knew the facts, it would make perfectly good sense for the Millers to have those kids. Maybe they're their grandchildren."

"Nonsense! They never had any children, so how could they have grandchildren? Besides, I'm a little put out with them. I've been shopping there at least once a week for years, and when I stopped there Saturday, Hilda Miller never told me anything about any kids."

"Maybe," her spouse replied, emphasizing his words with short shakes of his head, "Because it isn't any of your business."

There was a moment of strained silence, broken by the loud voice of little Herbie. "I gotta new playmate in my grade, too, name a' Timmy Markum," blabbed the Cute One.

"Is that so!" exclaimed his mother. "He must be the little brother Danny mentioned. Honey, tomorrow why don't you ask your new friend if he can come over after school to play?"

"Oh, for Pete's sake!" Ray Van Kuyper tossed his fork down disgustedly. "Elsie, what's the matter with you?" Then turning to Danny, he mimicked his wife's voice and words: "And Honey, tomorrow why don't *you* ask your new little friend if *she* can come over after school and play?"

Now it was Mrs. Van K's turn to be annoyed. "That'll be quite enough, Ray," she said coldly.

"I'd say there's already been way too much," he replied. "Why don't we just leave those little total strangers alone?"

"They need friends."

"Fine. Let them make them around the bakery."

"The bakery's not that far from here!"

"Must be eight or nine blocks. Would you let our first grader go that far alone? And in a strange town yet?"

"Of course not," Elsie snapped.

"That's one of the things I love about you, Elsie," Ray beamed as he got up to leave the room. "You're such a conscientious mother."

"Humpf!" Elsie Van Kuyper stewed silently for a long moment, then got up to follow her spouse. "Daniel, you may do the dishes alone tonight. I'm sure that Doris has plenty of homework to do," she said, departing.

Doris smiled at her brother's stupefied expression. "Well, you know mother," she comforted him. "She's got to blame somebody, and she figures you started it. But just stack the dishes, and I'll wipe them later."

Sighing resignedly, Danny resumed his dinner. But he had to admit to himself that for being a girl, his sister Doris certainly could be gentlemanly at times.

CHAPTER 4

The Accidental Hero

The first few weeks of school quickly and relentlessly re-established for Danny the old familiar pattern of past years. Dutifully he attended class every school day, and ignored as much of the proceedings as he possibly could. But he did manage to absorb a little learning in spite of himself. Miss Hecker was not one to give up easily.

The sensation which had rocked Hornville on the first day of school, the murder of Doggie Blodgett, had long since ceased to be of any local interest. The unlamented hoodlum's funeral had been held as scheduled at Rydzik's Funeral Parlor, well attended as predicted by Ray Van Kuyper, but without a damp eye in the house. The remains had been interred in an unmarked grave at the far end of the county, destined to be forever forgotten.

"Person or persons unknown", presumably rival Chicago gangsters, were given credit for the murder, and since the local police's jurisdiction fell far short of that distant city, the Hornville police department's file on D. Blodgett soon sifted to the bottom of the pile.

True, a pair of Chicago detectives had come up the day after the murder to nose about briefly, and had lunch with Chief Lathrop, and had favored the news reporter/sports editor/classified ads manager of the Hornville Bugle with several cryptic "no comments" in response to pointed questions. Evidently the Chicago police didn't know anything either.

So as no new factors developed and local interest in the crime waned, the Bugle's editor reluctantly let the story die. At least one infrequent reader of the paper, Danny Van Kuyper, shared the editor's grief. It seemed a shame to have the late Mr. Blodgett depart so spectacularly without turning up a clue or two or perhaps a suspect in his wake.

Miss Hecker's seating chart had placed Danny fifth and last in the row farthest from the windows, the good lady's intention being to minimize distraction for the boy by the outdoors. The result was eyestrain; due not to the chalkboard up front, but the far windows and their limitations on scenery from Danny's point of view. Still, the top of Hickory Hill was easily visible to Danny's roving eyes; day after day its vibrant crown of hardwoods in autumn colors danced invitingly in the bright afternoon sun. In body, the boy was desk-bound. But each day his spirit spent considerable time roaming the familiar byways atop Ol' Hickory.

Danny's gaze occasionally fell upon the quiet face of Jennifer Markham, seated near the front center of the class, who daily became more and more familiar to those around her, and less and less of a curiosity.

She was studious, better than most at recitation, and had made friends with a couple of girls who also were quiet types. Still, he was sure he frequently saw sadness, possibly loneliness or even fear in that small oval face. It might have been a pretty face except for that.

Most of the initial questions concerning the girl and her little brother still remained unanswered. Not that Danny cared, but his mother's curiosity was slow to abate.

Herbie was no help, either. All Mrs. Van Kuyper could learn from him was, "Timmy Markum busted my red crayon," and "I kin run faster'n Timmy." As for Danny, he had not exchanged a single word with Jennifer, nor was he in any hurry to do so. All of which did little to assuage Mrs. Van Kuyper's curiosity, and possibly prompted her remark to Danny that he "really shouldn't be so backwards about talking to girls".

Watching Jennifer in class now, Danny recalled his parents' conversation of the previous evening:

"Ray, Mrs. Price is a member of my Women's Club, and the school transfer records would probably tell quite a lot about those Markham kids; where they came from, who -"

"Honey," Danny's dad had interrupted, "Would you want the principal's wife answering other people's questions about our kids?"

"OUR kids? Of course not. Mrs. Price wouldn't dare!"

"Exactly. So why don't you forget about those Markham kids? They probably belong to relatives or friends of the Millers; maybe they're from a broken home, and you'd just embarrass them by forcing the issue."

Danny admired his dad's live and let live attitude. Danny never bothered him and he seldom bothered Danny. Consequently there was no pressure to get involved in Boy Scouts or the Little League, making it easy for Danny to avoid entanglement in anything that looked organized or supervised. For his part, Ray Van Kuyper was happy to have more free time for bowling, poker, and beer league baseball.

One of the privileges of being an eighth grader was the ability to spend part of Tuesday and Thursday lunch hours in a room off the gym attending dancing classes supervised by Miss Quince, the girls' athletic teacher. It was a privilege which Danny forsook with no hesitancy. So did most of the eighth grade boys, for that matter. Nevertheless, on those days Danny was slow getting back to school after lunch to avoid possible recruitment by Miss Quince, who was frequently short on eighth grade males for her dancing class.

It was about two minutes before the afternoon bell one Thursday in October when Danny warily approached the front lawn of Lincoln School. The area appeared deserted. Free time activities were confined to the playground in back of the school, and the usual din from that quarter indicated plenty of activity back there. But sounds of scuffling emanating from one of the broad clumps of bushes decorating the front lawn indicated some unauthorized activity in that direction.

Curiosity bloomed in Danny. Silently he trotted across the clipped lawn and ducked into the labyrinth of tunnels formed through the bushes by kids during numerous summertime games of cowboys and Indians. The scuffling took on the sounds of a struggle. Then he heard the stifled cry of a girl, breathless, half pleading, half in anger.

Danny slid through a thick screen of branches into a tiny clearing. There Butchie Brockman sat astride Jennifer Markham's stomach, pinning her wrists to the ground spread-eagle fashion. He was trying to kiss her. The girl kept twisting her head violently, matting her hair with twigs, leaves and dust, while Butchie tried to trap her head with his own.

"Aw, c'mon," he growled. "Don't play so hard to get, Miss Hoity-Toity."

Stupified, Danny crouched silently watching the battle. Nearly a minute passed before his presence was noticed. The sobbing girl suddenly fixed her wide eyes on him and tried to raise her head. Startled, Butchie swung his head around, following her gaze.

Fear left his face as he spotted Danny, and he flushed angrily instead.

"Beat it, skinny," he hissed. "Go mind your own business."

Danny trembled, but hesitated. The exhausted Jennifer gazed at him pleadingly. Danny swallowed his fear, partly.

"I think you should let her go," he said. "The bell's gonna ring pretty soon."

Randolph "Butchie" Brockman was the long-established champion battler of Danny's class. He wasn't much taller than Danny, but outweighed him by a solid 20 pounds. He took advantage of every opportunity to uphold his reputation and had even been known to create additional opportunities for himself, usually over fancied insults about his given name of Randolph. He detested it.

"Bean-pole," Butchie snarled. "You want another treatment?"

Dating back to Kindergarten, Butchie had trounced Danny at least once each year. Danny worked hard to avoid contact, and trouble, with the domineering butcher boy, but whenever Butchie felt like it, he managed to dream up a grievance against Danny and create an opportunity to exact vengeance for it.

Danny was sure that his witless intrusion into the present situation foredoomed him to another thrashing. He decided to merit it for a change. Screwing up his limited supply of courage, he smiled with exaggerated sweetness at Butchie, raising his eyebrows and shaking his finger at him. "Miss Hecker ain't gonna like this, Randy-baby!"

In a flash, Butchie was off Jennifer and all over Danny. The girl rolled under a bush opposite just as the combatants bounced off the surrounding thicket and fell wrapped together into the clearing. Danny, fighting with the ferocity of a trapped animal, held his own briefly, but the stronger and more practiced battler soon was astride him, pummeling him furiously. Danny clawed frantically at Butchie, trying to protect his face and wrench himself free.

Suddenly Jennifer was standing over them, a dry branch in her hand, furiously whipping the butcher boy about the head. Swearing, Butchie grabbed the branch and engaged the girl in a tug-of-war for it. The desperate Danny sensed his opportunity. Doubling his fist, he swung hard, and was rewarded with a satisfying crunch as he mashed Butchie's face.

"Oowah!" Butchie tumbled off, clutching his bleeding nose. In an instant he was gone into the bushes.

Slowly Danny raised himself to a sitting position. Jennifer sank down beside him. They sat wordlessly, panting for breath; the silence was heavy about them.

By now the afternoon bell had rung and the other students were all in school.

"You're hurt." Jennifer eyed Danny's bleeding lip and scratched face. She pulled a handkerchief out of her pocket and began to dab the dirt off his wounds. He looked at her. Her clothes were dirty and rumpled, her face swollen and streaked from crying, and she was matted with dust and debris. But she appeared to be unhurt.

"How come you were in here with Butchie?" Danny didn't really care, but he was embarrassed at being alone with Jennifer, at having this first exchange of words with her. He felt compelled to say something.

For her part, Jennifer was annoyed at his choice of words, and her expression showed it. "After lunch, he walked with me to school, not that I wanted him to," she explained. "When we were passing the bushes, he twisted my arm behind me, put his hand over my mouth and dragged me in here."

"Are ya gonna tell Miss Hecker?"

Jennifer chewed her lip thoughtfully. "I don't think Randolph will bother me anymore," she said. Plainly, she didn't want any more trouble. Danny recalled that Heinie Brockman's butcher shop wasn't too far from Millers' bakery. Maybe the butcher boy would let her alone, and maybe he wouldn't.

"What will you say to ol' lady Hecker 'bout how you look?"

"I think... I think I'll just go home... and bring some sort of excuse tomorrow."

"Yeah? Well, when you get home, what you gonna tell yer... yer..."

Danny hesitated, and Jennifer flushed. "I'll just say I fell down the creekbank on the way to school." A sudden thought disturbed her. "You're not going to tell Miss Hecker, are you?"

"Naw." Danny paused to consider his own situation. He'd be late getting into class, and Miss Hecker was tough on the tardy. Also, she knew the loser in a fight when she saw one.

Of course, Danny didn't really lose this time but he'd have to admit to being helped by a girl. To claim single-handed victory over Butchie Brockman would be tantamount to suicide. Danny may not have been able to define discretion, but he knew when to practice it.

"Butchie went home with that nose, I bet," he said. "I think I will, too."

"Good," said Jennifer. "I think we'll all feel better tomorrow." She was on her feet now, looking around.

"Whatsa matter? Lose something?"

"My purse," she said, frowning. "I was sure I had it when Randolph... took me in here."

Danny turned over on his knees and crawled toward the sidewalk. He quickly located the shiny red purse and brought it back to Jennifer. She was busily straightening her skirt and tucking her blouse back into it.

"Thank you," she smiled as he handed her the purse. She has a nice smile, Danny thought, even with a dirty face. She opened the purse and gazed at a tiny mirror glued to the lid.

"Oh, my, what a sight," she giggled, using her handkerchief, now stained with dirt and blood from Danny's face, to wipe the dirt streaks off her own. Then she took from her purse a large, clear plastic comb. It did a pretty fair raking job on her hair, Danny observed as he slowly brushed himself off. She offered the comb to him, but he shook his head no. Then she took another critical look at his bruised face. Her matter-of-fact manner muted his discomfort considerably, but the proximity of her face to his still made him feel ill at ease.

"You've stopped bleeding," she told him. "But you wash as soon as you get home, and put medicine on those scratches."

"Okay."

"Shall we go?" She started toward the sidewalk, but he grabbed her arm and pointed in the direction of the street.

"We better keep the bushes between us and the school 'til we're out of sight," he said, taking her hand to lead her. Together they ducked and weaved their way through the bushes to the edge of the street. They waited for a car to pass, then, crouching low, darted across the street into an alley. By walking close to the fence they were able to stay out of view of the school.

Danny was suddenly aware that he still had hold of the girl's hand. He let loose of it and unconsciously wiped his hand on his shirt. Jennifer smiled quietly to herself, but said nothing. Finally, as they neared the end of the alley, she spoke:

"You're Danny Van Kuyper, aren't you?"

"Yeah."

"I haven't got to know many of the boys in our class, mostly just those sitting around me. I'm Jennifer Markham."

"I know."

"I think your little brother and my little brother are in first grade together."

"Yeah."

They had reached the end of the alley. Miller's bakery was south, several blocks down the street. Danny gazed northeast toward the crest of Hickory Hill. A splendid place to spend the rest of the day, he decided. They paused for a moment before parting company.

"Will Randolph give you any more trouble?" she asked worriedly.

"No, I don't think so," Danny lied.

"If he ever does, I'll help you."

The offer humiliated Danny, and his face showed it as he started to walk away. "I can take care of myself."

"Danny."

He stopped and looked back. Jennifer's lips were trembling.

"Thank you for what you did," she finally managed.

"Yeah."

He turned north again, and began to trot. It was four blocks to the edge of town, then straight up the hill. Once he made the mistake of looking back. She was watching him, and when he turned, she waved. He began to raise his own hand in reply, then, disgusted with himself, faced away again and continued to run. Only faster.

****

Danny eased the throbbing in his face and head by soaking that entire end of his anatomy in the tiny pool of the spring that seeped out of the side of Hickory Hill. Then he seated himself against a sun-warmed boulder and examined his town. Most of Hornville lay on the south side of the broad Wausupee River, across from the paper mill and railyard. Then the river flowed over a mile or so before hitting a stretch of rapids and into Lake Michigan. Right then, from well up the side of Hickory Hill, its nearly 2,000 souls seemed an inactive lot. A few cars were moving on Central Avenue, and the kids were out for afternoon recess at the Lincoln School on the north side and the Washington School on the south side. A few puffs of smoke from the paper mill indicated some life there. Otherwise, all looked quiet.

At the moment, however, Danny's thoughts were centered on just one citizen of Hornville. From his vantage point, Danny had little trouble picking out the red brick front of Heinie Brockman's butcher shop, and he could easily picture Mr. Brockman's little boy Randolph sulking in his room upstairs, nursing his cracked and bleeding nose and plotting to wreak horrible vengeance upon the person of one Danny Van Kuyper.

Danny wracked his brain for a way to avoid further disablement. Running away was impractical, with the October nights getting so chilly. He couldn't feign sickness forever. Butchie wouldn't stand still long enough to be bribed; besides, he probably wouldn't stay bribed for very long, no matter what valuables Danny might give him. And eight years of practice at avoiding Butchie had taught him that even this tactic couldn't work indefinitely.

The boy sighed resignedly. "Guess he won't work off his feelin's until he gives me more lumps," Danny moaned to himself.

His feelings! A tiny glimmer of hope kindled in Danny's brain, and grew brighter as he mulled over his thought. Butchie's feelings – they weren't particularly hurt. It had taken two kids to best him, even if one of them was a girl; enough to make him mad, and sore, but not hang-tail.

Danny strained to remember a recent dinner table dissertation by his sister Doris on something she'd called "sy-kology". One particular thing she had said seemed to make sense: "A person whose pride has been hurt is usually aroused, and will fight; but if he has *really* been humiliated, he's defeated, and will usually seek to avoid more of the same." There was an answer there, but what? How could he turn Butchie Brockman from a fighting mad hound into a hang-tail pup?

In school tomorrow, Butchie would quickly guess that nothing had been said to anybody; in fact, he was probably figuring that way already and would be certain of it if he spotted Jennifer coming home early to the bakery down the street. This would bolster his confidence, and he'd waylay Danny first chance he'd get, probably in the boy's restroom.

Idly Danny's eye scanned the town. It came to rest on the barn loft back of Chet Murphy's place. Chet was a regular candidate for county commissioner, third district, and between elections his huge oil cloth election banners lay rolled up in the loft of his barn, along with the jars of poster paint used to refresh the banners' colors and update them for display at various picnics, across Central Avenue, and at other prominent locations. Danny had been in Murphy's loft many times; it was easy to access from the alley and a great place to eat borrowed apples and play cards on rainy summer afternoons.

Best of all, the sight of it now gave Danny the answer he was seeking! Not absolutely surefire, but a good bet, anyhow. He jumped to his feet and jogged downhill, planning as he went.

He would use the back of one of Murphy's banners. The sign would need a couple hours to dry. He couldn't smuggle it out until after dark anyhow, and he would require help to hang it right. After school he'd recruit his number one buddy, Homer Peckley, for the job. Homer was always ready to try anything twice; the second time to see why it didn't work the first time.

He'd need rope. Homer could get plenty from his dad's boatyard. And Homer could climb like a monkey; so much so, in fact, that sometimes Danny couldn't help but wonder about him.

* * * * * * *

Teaching proceeded poorly at Lincoln School the next morning, and not just because it was Friday and the students were eagerly anticipating the weekend break. The entire student body was abuzz with questions, speculation and wonderment. So, in fact, were the teachers. It was nearly an hour after the bell before Mr. Jelinec, the school custodian, could remove the huge white oilcloth banner securely fastened at the second floor level of the school's front door colonnade. Emblazoned in bold red letters on the banner were the words "RANDOLF BROKMAN KISSES GIRLS".

Several students swore that Butchie Brockman, upon seeing the sign, turned and fled homeward; the number who claimed to have witnessed this amazing phenomenon grew hourly. The fact that Butchie's nose was seen to be taped gave substance to the rumor that some girl had bitten him. All the young ladies of the eighth grade eyed one another suspiciously; the smarter ones smiled mysteriously, but inwardly churned with the frustration of not being "in the know".

Jennifer Markham managed to sneak a glance back toward Danny Van Kuyper, but he was studiously engrossed in his textbook, his hand shading the tincture stains on his face. But when Homer Peckley caught her eye, he winked knowingly. And grinned like an idiot. His familiarity was most disturbing.

Miss Hecker shuffled the vague absence excuse signed by Mrs. Miller with the obvious forgery submitted by Danny Van Kuyper, and suspiciously eyed the vacant desk of Randolph Brockman. Miss Hecker was a very capable logician. But she said nothing.

CHAPTER 5

Halloween High-Jinks

"Now, son, I don't often put my foot down regarding your free time activities, but if you go out at all tomorrow night, it'll be to take part in the Halloween costume parade. Otherwise, you're confined to the house, and no tricks, or else!"

Ray Van Kuyper, seated in his favorite chair, was working hard at the unaccustomed role of "stern father". He felt uncomfortable at it, and a little hypocritical, but his wife, Elsie, had given him the word.

"Can't I just go watch the parade, Dad?" Danny tried.

"Nothin' doin'," the man smiled wryly. "It would take you all of two seconds to cut out of there and rejoin the alley-box dumping crowd. I had enough trouble with the police and neighbors about that last year. And didn't you get a little tired re-filling those garbage cans and alley boxes?"

"Yeah, but nobody *proved* I was in on it."

"But you and I know better, don't we?"

Glumly, Danny stared at his scuffed shoes. Last year he had been sentenced, so to speak, strictly on circumstantial evidence – ashes and coffee grounds on his shoes. A patrolman had come to the door that night, long after Danny was in bed, stating that a neighbor thought he had recognized Danny amongst the pranksters who had tipped over his alley-box. Ray Van Kuyper had assured the officer that he would investigate the situation and make any necessary corrections.

After finding the telltale residue on Danny's shoes, his father had given the boy this option: a full month of strict curfew, or a clean-up job in the neighborhood alleys next day after school. Danny chose humiliation over solitary confinement, and the following evening had made the rounds shoveling as discreetly as possible. Without help, this time.

"We're not going to have any repetition of last year," Danny's father broke into the boy's thoughts. "Besides, people will be looking for the trouble-makers this year, and any kids who get caught are likely to be made examples of. Now, what'll it be? The parade, where your sister Doris can keep an eye on you, or home, where your mother and I can?"

"I dunno, Dad," Danny replied gloomily. "I'm not much on bein' in parades."

"Well, I'll give you until after dinner to make up your mind. 'Cause if you're going to be in the parade, you'll have to get started on some sort of a costume tonight."

"Yes sir."

Danny rose and shuffled quietly through the swinging door into the kitchen. His mother, busy with dinner over at the stove, eyed him with a stern but satisfied look. Evidently she had overheard the conversation.

"I'll finish rakin' those leaves before dinner, Mom," Danny volunteered as he continued into the back hall, where he lifted his jacket off the wall hook. He needed an opportunity to think.

Outside in the fading daylight, Danny swiped at the leaves a couple of times and then leaned on the rake thoughtfully. One thing was already settled as far as he was concerned. He had heard rumors of the watch some neighbors would be keeping over their garbage cans and alley boxes. He wasn't about to walk into any trap. This year, at least, the neighborhood dump-and-run routine was not for him.

How about that "sane Halloween" costume parade the local Junior Chamber of Commerce was promoting for Hornville's youngsters? The kids were scheduled to parade from Hornville High down Central Avenue to Sheridan Park. Under the lights at the bandstand, there'd be prizes awarded for "the most original costume", "the scariest costume", "the cutest costume", and so forth. And each participant was to be given a bag of candy, courtesy of Blumgren's Arcade. Miserable!

The last thing Danny wanted was for his friends and enemies to recognize him as one of the paraders; their taunts and jeers would be unbearable. But it was the parade or solitary confinement. A crummy choice either way, Danny concluded woefully as he studied the setting sun. Veiled by lacy clouds, the sun reminded him of a huge pumpkin; very stylish, considering the season. Some of the farms south of Hickory Hill were sporting some pretty good-sized pumpkins in their fields, last time he had been that way.

"Hey, industrious, c'mon in and wash for dinner," Doris called cheerily from the back door. Danny turned loose the rake handle and strolled toward the house, nodding at no one in particular. He had an idea – part of one, at least – and he was agreeing with himself.

* * * * * * *

Danny caught the family by surprise by launching the dinner table conversation himself. "I'm gonna be in that parade tomorrow night," he announced matter-of-factly. "Dad, could I please have four bits for a pumpkin?"

"Fifty cents for a pumpkin?" protested the senior Van Kuyper.

"A big one. That's what they want for 'em at the produce market."

"Well, O.K." The man fished in his pocket. "Here," he said, handing the boy a half-dollar. "Jack-o-lantern on a stick, huh? Is that gonna be your get-up?"

"Uh, I'll show you when I'm done," Danny replied as he pocketed the coin.

Mr. Van Kuyper was satisfied. Danny was demonstrating a co-operative attitude, he thought, and surely a boy with a large pumpkin on his hands was in no position to dump alley-boxes!

Danny then proceeded to engross himself in his dinner and his plans for Halloween night, paying little attention to the rest of the family's chatter, until someone mentioned the Hornville Happy Daze Club.

"Those bums!" snorted Mrs. Van Kuyper, an opinion shared, and for good reason, by many of the local citizenry. The Happy Daze Club was a loosely organized drinking fraternity of young adults, mostly the college kids, who periodically subjected their fellow townspeople to all sorts of pranks in the name of good fellowship and adult humor, so-called.

This spirited bunch numbered among its members several of Hornville's social elite, which gave the club an air of respectability and a degree of immunity. With the police court judge their vice-president, how could they lose?

The club justified its existence in a small way (and also smoothed feathers they periodically ruffled) by occasionally sponsoring a charity event of some sort. Besides affording another opportunity for excessive partying, these events sometimes actually did raise a small surplus of cash over and above their considerable expense, which was forwarded, in time, to the charitable institutions honored.

It seemed from the conversation, as Danny tuned in, that one of the club members had tried to sell Ray Van Kuyper two tickets to the club's Halloween dance, in the name of some obscure welfare society.

"Of course I didn't buy any," Ray waved down his wife's protests.

"I hear their dances are real wing-dings," Doris chimed in.

"Brawls," corrected her mother. "It wouldn't be so bad if they'd keep their "fun" to themselves. Why if mere boys were guilty of the squirt gunning, stink bombing, and other pranks, they'd end up in a reform school."

"I thought the time they all wore maternity smocks on the day before Mother's Day was kind of funny," Ray smiled.

"Maybe so," sniffed Elsie. "But their jokes sure weren't."

"College humor, raw, raw, raw," quipped Ray.

"Darling, the children are present!"

Danny pushed back his chair and stood up. "May I be excused? I wanna go get that pumpkin now. I wanna work on it tonight."

His parents nodded and resumed their conversation. Danny left by the back door, zipping up his jacket as he trotted into the chill night, and headed towards Hickory Hill. An hour later, a huge pumpkin cradled in his arms, he took a slow turn around the Happy Daze clubhouse, taking care to stay out of sight of the several members strolling into the downstairs bar. Then he borrowed a coaster wagon some thoughtful child had abandoned along the sidewalk. The pumpkin was getting awfully heavy.

Home again, he covered the kitchen table with newspaper and began to carve and clean his large prize by cutting the bottom out of it.

"Yer gonna wear it on yer head," little Herbie guessed.

"Yeah," Danny said amiably. "I'm gonna need a bed sheet from you, Mom."

"Oh, a ghost with a pumpkin head," Doris teased him. "You'll be *so* cute."

"Yeah. I'm gonna shine a flashlight up here this way under my chin," Danny demonstrated. "Like candle light, sort of."

Ray rumpled his son's hair and retreated toward the parlor with his newspaper. "Who said my kid ain't got no imagination?" he chuckled. He was as pleased with himself as he was with Danny. His firm posture with the boy was obviously paying quick and sure dividends.

Before going to bed that night, Danny slipped his newly acquired half dollar into the cigar box underneath the comic books stacked in his closet. Here was the depository for his unofficial working capital. His mother kept too close an account of the funds in the coin bank on his dresser, a practice which put a crimp in projects which called for a little ready cash if a fella had no other financial resources.

* * * * * * *

Down went the sun, up came the moon; it was Halloween! Danny left home shortly before 7:30, well-disguised by a bed sheet from the neck down and a pumpkin from the neck up. He hurried through the alleys toward Hornville High. If things worked out as he hoped, he'd arrive just as the parade was getting underway and would wind up in the last row of the paraders.

Doris had agreed to take Herbie directly to Central Avenue to view the parade, rather than accompany Danny to the school. Not that he'd mind their company so much; he just didn't want to be recognized. Not in that get-up. He shuddered at the thought.

His timing was excellent. Most of the costumed children were already marching up Barnard Street toward Central Avenue when he arrived. The tag end of the group was being lined up on the school lawn by an officious-looking young man wearing a paper badge.

"Right there at the end of the row for you, pumpkin-head!" the young man directed with a laugh as Danny jogged toward him. "My, you certainly are a handsome looking vegetable!" He thumped the pumpkin as Danny passed him

Moving to the end of the line, Danny did a double take at one shroud-wrapped figure, spotted on the front by six large, red "bullet holes" and labeled on the back by a sign reading "The Ghost of Doggie Blodgett". Life-sized cardboard "concrete blocks" dangled from each wrist and dragged behind each ankle. A sure prize winner in some division, Danny mused, filled with a mixture of admiration and revulsion for the macabre imagination displayed.

A little hobo wearing a battered derby and a sad clown mask dropped back two rows and elbowed in beside Danny. Together they lagged a little to form a rank of their own.

"Dat you, Danny?" whispered the hobo.

"Yeah, Homer," Danny replied softly. "Got the matches and candles?"

"In my pockets. I could hide a bowlin' ball in my Pa's old clothes. Got duh film?"

"After school I fished some old negatives out of the alley-box back of Benger's photo studio. I didn't wanna take any of my folks'. My picture might be on 'em!"

"Good tinkin', Danny!"

"Where'd ya put the board?"

"Next to duh garage, right where dey keep duh ladder."

"Fine!"

Several other late comers were now trooping along behind Danny and Homer, but the two friends continued to march along as a pair. The front line of the parade had already turned the corner and was marching down brightly lit Central Avenue. Knots of noisy spectators lined the curbs. Shouts, laughter, waves and whistles were exchanged by the viewers and the viewed. It was hard to say which group was having more fun, except for the pumpkin-head and the hobo in the rear ranks. They marched along quietly, seemingly oblivious to everything except each other. Their conversation certainly appeared to be an earnest one.

"Hey," the hobo suddenly jerked his head around. "Dere's yer brudder'n sister wavin' atcha. Ya better wave back."

"Where?" Pumpkin-head had to turn his whole body to get a change of view.

"On yer side, in fronta duh dime store. Hurry up; we're almost past 'em."

Danny turned and walked sideways several steps. Herbie sat on the curb, Doris standing in back of him, and both were waving frantically. Danny, hugging his sheet closely about him, nodded his pumpkin head in their direction, but turned away hastily as he heard them call his name.

"Rats!"

"What'sa matter?" asked Homer. "How kin anybody tell who's who in dese outfits?"

"I don't want *anybody* to know I'm in this stupid parade," Danny grumbled. "And I 'speshly don't want anybody to know I'm in this pumpkin!"

"Relax. There's a girl way up front wit a outfit jist like yers. I t'ought she was you at first," Homer chuckled.

"Yeah?" Danny sniffed, a trifle indignant at his friend. "How couldja tell it wasn't?"

"By duh silly voice. An duh shoes, when I looked, an' she's taller'n you are. An' how she walked. An' she was wit' some udder girls, which I figgered you would'n be…"

"Never mind," Danny interrupted. "We're getting close to the park. Soon as we get to the big bushes, we cut out. An' stick to the creek bottom 'til we're outa the park. I don't want Doris and Herbie spottin' us takin' off."

The shrubbery flanking the gravel walkway winding into the center of Sheridan Park narrowed the file of marchers to two abreast. At a convenient parting in the bushes, Homer and Danny detoured to the left.

Danny slipped off his pumpkin and carried it by the stem as he followed Homer down the dark, familiar trail to the creek bottom. There they paused briefly while Danny fashioned a sack out of his mother's bed sheet for the pumpkin. Then, with Danny shouldering his bundle, the boys hastened quietly up the nearly dry creek bed back toward the center of town.

Above them, they could hear the voices of the parade spectators moving in the opposite direction and crowding into Sheridan Park to watch the costume judging contest. Doris and Herbie Van Kuyper were part of that crowd...

* * * * * * *

The Hornville Happy Dazers had converted a large, old-fashioned but substantial two-story brick residence just off Central Avenue into an elaborate party house with a ballroom, bar, meeting room, a den and two card rooms, with a billiard parlor in the basement. This Halloween found the place ablaze with lights as the Happy Dazers and others who had invested in the latest batch of charity dance tickets proceeded to make merry in their typical fashion.

The October chill was alleviated by a cheerful blaze in the ballroom's great stone fireplace; on the roof above, the thin smoke rising from the massive twin-funneled chimney curled gracefully upward toward the stars.

Also on the roof above, two small figures crept along the steep gable. The first, burdened with a large white bedsheet, appeared to be cradling a substantial-sized pumpkin within its folds. The second figure, a hobo lookalike, was burdened by a short, wide board.

"Easy now," Danny cautioned as he propped his feet against the inward side of the chimney. "Some of 'em are upstairs, I think in the room right under us."

Homer gingerly settled himself against the chimney, panting more from excitement than exertion. "Well, what are we waitin' fer?" he whispered. "Got the film? Let's get started!"

"No, we'll wait."

"Fer what?"

"'Til they pile on some more wood."

"I getcha. We want lotsa smoke in a hurry."

"Right." Danny winked at his fellow conspirator, and Homer hugged himself in suppressed anticipation. From the street below came the sound of slamming car doors. Each boy peeked around his corner of the chimney. Two couples were sauntering across the street to the clubhouse, chatting happily.

"More victims," chuckled Homer.

"Ssh!" warned Danny. "If they spot us, we'll be cooked." The boys ducked back into the protective shadow of the chimney. They sat quietly, listening to the laughter and music piped up to them from the ballroom two stories below. A chilly breath of wind set them to shivering and made the thin wisp of smoke rising in front of them curlicue in the air. But they sat patiently, almost breathlessly, listening to the ebb and flow of the party below.

Homer finally broke the stillness. "Bet dere's a hunnert people down dere," he whispered.

"Hunnert an' two," Danny whispered back, peeking around the chimney. "Here comes a couple more."

Suddenly the boys sat erect. New and louder sounds came from the chimney – grating, scraping, thumping. A stream of sparks rose and winked out in the darkness, the smoke wavered and thickened.

"That's it!" Danny shivered excitedly. "They're stokin' the fireplace. First let's light the candles!"

Acting as he spoke, he struck a large wooden match against the chimney and began lighting the half-dozen short, thick candles bunched in the center of the board on Homer's lap. He even tried to light the point of one of the nails on which the candles were stuck.

"Calm down, yuh ninny," Homer chided as the half-dozen illumined his freckled face. "I guess yer more nervisser'n I am!"

"Just shuddup'n hold still," whispered Danny, reaching for the pumpkin wedged against the chimney. He set the bottomless pumpkin carefully over the burning candles. "Gotta have it facin' the street. After I drop the film, I'll handle my end of the board. We gotta put it on easy an' careful-like, cover both chimney holes, an' not drop the pumpkin."

Homer nodded impatiently. "Gotcha."

Silently Danny stood up. From his pocket he drew a thick wad of photo negatives, stacked like a deck of cards. He divided the stack in two and simultaneously dropped a handful down each chimney funnel. Swiftly he reached down for his end of the board. Homer rose unsteadily, supporting his end. The pumpkin teetered, but didn't shift. The board fit neatly over the smoking twin funnels, sealing them completely.

"Let's go!" urged Danny needlessly; Homer was already scrambling across the roof ahead of him.

Even as the stacked negatives fluttered apart in the chimney, some drifting down into the fire, the culprits were skinning down the Happy Daze Club's ladder to the roof of the attached garage; even as the sweet-smelling hardwood smoke belched backward into the ballroom and turned foul with the acrid odor of burning celluloid, the boys slid on their stomachs over the edge of the garage roof, clung briefly to the rain gutter and dropped into the alley.

The noise from the club was much louder now, and much less joyous. Doors were opening, people were coughing and cursing, some were running around the yard.

"Look! A jack-o-lantern! Some jerk plugged up the chimney with a big ol' pumpkin!"

Danny paused just long enough to secure his bundled bed sheet and raced down the alley after the fleeing figure of Homer

"There they go!" someone behind them shouted. "One of 'em's got a white jacket!"

Heavy footsteps thundered down the alley behind the boys. Homer led the way into a narrow passage between two store buildings.

"They're headed toward Fir Street! Cut 'em off!" The boys darted across dimly lit Fir Street, glancing only briefly at the ominously large figures racing toward them from the direction of the club. They hurdled a hedge, dashed between two houses, over a fence, down an alley and across another street, and into yet another alley.

Somewhere a siren wailed. Several cars were now racing and tooting up and down various streets and alleys, but the sound of pursuing footsteps was gone. Gratefully the gasping boys slowed to a walk, secure in the darkness of the alley.

A car suddenly swung into the end of the alley in front of them. Quickly the boys ducked behind an alley box, crouching lower and lower as the cruising car approached closer and closer. The car was equipped with a spotlight, which swung back and forth probing the shadows of the houses and shops backing on the alley.

"It's duh cops," whispered Homer, frightened.

"No, I don't think so," replied Danny, hopeful.

The car stopped directly opposite them. The boys hugged the ground on their side of the alley-box. The spotlight beam swung over their heads and reflected off the bricks of the building in back of them. It stopped.

"Hey buddy," came a husky voice from the car. "You seen two punk kids run through here?"

"No," replied an even huskier voice from the direction of the building. "Now get that spotlight out of my face."

Equally slack-jawed, equally speechless, equally amazed, Danny and Homer turned their heads as one toward the second voice. A tall man in a brown overcoat and hat stood in the back doorway of the shop. The spotlight ringed him from the waist up, but his upturned collar and hat brim obscured his face.

"What're you doin' here, Bud?" asked the voice in the car.

"What are *you* doing here?" replied the man in the doorway. His tone was angry, ominous. "Now kill that light before I do." He stepped down from the doorway, and the spotlight swung away.

"Take it easy, Mac," said the voice in the car. Gears clashed, the motor raced, and the car sped away and out of the alley. So did the boys – in the opposite direction.

"Wait!" the husky voice called after them, but the boys paid no heed. If anything, they ran faster.

"Rats!" gasped Danny after they had run for several blocks. "I forgot my Mom's bed sheet back there!"

"Well, yuh kin go back an' get it alone, if yer dat crazy," Homer puffed as he veered off toward his own home. "I'll see ya in school inna mornin'."

Danny waved a silent farewell to his companion, but Homer wasn't looking back, even now. Danny maintained a trot until he neared home, then slowed to a walk to catch his breath. He let himself quietly in the back door, hung up his jacket, turned on the kitchen light, and then with as much nonchalance as he could muster, proceeded to supply himself with a glass of milk and several cookies. The swinging door to the parlor opened. In came his father, followed by the two women of the household.

"Son, Doris says she couldn't find you after the costume judging contest," Ray Van Kuyper said quietly.

Danny studied the cookies in his hand. "Someone swiped my punkin right off my head," he lied, inspired. "I bet I chased him half-way home."

"Who was it?"

"I dunno. Some punk kid from the south side. I seen him around Washington school once."

His mother was suspicious and angry. "Where's my bed sheet?" she demanded.

"I - I lost it chasin' the kid."

"A likely story!" Mrs. Van Kuyper snorted.

"He *was* in the parade, Mother," Doris defended.

"And he's obviously been running," added Mr. Van Kuyper. "Look at that sweat."

"From trouble, I'll bet," guessed his wife.

"Cross my heart, Mom," Danny vowed, crossing his heart. "Never tipped an alley box, never soaped a window. You get any complaints about me tomorrow, I'll give up my allowance for a month."

"You'll give up more than that," his mother promised grimly. "And I'm charging you two dollars for that lost sheet, young man. You've *got* to learn responsibility! Now get to bed."

Danny got. Lying there staring into the darkness, Danny sadly mulled over the prospect of parting with two dollars to pay for the lost bed sheet. Could he go back and retrieve it?

Mentally he retraced his and Homer's route from the Happy Daze Club, pausing only briefly to savor their coup over the town's self-appointed chief tricksters. He shivered at the thought of their near-capture and the sudden appearance of the man in the brown coat and hat.

That's where he had lost the sheet. In the alley back of Packard Avenue, by the alley box back of… of Miller's Bakery!

But who was that guy standing there? It sure wasn't ol' man Miller, or anyone else Danny could remember seeing around town. He *must* have seen Homer and Danny hide behind the alley box. So why did he lie to the guy in the car? That's what Danny wondered as exhaustion rushed him into sleep. Why did that guy lie?

CHAPTER 6

Tall Stranger, Short Thief

"HALLOWEEN GHOSTS SPOOK HAPPY DAZE BALL," boomed the front page headline of the Hornville Bugle's November 3rd edition, obviously thrilled at again having some excitement to report since the oft rehashed demise of the late Doggie Blodgett had ceased to be good copy.

"A good time was *not* had by all," the paper went on to say. "Several not-so-Happy Dazers were heard to mutter dire threats of revenge against the pumpkin planters who smoked out the Club's Halloween dance. However, a major obstacle thwarts their just vengeance, namely, just who were the culprits?

"Rumors of suspects range from two small boys (unlikely), to a pair of ex-Happy Dazers (impossible; there are no ex-members), to several of the more athletic members of the Hornville Women's Club (outrageous thought!), to members of the local clergy (sacreligious!)!"

"In short, there are no hard clues, but our esteemed Chief of Police, Pat Lathrop, has promised to pursue the case diligently . . . when he gets around to it.

"In the meantime, the villainous pumpkin which leered down at the Happy Dazers from the heights of their chimney pots sits ensconced in the club's meeting hall, waiting to be thrust down over the ears of any of its accomplices who happen to fall into the clutches of the pumpkin's furious victims.

"But the general feeling around town is that the jack-o-lantern will putrefy long before the Happy Dazers determine the identity of the anonymous mischief makers. Whoever they are, only their own boastfulness would likely lead to their discovery, and no sensible being in this community is likely to lay false claim to the deed. For the Happy Dazers are much too well known for their insistence on dishing out far more than they take."

The two boys who read these words together on the back porch steps of the Van Kuyper residence shared mixed feelings of satisfaction and trepidation.

"Boy, if dey ever finds us out, we're in fer it," murmured Homer, trembling.

Danny shifted his seat and glanced back over his shoulder. "Just like it says in the paper, Homer, all we gotta do is shuddup an' no one will ever know we did it. But if we ever start braggin', we're *cooked*."

"Yeah. It's a shame, d'ough. Best gag we ever pulled, an' we can't get duh glory! Wouldn' duh udder kids turn green, hey? 'Speshly Butchie Brockman. He t'inks he's such hot stuff!"

"He ain't bothered me since we hung up that sign 'bout him at school. An' he knows yer my best friend."

Homer looked dissatisfied. "I'd still like tuh let 'm know personal dat I helped hang dat sign."

"He knows," Danny assured his chum. "He knows it took more'n one guy to hang it up. Sometimes people know a thing without actually knowin' it, ya know what I mean?"

Homer nodded. "Yeah, I guess," he replied vaguely.

Danny stretched out to soak up more of the Saturday morning sun. The warmth of it on the wooden steps was a pleasant contrast to the chill northern breeze.

"It's gonna snow one a' dese days," Homer observed, shivering. "Let's get doin' sumpthin, 'steada sittin' here freezin'."

"Okay. Let's hike over to Packard Avenue," replied Danny, rising to his feet. He led the way toward the alley.

"Dere? Butchie Brockman lives dere!"

"I know." Danny paused at the alley box long enough to dispose of the Hornville Bugle. He hoped the rest of the family wouldn't miss it. "But the mornin' after Halloween – before school – I went an' got my mom's bed sheet back."

"So what? Yuh tol' me dat yestiday."

"Remember where we was, when I left it?"

Homer's brow wrinkled as his mind labored to retrace their escape route three evenings past. "It was . . . backa Miller's Bakery, wasn't it?"

Danny nodded.

"So like I said, so what? Dat guy dere – whoever he wuz – din't hardly get any kind of a look at us; *he* wuz in duh light, remember? An' if we din't know him, betcha he don't know us, eider. So stop worryin', pal."

The boys' conversation continued as they ambled from alley to alley. Danny snapped off a withered hollyhock stalk and idly tore apart the seed pods as they walked.

"Well, maybe he don't *know* us, but he sure can *rekanize* us," Danny said, looking at his friend meaningfully. "Me, at any rate."

"Whaddayamean?"

"That mornin', when I went an' got my Ma's sheet…"

"Yeah?"

"I'm comin' outa the alley, an' there he is, standin'."

"Yeah?" Homer's eyes widened with wonderment. "Who is he?"

"I dunno. Big guy -- still had his face pretty much hid with his hat 'n coat collar. But I'm positive he ain't no one we seen aroun' town before."

"Whaddee say?"

"Nuthin'."

"Whaddee do?"

"Nuthin'."

"Whatchu do?"

"Whatcha think I did, ya ninny?" Danny jabbed his friend with the hollyhock stalk. "I just kept goin'. An' every time I looked back, he was just lookin – an' lookin'. He gimme the creeps."

They crossed another street in silence before Homer spoke again. "So let's stay outa his neighborhood. We don't bodder him, he don't bodder us. After all, he still don't know yer name."

"No, but he knows what I look like. An' he knows the Happy Dazers are lookin' fer us. All he has to do is describe me, an' sooner or later we're tagged."

"So why let 'm maybe get anudder good look atcha?" Homer persisted, throwing up his hands. "An' at me, too? What if…?" A tinge of fear shaded the redhead's words. "What if he's duh guy what kilt Doggie Blodgett? Duh cops ain't got no idee, yuh know."

"Nah," Danny scoffed, dismissing the supposition with a wave of his hand. "If he was, he'd a left town long before now."

"Den why bodder duh guy when yuh don't t'ink he ain't done nuttin'?"

"You don't understand, Homer. Point is, he's got somethin' on *us*, but we don't know nuthin' 'bout *him*! I don't like that."

Homer was silent for a moment as he pondered Danny's words. Then he said, "Yer worried fer nuthin', Danny. This guy fer sure ain't no Happy Dazer, an' prob'ly don't even live in Hornville if yuh don't 'member ever seein' 'm aroun'. He's prob'ly jist visitin' somebody, an' no Happy Dazer eider, I betcha, else he'd a been at dat dance."

"Well, I'm sure he's new in town, else we'd've seen him aroun' before. But I'm sure he ain't visitin', either."

"How da yuh know?" Homer asked dubiously.

"Cause he ain't visitin', that's how."

"Dat's whatcha said! An' I sez, how da yuh know, big brain?"

"Like I said, 'cause he *ain't* visitin'. Visitors stay at the people's house where they visit, or go aroun' doin' things with them people. *They don't stand around in alleys by their selves,*" Danny concluded emphatically.

Homer trudged along silently, scratched his freckled nose, lifted his cap and scratched his red head. Finally he said, "I gotta idee yer more intrusted in dat guy fer hisself den fer what he might do 'bout us. After all, he coulda turned us in dat night in duh alley, if he'd a mind to."

"That's the point, Homer. Why didn't he? Don't that bother ya?"

"No. I ain't no curious cat. He let me be, I'm fer lettin' him be."

"What was he doin' backa the bakery? Don't <u>that</u> bother ya?"

"No, not 'tic'larly. Danny, why yuh lettin' dat guy bug yuh so?"

"'Cause he's up to no good, Homer. I got a feelin'."

"So call duh cops."

"And tell 'em what?"

"Yeah," Homer smiled wryly. "Not much. But if he's up tuh no good, den dat's trouble. I'm here fer fun, ol' buddy, but gone fer trouble. Let's go up Hick'ry Hill instead."

"No. I figure we ain't got nuthin' to worry 'bout if we're lookin' fer him fer a change, 'steada him lookin' fer us. Then if we can figure out what he's up to, we can turn him in, an' *this time* get our names in the paper fer what we done."

Homer's nose wrinkled skeptically. "So what if he's casin' duh bakery tuh steal a jelly roll? I kin see duh headline now: "Two Boys Save Jelly Roll!" Danny, yer nuts."

"*Yer* nuts. Guys like that don't go aroun' swipin' jelly rolls."

"Okay, okay. But dere ain't no store roun' dere what's big enough tuh make a real crook itchy. Duh bakery'? Brockman's butcher shop? Ol' man Ortman, duh tailor? Why, duh bank's clear up town, on Central Av'noo!"

"Yer right. Hunnert percent, Homer."

"So what's he up to?"

"That's the question, all right. What is he up to? Don't it bother ya?"

"No."

"Then why don't you go chase a rabbit? I'll go see fer myself."

"If yer gonna get intuh trouble, I better be dere tuh getcha out."

"That's what I like aboutcha, Homer; yer a true friend."

The boys had traversed the several blocks leading up to one of the alleys paralleling Packard Avenue. Now they turned south and walked behind the row of homes and small business places lining the north side's only commercial street. As they traveled the two blocks to the alley behind the bakery, they found themselves walking single file, Danny in the lead, hugging the shrubbery and the fences.

At the last cross street, they stopped and gazed at the usual scattering of Saturday morning shoppers scurrying back and forth in the thin November sunshine. All seemed to be contentedly pursuing their business, unaware of the close scrutiny they were undergoing. There wasn't a single suspicious stranger among them. Not even an unsuspicious one.

The silent watch continued for nearly four long minutes before Homer began to fidget. "Whoever he is, he ain't out buying' groceries or hardware dis mornin'," he commented. "He's pro'bly home in bed."

"Where does he live?"

"Jeez, how would I know?"

"'Course you don't know. Me neither. That's part a' the problem. But if he walks aroun' here, he must live aroun' here. Let's float aroun' the neighborhood a little."

"What if he sees us?"

"If he's where he kin see us, chances are we'll see him first. After all, *we're lookin' fer him*. He's not lookin' fer us."

Slowly, warily, the two boys scouted the sidewalks, alleys and shops on the block where Millers' Bakery fronted, and two blocks north and south of it. Their stealth wasn't entirely unobserved:

several shopkeepers viewed their odd actions with misgiving, and marked them as potential shoplifters.

Consequently, the proprietress of the variety store made them turn their pockets out before she would allow them to leave the premises. This humiliation prompted the lads to declare "we won't shop *here* anymore", spoken indignantly by Danny and Homer to the closed door after they had been ushered from the shop.

Together they skulked down Packard Avenue, forgetting momentarily their self-appointed task of the morning. Presently they approached the front of the bakery. The aromas lingering about were enticing, and the sight of the various delicacies was positively tantalizing. The boys found themselves drawn hand and nose against the large plate glass windows.

"Man oh man, lookit dem cream pies!" drooled Homer ecstatically as Danny smacked his lips. "An' duh frostin' on dat birt'day cake! Wonder who's havin' a party?"

"It says 'Happy Birthday Mother' on it," Danny read. "If it ain't yer Ma, I don't think yer gonna get invited, ya meat-head."

"I don't need any invite. Jist gimme about two seckints wit' Missus Miller lookin' duh udder way…"

"Well, hi!"

The boys turned toward the voice. It was Jennifer Markham, standing near the walkway leading back to the bakery's family entrance. She was smiling broadly, causing the embarrassed boys to speculate silently that perhaps they had just been speculating a trifle too loudly.

"H'lo, Jennifer," Danny replied.

Homer raised a limp hand and waved awkwardly. "Hi, Jenny," he said.

Jennifer approached them slowly. "Did you come over to see me?" she asked, hopefully it seemed. She was dressed in dark corduroy pants and a green bulky knit sweater, and her hair was done up tightly with a small ribbon. The boys had never seen her look so tomboyish.

She almost looked like she might be fun, Danny thought, but he was already shaking his head no in reply to the girl's question. A faint cloud of disappointment shadowed her face.

"Just doing some shopping, I suppose," she guessed, and this time Danny nodded agreement to the proffered excuse.

"My, uh, my Ma wants some . . . t'umb tacks," Homer fibbed unskillfully. He lacked Danny's ability to lie with conviction.

"I'm afraid we don't sell thumb tacks," the girl smiled quietly.

Homer laughed – tried to. "Oh, I know dat," he replied, his voice unnecessarily loud. "We're goin'… tuh duh variety store." He jerked his thumb back over his shoulder. Danny raised his eyes to study the sky, saying nothing. He would let Homer dig his own grave.

"Didn't you just come from that way?" the girl asked.

Homer looked back as if to make sure. "Oh. Well, we're in no hurry, he tried another laugh. "Jus' killin' time."

Jennifer's face brightened. "Well, if you're in no hurry, come on in," she said, taking Danny's elbow and leading the weakly protesting lad toward the shop entrance. "My aunt and uncle said I should introduce them to any of my school mates who come around."

"We buy bakery here once inna while," Homer said as he tagged along unwillingly. "So we has met yer folks… er, duh Millers."

"Maybe so," Jennifer overruled them as she opened the shop door and ushered them inside. "But they don't know you as my classmates. In fact, they probably don't even know your names!"

Mrs. Miller had just finished waiting on a pair of customers who were leaving the store together, well-burdened with interesting bags and boxes. Homer sniffed hungrily, and the second customer was saved from what might have been a disastrous collision when Danny yanked his entranced buddy out of the way.

"Auntie," said Jennifer, leading the boys to the counter. "I want you to meet two of the boys in my class. This is Homer Peckley, and this is Danny Van Kuyper."

"Ach, ja, I haf zeen dem here mitt dere mudders," the portly old German woman beamed at the boys over her spectacles.

"H'lo, Missus Miller," said one boy.

"H'lo Missus Miller," said the other.

"And Danny's little brother, Herbie," Jennifer continued, "Is in the first grade with Timmy."

"Ach, how nize!" Mrs. Miller beamed a brighter pink. "I haf heard Dimmie zay dot Herbie's name. Soch nize boys you are, to come play mitt our liddle Chennifer. You vant maybe a nize chucklid doughnut?"

The boys were only too happy to accept the offer. Both examined the doughnut tray carefully and each selected one of the larger specimens with an extra thick layer of chocolate icing. The brass bell on the shop door rang, signaling the entrance of another customer.

"Goot mornink, Miz Brewster," Hilda Miller's accent boomed to greet the new arrival. "Chennifer, you plizz take your frents ofer dere on der bench for ein minute, ja?"

The old woman hurried around the showcase to wait on her customer. Jennifer led the boys to a bench near the front of the store. The boys sat with their backs propped against the wall, munching greedily on their unexpected treats. Jennifer sat on the end of the bench, her legs crossed and her hands clasped over her knee, enjoying the spectacle of two healthy appetites.

"Gee, it's too bad," Homer managed between bites.

"What's too bad?" the girl asked curiously.

Homer gulped. "Why, dat yer a – well, dat yer not a – nuttin'… never mind," Homer concluded hastily, and silenced himself with a huge bite of doughnut.

"My girl friends don't mind," Jennifer said knowingly. "And I hope that Danny doesn't…"

She switched her attention to the other boy. Danny, seated nearest the large front window, sat as though frozen, staring out of it, his jaws unmoving, the remainder of his doughnut poised in mid-air.

"Danny?" At the sound of his name, the boy swiftly turned his head to face her. "What's so fascinating out there?" she asked.

"Oh, jist a fancy new Buick went by is all," he lied glibly, and smiled as he nibbled at his doughnut. "Boy, these are great. Can we see where yer... ah... uncle makes 'em?"

"Why sure," the girl jumped lightly to her feet. "Uncle Karl will be pleased to meet you, and I'll bet you've not seen the big bake ovens before."

She led the boys around a cake-laden showcase and back through two sets of swinging doors connected by a short hallway. The bakery itself was very warm and bright, and heavy with heady fragrances. Bags of flour and sugar were stacked high in the corners, flanked by shelves and racks bearing canisters of spices and other ingredients.

Flour-dusted Uncle Karl was just as old, just as chubby, and just as pleasant as Aunt Hilda and his accent just as pronounced. He showed the boys the ovens and let Homer switch on the mixing machine. Homer was fascinated by it. Danny, however, appeared to be more interested in the back door. Specifically, to go through it. He wanted to leave.

"Ach, so soon you must leaf yet?" Mr. Miller seemed genuinely disappointed.

"'Fraid so," said Danny. "My mom wants me to clean our garage today."

"She does?" asked Homer unhappily.

"Yeah," replied Danny emphatically.

"I'm sorry you have to leave," said Jennifer sadly. "Please go out the front. I'm sure Aunt Hilda would like to say good-bye to you."

"Aw, she's prob'ly busy with lotsa customers," Danny replied as he edged toward the back door and opened it. "We'll see her again soon."

"Yeah," agreed Homer, suddenly as anxious to leave as Danny seemed to be. "Tell yer Antie goo-bye fer us, an' t'anks fer duh doughnuts."

"Ja, here, ein chelly roll for you yet," said Uncle Karl, pressing a fresh pastry into each boy's hand.

"Thanks, Mr. Miller," the boys said in unison as they shuffled out the door. "'Bye. 'Bye, Jennifer. See ya in school Monday."

Danny shut the door behind them even as Jennifer bade them farewell. He looked about warily, then peeked around the alley box behind which they had hidden that eventful Halloween night, checking the alley.

"All clear. C'mon, Homer," he said, hooking his friend by the arm and hastening northward up the alley.

"Take it easy, pal," protested Homer. "I'll keep up wit'cha. Why are you in sich a sweat?"

"You know our big friend?"

"Yeah?"

"I saw'm!"

"No kiddin'! Was he headed dis way?"

"No. You know that upstairs sun porch on that big house across the street from the bakery? Down a ways?"

"Ol' lady McClatchy's boardin' house? He was up dere?"

"Yep! No hat this time, but I rekanized the coat. He was just standin' by the sun porch rail, lookin' up and down the street."

"T'ink he saw us?" Homer was suddenly worried.

"Naw! If he had, I'm sure he wouldn'ta stood out there like that."

"So dat's why yuh wanted to get outa duh backa duh bakery!"

"Yer gettin' sharper every day, Homer. An' now we know where that guy lives."

As they reached the end of the alley, Homer paused. "Yer not circlin' aroun' to dat place now, are yuh?"

"Nope. We kin look him up after dark sometime. There's somethin' else we gotta do first. Why?"

"'Cause I ain't pre-pared. Dere's sumpthin' else I gotta do first. Here, have anudder jelly roll."

Danny took the pastry gratefully, but frankly puzzled. "You don't want a jelly roll? Whatsa matter, you sick er somethin'?"

"Nope. I jist got sumpthin' better tuh occupy me." Homer stepped back into the protective camouflage of some shrubs and pulled a pie carton out from under his jacket.

"You crook!" Danny exclaimed, "When didja swipe that?"

"When duh ol' man and duh girl was practicully kissin' yuh goo-bye an' beggin' yuh not tuh leave. 'When oppertunity knocks, answer duh door', like my ol' lady sez." Homer opened the carton. The dented cover had mashed the cream topping, but the calories were all still there.

"B'nana cream," he declared after dipping a soiled finger into the gooey mass and transferring the sample to his mouth.

"C'mon, ol' buddy. Dibs. Even-steven," Danny insisted wistfully.

"Why? You got two jelly rolls, and I even give yuh one of 'em!"

"Homer, if I even thought you was fer real, I wouldn't letcha in on my plan. Not one bit."

"Well… okay, half duh pie is yers when we get tuh Hick'ry Hill, and gimme back my jelly roll. Now, what's yer big deal plan?" Homer asked as he closed the pie carton.

"No. No Hick'ry Hill, I mean. We'll split the pie in my garage loft."

"Why?"

"'Cause we gotta read newspapers, that's why."

"Why? What papers? Duh Milwaukee daily?"

"No, the Hornville weekly. We should have mosta the latest ones stacked with the old dailies in our garage." Danny scanned their surroundings again while Homer once more secreted the pie carton under his jacket. "All clear, as far as our friend is concerned," announced Danny. "Let's go." He led the way across the street, followed by a puzzled Homer.

"Danny, maybe you 'member sumpthin' yuh read about dat guy in duh Bugle?"

"Naw, but sometimes I read the little ads to see if anybody's sellin' some good stuff.".

"So what?"

"So remember how Mrs. McClatchy useta have that 'Room fer Rent' sign on the front of her house? Well, it's gone. I saw that when I saw that guy upstairs. Well, she also useta have a ad in the Bugle, 'bout the room for rent. Ya catch on, now?"

Homer mulled it over. "Uh, no," he finally admitted.

"Well, I figure this guy musta rented the room. Ol' lady McClatchy takes down the sign, an' stops advertisin' in the Bugle. We find the paper when she stopped advertisin', like I 'spect she did, an' we know when this guy came to town. Can't be too long ago, I figure."

Homer was still perplexed. "Look, Danny, I ain't no ninny, but I can't see what's so darned important 'bout knowin' jist when dat guy blew intuh town."

"What if he's been here a year an' we just never saw him before? Ain't likely, but I wanna be sure. I figure if that ad is gone, like the sign on the ol' lady's house, then he's the reason fer it. An' we'll know how new he is aroun' here. It'll be a start."

"Okay, G-man; when we get tuh yer garage, *you* kin shuffle papers, an' I'll divvy up duh pie," declared Homer. He intended to concentrate on what, in his estimation, was the more important project.

And so it was done. The back issues of the Hornville Bugle were exhumed, the pie was divided and consumed, and Mrs. McClatchy's weekly classified ad last appeared in the September seventh issue, not quite two months' previous. Both boys were thoroughly satisfied with the results of their respective projects.

CHAPTER 7

Mrs. McClatchy's Boarder

Danny parked his bike in the rack next to City Hall and sauntered slowly up the south side of Central Avenue. It grew dark early these November evenings; it was barely 5:30 by the bank clock, and already all the street lights were on. All the shops on Hornville's main commercial thoroughfare were brightly lit, too, but Danny's interest was focused entirely on just one business place - the Little Bavaria Restaurant, on the northeast corner of Central and Packard Avenues.

As he approached the intersection, Danny favored the shadowy corners created by the bank's massive stone masonry. He paused when he reached a point where he could see clearly into the restaurant.

Sure enough. There sat the object of his interest, Mrs. McClatchy's mysterious roomer, eating alone as usual. And, as usual, Danny noticed, the man sat with his back to the wall, where he could keep an eye on everybody in the restaurant as well as the street. And again as usual, the man appeared to be reading a folded newspaper propped against the short vase of flowers in the center of the table. Idly Danny wondered if it might also be the same newspaper.

For nearly two weeks now, ever since he had discovered the stranger's place of residence, Danny had spent a part of each day, both morning and evening, shadowing him. Each morning he left extra early for school, much to Mrs. Van Kuyper's amazement, and had taken to riding his bike the short distance.

"To play ball," Danny lied to his mother when her curiosity finally prompted her to inquire after his sudden zeal for school. Mrs. Van Kuyper was content to accept this explanation of his unusual punctuality; she didn't enjoy the job of rousting Danny out of bed on school mornings any more than he did.

Evenings were a little stickier. Sometimes Danny would be "helping Roger Zaborski with his paper route", or "playing some football down at Sheridan Park". His occasional late arrival for dinner had created a few awkward scenes, and when Homer would call for him after school and find him gone, his best friend's annoyed look would puzzle Mrs. Van Kuyper, but only briefly.

Homer had tired quickly of Danny's shadow routine. He had accompanied Danny exactly one evening, and found watching the mystery man eat his solitary dinner in the Little Bavaria and then following him back to Mrs. McClatchy's to be terribly boring. To say nothing of chilly.

"In the morning, he eats breakfast at Tiny's Waffle Shop," Danny had since informed him.

"Big deal!" Homer had replied sarcastically. "All dem waffles'll make him too fat tuh chase yuh."

"No," said Danny solemnly. "He usually has scrambled eggs, I think."

Now shivering in the chilling dusk, Danny watched as the man arose from his table and prepared to leave the restaurant. Slowly Danny backed off until he was out of the man's line of vision, then turned and trotted the block and a half to City Hall, weaving deftly through the scattering of shoppers on Central Avenue. Retrieving his bike from the rack, Danny crossed Central and went north one block to dimly lit Pine Street before turning west toward Packard Avenue.

There, as usual, Danny would intercept his quarry in his now-familiar brown hat and coat, folded newspaper under his arm, strolling the four blocks back to Mrs. McClatchy's rooming house. As usual, Danny would follow him at a discreet distance, hoping to learn – what?

The boy wished he had even the remotest idea. The man's seemingly purposeless existence was puzzling, to be sure, but even Danny's interest in him would have quickly waned except for one curious thing; the man never went directly down Packard Avenue to Mrs. McClatchy's. Invariably, he would detour half a block and then disappear into the alley which passed behind Miller's Bakery!

Danny never had the courage to follow the man into the darkened alley, but from a vantage point further up Packard Avenue, he would eventually see the man emerge at either the near or far end of the block and then cross over to Mrs. McClatchy's.

"What does he find so int'rustin' in that stupid alley?" Danny wondered to himself again for the thousandth time as he coasted to a halt behind a parked car in one of the darker stretches of shadowy Pine Street.

Right on schedule, the object of his curiosity strode into view at the corner, paused to permit a car turning into Pine Street to pass, and then continued his stroll down Packard Avenue. Silently cursing the bright headlights on the oncoming car, Danny ducked as low as the handlebars of his bike would allow, hoping that the parked car would provide him sufficient concealment. The headlights passed. Danny looked up. His man was already out of sight.

Pedaling quickly to the corner, Danny again sighted his man. He was the only pedestrian in sight on the lower reaches of Packard Avenue, except for a boy coming toward him from the opposite direction. Danny thought he recognized the boy.

Content merely to keep his quarry in view, Danny watched as the man and boy approached each other, nearly a block away. The approaching boy looked up at the man and, as they passed each other, raised his hand in silent greeting.

Danny's eyes popped in amazement. He sucked in his breath. "He nodded back!" Danny exclaimed to himself. "I'll swear he nodded at the kid!"

Danny's eyes narrowed as they focused on the oncoming boy. Sure enough. It was Henry Rydzik, Jr., son Henry Rydzik, Sr., operator of Rydzik's Funeral Parlor. Henry was Danny's social inferior. He was a seventh grader. But suddenly Danny felt an interest in the boy.

A friendly smile lit Henry's face as he recognized Danny, still leaning on his bike at the corner of Pine and Packard.

"Hi, Danny! Watcha up to?" he asked hopefully. Everything Henry said or did was hopeful. He had to be the loneliest kid in town. Being the son of an undertaker made him an object of curiosity, and Henry could spellbind his schoolmates with fascinating answers to morbid questions, but somehow this never seemed to win him any friends. And nobody ever wanted to play at his house.

"Oh, nuthin' much," Danny answered the younger boy's question. A hopeful light flashed in Henry's eyes.

"Why don'tcha come over to my house? I've got a brand new Green Bay Packer football uniform…"

Danny was shaking his head no. He remembered that the Rydzik place was only a couple of blocks away, just off Central Avenue. The only time he had ever been there was when his Grandma had died.

"You kin try on the helmet," Henry was still hopeful. "And the shoulder pads. They're neat!"

"I gotta get home for dinner," Danny interrupted, truthful for a change. "You shoulda asked yer big friend there," he smiled. Craftily, he thought.

Henry looked puzzled. "Who?"

"That big guy I saw you talkin' to down there," Danny pointed at the man, still visible well down the street. Henry turned to look.

"Oh, him," he said disappointedly. "You can't ask a *man* to come play at yer house," he continued, turning a hurt look toward Danny.

"Oh, I just meant I thought maybe you knew him, is all."

"Do you know him?" asked Henry.

"No. Don't you?"

"Well, kinda. Leastways I met him once."

"Oh?"

Henry shifted his feet uneasily.

"Where?" Danny persisted.

"Oh, at my place once..." Henry wanted to change the subject. Here he was, getting into his father's business again...

Danny's curiosity was welling upward now. "When?"

Henry answered reluctantly. "At Mr. Blodgett's funeral."

"Doggie Blodgett? You mean the guy what was murdered?" Danny tried to keep his tone matter-of-fact, but excitement fairly bubbled in his veins, like so much ginger ale. "Probably a friend of the family, huh?"

"Uh – I don't think so."

"Why not?"

"Well, it was kinda peculiar."

"Peculiar? How peculiar?"

"Jeez, I'll tell ya, if ya let me!" Henry bristled slightly at Danny's constant interruptions. Danny bit his tongue.

Henry proceeded. "He din't sit out front with the rest of the people. There were lotsa people . . ." Danny remembered the news stories about the crowds of curiosity seekers who attended Doggie's funeral. Unfortunately for Danny, it had been held on a school day.

"This guy," Henry pointed toward the now vanished party in question, "he stood behind the screen partition back of the casket, where my daddy always stands to keep an eye on things. And he was takin' movies of everybody…"

"What?"

"Yeah! He was where nobody could see him at all, but he had this little movie camera, and he was takin' movies of everybody right in their faces. And I watched him. And when my daddy came, I asked what's he doin' and my daddy says never mind, go sing. That's why I get to stay home on funeral days."

"Why?"

"To sing! Would you like to hear 'Nearer My God To Thee'?"

"No, thanks. Did you talk to that guy at all?"

"Later on, he was upstairs in my room, takin' movies of the people outside through my bedroom window. But he din't go out to the cemetery. When I asked him was he gonna come to the cemetery with us, he said no thanks, but that I was a good boy and that it'd be best I din't say nuthin' 'bout him bein' there, fer my Daddy's sake."

"He threatened you?" Danny asked, incredulous.

"Why, no," Henry replied, slightly indignant. "He said it nice. He even smiled."

"Oh. Whatcha say his name was?"

"I dunno. I ain't never heard it."

"Din't yer Dad tell ya?"

"I ain't never asked my Daddy anymore about him. Why do you care so much about him?"

"Oh, I don't, really," Danny tried to be casual. "It's just that I don't remember seein' him around before, is all."

"Come to think of it," Henry said, "I ain't seen him much, either. I don't even know where he lives."

"Mmmm. Well, I gotta go now, Henry. I'm gonna be late fer dinner." Danny wheeled his bike into motion.

"Sorry you couldn't come try on my new shoulder pads."

"Yeah. Maybe next time."

"Gee, I hope so," said Henry, hopefully.

Danny never heard the boy's parting remark. His brain churned with questions. Why was the man so interested in Doggie Blodgett's mourners? And what influence did he have with little Henry's father to permit him such liberties at a funeral?

Once before, Danny had dismissed any connection between the mystery man and the late departed Mr. Blodgett. Obviously he had been wrong. But what could the connection be?

And then there was the more immediate problem facing Danny, namely, arriving home late for dinner. It would be the third time this week. What could he tell his folks that would sound convincing?

CHAPTER 8

Sneakin' Out

"I – I was playing with Henry Rydzik," was the best Danny could manage as he confronted his questioning parents. They were having coffee in the living room. Dinner was long over; in fact, Doris was just finishing the dishes when the Danny had eased himself in quietly through the kitchen door.

"Mom and Pop are looking for you," was all Doris had to say after fixing him with a quizzical eye. His mother's expession clearly showed her anger. His father eyed him suspiciously.

"You mean the undertaker's boy?" Mrs. Van Kuyper took up the questioning.

"Yes'm."

"Where?"

"Over by his house."

"Doing what?"

"Oh, he got some new football stuff."

"Since when have you and Henry become friends?"

Danny shifted his weight uneasily, fearful of trapping himself with his tongue. "I see him at school once in awhile. He asked me to come over an' try on his new Green Bay Packer suit."

Now it was Mr. Van K's turn. "Did you like it?" he asked.

Danny's unease increased. He felt, if not a kinship, a similarity of minds with his father, which made the elder Van Kuyper that much harder for him to fool. "Oh, its okay, I guess," he finally managed.

"I understand you're playing a lot of ball at school these mornings," Danny's father continued.

"Some," Danny shrugged.

"And football at the park after school."

"A little," Danny shrugged again. Danny's father knew that the boy was not inordinately fond of team sports. And Danny knew he knew. He tried to read his father's face, but the senior Van Kuyper's features remained inscrutable behind his poised coffee cup.

Mrs. Van K took over the inquisition. "What's the matter with Homer Peckley nowadays? Aren't you and he friends anymore?"

"Sure we are," Danny replied, happy to return his attention to his mother. He could cope with her much more easily.

"When he comes over after school to call for you, he doesn't find you home anymore."

Danny said nothing, but his mother was obviously awaiting an explanation. "Guess he doesn't care much fer football," the boy finally managed, avoiding his father's stare.

Mrs. Van K turned to her husband. "He's your son, Ray," she said, neatly shifting the responsibility. "What are you going to do with him?"

Danny's father rocked thoughtfully in his corner chair. Without looking at him, Danny felt the man's eyes seeming to stare right through him. "Son," he spoke quietly, "if you're late again for dinner this month, it'll go hard on you."

"Yes sir," Danny mumbled.

"And you may do the dinner dishes alone for a week."

"Yes sir."

"Now go get yourself something to eat, and then plan on spending the rest of the evening in your room."

"Yes sir." Danny departed, relieved that his ordeal was concluded.

Mrs. Van Kuyper watched her son disappear behind the swinging door leading to the kitchen. "Ray, is he lying to us?" she asked her husband.

Ray Van Kuyper was sure of it, but he chose not to answer his wife directly. "Well, I'll tell ya, Elsie. I'm thinking maybe he's got a girl friend, but I just can't quite bring myself to believe it."

"Him? A girl friend? Don't be silly! Who?"

"How should I know?" Mr. Van Kuyper shrugged. "I'm not in the eighth grade."

* * * * * * *

Danny, burdened with a tray holding a cold beef sandwich, a bottle of root beer, four cookies, a salt shaker and two green apples, used his foot to slam shut the door to his room. He was grateful to have the premises to himself for awhile. He glanced at the clock on his desk; it was 7:30, an hour before his roommate, little brother Herbie, would be sent up to bed.

He set the tray on his desk, sat down, propped up the daily funny page, and proceeded to make inroads into his dinner. He was ravenously hungry; it had been a long time since lunch. But he couldn't concentrate on the comics. His mind was too full of what young Henry Rydzik had told him about the mystery man's odd behavior at Doggie Blodgett's funeral. Could the man possibly have been involved in Doggie's murder? If so, he was certainly acting most peculiar for a murderer.

Danny's head jerked up in response to a small, sharp noise, and his ears detected the sound of a pebble bouncing and rolling off the shingle roof. Quickly he strode to the front window and raised it quietly. Below, a figure was barely discernible in the heavy shadow cast by the largest of the four spruces lining the Van Kuyper front walkway.

"Hi stranger," came the quiet greeting. Danny recognized Homer's voice. He also noted the sarcasm.

"Whatcha up to?" he whispered back.

"What's wit'chu?" Homer demanded.

"I'm sentenced to jail up here fer the resta the night," Danny admitted disgustedly.

"Been out late playin' junior G-man again," Homer jeered.

"Yeah, well, *you* won't act so smart when I tell ya what *I* found out," Danny sneered back.

"That so? Well, ya kin tell me later t'night."

"T'night?"

"Yeah. Later. Kin yah sneak out?"

"I dunno. If my Dad catches me, I'll be dead. What time?"

"'Bout 11:30. Meet me under duh pier at our boat yard."

"What for? What are we…?"

"Shh!" The Van Kuyper's' front porch light flashed on. Homer had already slid to the ground and rolled under the spreading spruce. Danny quickly lowered his window and ducked below the level of the sill.

Ray Van Kuyper, newspaper in hand, emerged from the house, walked to the edge of the porch and carefully looked about. Then he looked up at the bright oblong of light coming from Danny's window. Glancing around at the still scene once more, he started down the steps, then changing his mind, he retreated slowly back into the house, muttering to himself. The porch light blinked out.

On hands and knees, Danny crawled quietly to the bedroom door. Carefully he turned the knob, eased the door open slightly, and placed his ear to the crack.

"I'll swear I heard voices out there," Danny heard his father say, his words barely audible above the din of the TV. "Herbie, go on upstairs and see if your brother is okay."

"Aw, can I wait fer the commercial?" pleaded the Cute Little One.

"Sure, son," replied the indulgent Mr. Van Kuyper. Danny smiled as he eased the door shut and crawled over to the window. Carefully he eased it open. Below the shadows swayed as a gust of November wind buffeted the nearest street lamp.

"Hey, Homer," came Danny's husky whisper. But there was no reply.

"Homer?" Danny tried once more. Utter stillness. Homer had obviously departed the scene at first opportunity. Again Danny eased the window shut and padded quietly to his desk, where he resumed his solitary dinner.

Munching on the second apple, Danny pondered Homer's invitation to a late hour prowl. Homer rarely initiated any nocturnal exploits, but the few he did had proved to be interesting and profitable. And the intriguing aspect about tonight's call to wander was that they would be meeting so close to Homer's house, under the pier at Peckley's boatyard.

Tiny footsteps charging up the stairs signaled the imminent arrival of little Herbie. Must be time for the TV commercial, Danny thought. He resolved that when his little brother did finally retire for the evening, he would keep the little chatterbox awake and talking until at least 10 p.m. That way Herbie would be more certain to sleep soundly all night long.

CHAPTER 9

Midnight Rendezvous

"Pssst! Homer!" It was a dark, moonless night to begin with, and underneath Peckley's pier it was positively black.

"Here!"

Homer's whisper startled Danny even though he was expecting to hear it. Homer switched on an electric lantern to illumine himself sitting in a small rowboat afloat at the side of the pier. Danny moved gingerly down the catwalk leading out under the pier, feeling for the board trusses which angled down to the supporting pilings. He ducked under a half dozen of these before he reached the boat. Homer doused the light as Danny eased himself into the stern of the craft.

"What the heck are we doin' out here?"

"Shaddap until I get us away from duh house," cautioned Homer. He pushed the boat away from the pier, silently slipped the oars into the black waters of the Wausupee, and with practiced ease rowed a soundless course toward the center of the river, angling upstream. The gloom was nearly total, making the river appear wider and deeper than Danny knew it to be. A few street lights were visible, particularly upstream where the Central Avenue Bridge crossed the river, beneath which the weighted corpse of Doggie Blodgett had been discovered. Across the river, on the north side, yard-lights dimly lit the exterior and the giant smokestack of the papermill.

"O.K., so what's new wit' you?" asked Homer, finally breaking the silence.

Quickly Danny detailed for his friend the curious behavior of Mrs. McClatchy's mysterious boarder at Doggie Blodgett's funeral, as recounted by Henry Rydzik, Jr. "So howdaya like them ashes?" he concluded smugly.

"Maybe he's wunna dem amachoor movie nuts," Homer cackled quietly as he continued to row.

Danny was miffed. "So ya think I been wastin' my time, huh?"

"Not anymore," Homer was suddenly serious. "That's why I come tuh fetch ya t'night."

"Huh?" Danny leaned forward intently. For tonight, at least, it appeared that Homer had no plans for fun and frolic hidden up his jacket sleeve. The redhead was apparently bent on serious business. "Whatcha been up to, buddy?" Danny queried his chum.

"Nuttin'. I ain't been up tuh nuttin'. I jist happened tuh hear sumpthin' is all."

Danny waited impatiently for his friend to continue, but Homer had paused his rowing and was intently studying the south bank of the river. Danny turned his head to peer in same direction. The darkness seemed to offer very little to see.

"I think I'll row upstream a liddle furder, get close to duh bank, den let duh current carry us under."

"Under where?"

"Dere." Homer pointed, and commenced rowing again.

Again Danny studied the south bank of the river. The view from midstream was strange to him, and the darkness didn't help any, but with the aid of the balefully flickering neon sign over the front door, Danny recognized the Snug Harbor tavern. The squat, shingled building occupied most of a short, wide pier extending out over the Wausupee.

"The Snug Harbor!" Danny exclaimed, and recollections stirred in his brain. Sensational newspaper articles in the not-too-distant past. "That's the place where Doggie Blodgett used to be the bartender!"

"Yeah. My ol' man guzzles dere. He sez itsa great place fer boat bizness contacts. Leastways, dat's what he tells my ol' lady."

"That's the last place Doggie was seen alive!"

"Yeah. Didja know he usta play bar dice wit' my ol' man?"

"Yer Pa knew 'im?"

"A liddle. 'Course, he weren't in town long 'fore somebody croaked 'im."

"Whatcha hear that gotcha excited enough to haul me out here t'night?"

"Sumpthin' at supper -- my ol' man ain't said much 'bout dis Blodgett murder bizness. He knows my ol' lady ain't keen 'bout him spending' time n' money at da Snug Harbor. But t'night he wuz worried."

"'Bout what?"

"Well, da way he tells it – an' I t'ink he's leavin' out a few t'ings - he sez he wuz havin' a beer at da Snug Harbor dis mornin', an' nobody dere but him n' Sharkey Bates, da guy what owns da place. Well," Homer abruptly angled the rowboat toward the south bank. "Dis strange guy comes in n' sits way at duh udder enda duh bar. Sharkey quick goes over by him, but first he loads duh juke box. My ol' man t'inks he done dis so he ain't supposed t'hear dem talk."

"But yer Pop heard 'em anyhow," Danny guessed.

"Yeah. My ol' man kin hear a trout surface at a hunnert yards."

Homer shipped the oars and let the boat begin to drift on an apparent collision course with the Snug Harbor pier. The sputtering red and blue neon trim over the tavern door cast a garish glow into the seemingly deserted parking area. However, the faint tinkle of canned music emanating from the tavern attested to some sort of activity within.

"Anyways, dis strange guy sez t'night at midnight comes da bagman wit' payday fer Doggie Blodgett…"

"Money for Doggie?" Danny interjected. "That's kooky, him bein' dead two months now."

"Geez, will yuh lissen? I t'ink dey mean it diff'runt." He lowered his voice to a whisper as they began to drift close to the Snug Harbor pier. "So dis strange guy sez any trouble wit da local fuzz? An' Sharkey sez no, dey figger outa town hoods what knew Doggie before done 'im in, an' dey ain't lookin' too hard. An' duh strange guy he sez good, dat winds it up. An' Sharkey says bad, dere's some stranger in town what was nosin' aroun' Doggie's funeral, which din't bodder him 'tic'arly, but dis guy was still nosin' around town, which bodders him plenty!"

The fascinated Danny sat immobilized by Homer's tale, but the alert Homer slid to the bow of the boat and caught the first of the oncoming pier pilings with his hands, thus silently arresting the motion of the craft.

"What else did yer Pop hear?" Danny whispered. He couldn't wait, but Homer could. Using his hands, Homer guided the small boat through the maze of pilings and trusses into the intense gloom beneath the pier to a point approximately under the tavern's main entrance. Some ten feet overhead, the boards creaked as somebody walked about inside the tavern. The tinny music quit, and several coarse voices could be heard distinctly as they debated the donation of a quarter to reactivate the record player.

"Wish dey'd leave it empty; we could hear better," Homer voiced his opinion on the matter. "T'ink it's midnight yet, Danny?"

"Pert near. Yer Pa hear anythin' else?" Danny persisted.

"Almost time fer duh bagman, whatever dat is."

"They must mean like a money bag. Now, darn it, Homer, finish tellin' me what yer Pa heard!"

"I did."

"Make sense, will ya?"

"Well, when Sharkey said what he said, dis guy got nervisser, an' he look mean at my ol' man, an' my ol' man, he got nervousser, so he quick finished his beer an' blowed da joint."

"Nuts!"

"Don't moan. My ol' man sez he's sorry he even heerd what he heerd, but it sounded so fishy he wundered should he call duh cops. An' my ol' lady tells 'im mind yer own bees wax and stop drinkin' in cruddy joints 'fore yuh finds yerself on duh river bottom like Blodgett, weighed down wit'cher own boat anchors."

"So yer Pa didn't call the cops," Danny surmised.

"Naw. He jist went down to duh boat shed n' got quiet drunk."

Overhead, the record player resumed its tinkling music. Sounds of ponderous stomping and shuffling might have been those of some lead-footed couple dancing. Once the steps seemed to stagger, and for a moment the din of coarse laughter dominated the chilly darkness beneath the pier.

Danny, his hands thrust deep into his jacket pockets, hunched his shivering shoulders and snuggled his chin deeper into the warm woolen collar. He could barely see Homer, seated in the bow of the boat with one arm wrapped around a piling, silhouetted against the distant glint of the paper mill's yard lights.

Both boys sat quietly now, wondering if the midnight hour had already come and gone. Danny also mulled over the fruits of Mr. Peckley's unintentional eavesdropping. Could the stranger in town that Sharkey Bates was concerned with, and the one that Danny had been shadowing, be the same man?

Suddenly Danny poked his head out of his jacket like a turtle and cocked an ear toward the front of the tavern.

"Shh!" Homer cautioned, unnecessarily. The crunch of tires sounded in the gravel parking lot, the noise growing louder as a heavy car rolled right up to the edge of the pier. The quiet rumble of a powerful engine suddenly ceased. Silence, then the sound of a car door opening, then gently shut.

A single pair of footsteps, first on the gravel, then striding quietly on the wooden pier toward the front door. Past the front door. Out on the pier clear around to the Snug Harbor's back door. The two boys listened breathlessly. Without knocking, without pause, whoever it was simply opened the back door and went in. They heard first the screen door and then the inside door eased shut.

"That's Sharkey's office back there," Homer whispered, putting the boat into motion with his hands, feeling for the trusses and the pilings. "Watch yer head."

Danny had confidence in Homer's information. What with Mr. Peckley being a steady customer of the bar, he was sure that Homer had been on the premises before.

Overhead, a single steady tread was heard to move from the area of the bar room toward the rear of the building. A door was opened and closed, the footsteps continued, then another door was opened and shut, even as the boys glided silently under the advancing sound. The bar room noises faded as they moved away from them.

Homer eased the boat to a halt, not ten feet from the end of the pier. Danny could almost feel it better than he could see it; a small platform, suspended between two stout pilings. The boat gently bobbed against it.

"Dere's like a step-ladder nailed to it," Homer whispered. "Goes straight up intuh Sharkey's office."

"Through the floor?"

"Trapdoor. My ol' man sez dat's how dey useta sneak in duh booze durin' pro'bish'n."

Thanks to TV, Danny had a rough idea of the doings of the prohibition era. It struck him that his present surroundings afforded a perfect setting to stage a liquor smuggling scene. Grasping the platform, Danny eased himself onto it and out of the boat.

"Whadaya doin'?" inquired the startled Homer.

"I wanna hear better," Danny whispered back, groping for the ladder. He found it, attached firmly to one of the pilings, running straight up toward the voices above. Cautiously, Danny began his ascent.

"Danny! Cum back here! We'll get caught!"

"Shhh!"

"Nice ta see ya again, Mr. Guzman," boomed an overly-friendly voice above.

"Nice to see you again, Sharkey," replied a quieter, sterner voice. "Here, I've got an early Christmas present for you." Danny heard a faint plop. "It's all there – five grand."

"Thanks, Mr. Guzman. Youse guys really deliver, as promised."

"Unlike your previous affiliation, our organization truly takes care of those who co-operate."

"Nice, real nice. But ya know I ain't been active fer years. Maybe that's the trouble. There ain't much lefta the ol' gang."

"True. You've pinpointed the problem precisely. The remnants of a decaying organization are easy prey for the law, and break down readily under the pressure of questioning. Something about rats deserting a sinking ship."

"Not me!" protested Sharkey Bates.

"No, not you," Mr. Guzman reassured him quietly. "You retired long before that particular ship started sinking."

"Yeah, that's what Doggie tol' me he was doin' – retirin' from the rackets. Even had a new ID, phony bartender's license, the whole bit. Me, I was more'n happy tuh help an ol' pal. But when I finally figgered out that he was jist hidin' out until the Chicago grand jury met…"

"His testimony would have been highly injurious to a great many of us. He *had* to be silenced."

"An' if the word got around I was harborin' a stoolie, I'da been just as dead. Doggie didn't do me no favor, comin' here."

"You were very wise to bring his whereabouts to our attention. It not only saved your life, but netted you a nice reward as well."

"Wish your boys had dumped him someplace else, though. I wasn't figgerin' on answerin' any questions."

"Blodgett gave the boys considerable trouble, and he had to be eliminated immediately. They were understandably reluctant to transport a body any great distance, even at night, and your river seemed most handy. Unfortunately, the boys aren't used to your clear northern streams. Had the body been a mere two feet deep in the Chicago River, it would never have been spotted. Was the questioning that much of an ordeal?"

"Not bad. The Chicago cops came an' went in two days. The local fuzz I know good. No problem. I been here over 20 years now. I just points to the phony bartender's license an' sez I hired this guy named John Wood. Who is this Doggie Blodgett yer talkin' about? All wide-eyed an innercent, ya know. They quit on me inna hurry!" Sharkey stomped his foot gleefully as he laughed, and the jolt of it made Danny jerk his ear away from the trap door.

The man called Mr. Guzman resumed the conversation, but now his tone grew more sinister. "I spoke with Duke after he talked with you this morning. I understand we might have a new problem."

"Yeah. There's this strange galoot hangin' round town. I figger him fer a hit man from the ol' mob."

"How so?"

"I go tuh Doggie's funeral, see? After all, the guy worked fer me fer three weeks, so I figger it's expected. Nobody claims the body, so the city's stuck wit it. Lotsa people there, but all just nosey types, or cops, or reporters. Doggie woulda been flattered by the turnout, but not a tear in the place. Anyways, I'm lookin' particular fer anybody from the ol' mob. I don't see anybody, or anybody what even looks like a hood, yuh know?"

"Yes. Go on," encouraged Mr. Guzman.

"So I'm lookin' the place over good. Then I see this shadow behind a screen. Outline, kinda. Not the undertaker – too big. Then Doggie gets carted out. Everbody else leaves. But not that guy behind the screen! I go sit in my car an' watch. Purty soon I spots 'im lookin' outa upstairs window. I can't tell what he's doin'. Anyways, he's really eye-ballin' the crowd. So I drive a block away an' wait. Finally he comes out, after everybody else is long gone. He's hoofin' it, so I do, too. I tailed him to a boardin' house on Packard Avenue."

Danny, near paralysis from clinging tightly to the steep ladder, could not restrain a gasp. They were talking about his man!

"Odd, but not particularly suspicious," Mr. Guzman put in. "Probably another cop or maybe a reporter."

"Wait. I ain't done. I gotta regular customer here who also boards at that place. So I feel him out, casual-like. That guy was there a week *before* Doggie was bumped! That's even before I called you guys about Doggie. An' remember, the fuzz was lookin' fer Doggie, too, so if he's a cop, why'nt he grab Doggie before you guys could get to him? An' my customer says this guy don't see nobody, or talk to nobody; he don't do nuthin'. Just walks aroun' town. Once I thought I seen him casin' my place from up the river, usin' spy-glasses yet! He gives me the creeps."

"Since you feel that he might be a member of your former group, did he look at all familiar to you?"

"Naw, I didn' get a real good look at 'im, but I'm sure I don't know 'im. I figger he's gotta be somebody hidin' out with Doggie. Nuthin' else figgers."

"You'd think that upon hearing of Blodgett's fate, he'd promptly leave town."

"Why should he? Nobody went after him. So he figgers nobody knows he's here. He's figgerin', after what happened to Doggie, who'd figger another stoolie to hide out in this burg? I don't like him. Even from a distance, he looks too smart. But he don't know I'm onto him," Sharkey chuckled.

"If he did, you just might be…"

"Yeah, I know." Sharkey made a choking sound. "Like I said, he gives me the creeps."

"I'll send Duke back tomorrow to investigate this fellow. With the grand jury convening next week, we can't afford to have another possible informer running around loose."

"Fine. But this time, give 'im a ride clear back to Chicago, okay?" Sharkey pleaded.

Mr. Guzman chuckled. Once. Quietly. There was the sound of chair legs scraping on the floor.

"What the heck?" The chair and its occupant went crashing to the floor. The trap door thumped lightly as it bopped Danny's pressing ear. "How clumsy of me," it was Mr. Guzman. "My chair seemed to have caught on something."

"Look out!" Sharkey shouted, his own chair tumbling as leaped to his feet. Kicking Mr. Guzman's chair aside, he yanked open the trap door.

CHAPTER 10

"Sharkey" Bait

Their faces were a mere four feet apart. They stared at each other, startled. Sharkey Bates was startled and enraged. Danny Van Kuyper was startled and petrified. The boy blinked rapidly in the sudden flush of yellow light.

Despite his 60-plus years and his considerable bulk, Sharkey Bates could still move with fair agility. He dropped to his knees and grabbed at Danny's jacket collar. The grasp of that huge, hairy paw spurred Danny into action. The boy jerked violently to one side, pushed off from the ladder, and felt himself arch out into the blackness. His shoulder struck something. An instant later he was totally immersed in the black ink of the Wausupee.

Danny surfaced, gasping for breath. From overhead there came furious scrambling sounds, angry voices. The yellow shaft of light shining through the open trap door lit the scene dimly, centering on the tiny platform at the foot of the ladder. Fighting the weight of his soaked clothing, Danny strained to see through the forest of pilings. No rowboat. No Homer.

The light suddenly disappeared as the bulk of Sharkey Bates filled the trap doorway. It reappeared again as he cleared the doorway and rapidly descended the ladder. Then Sharkey was on the platform, the long tube of a six-cell flashlight visible in his hand. He flicked it on. Its bright beam shot through the darkness, dancing crazily amongst the pilings as he played it about. He concentrated on Danny's area, having observed the direction of Danny's fall.

"Do you see anything?" It was Mr. Guzman's voice, coming down through the trap door.

"Not yet. But it was just a kid, I tell ya', just a kid."

"Nevertheless, this is a most serious turn of events. We have to assume he heard enough to be dangerous to us."

The bright flashlight beam continued to probe the darkness. Danny, for a change grateful to be as thin as he was, clung to the dark side of a piling, his submerged arms wrapped around it for support. He gauged himself to be no more than 15 feet away from Sharkey. He didn't dare move.

"Did you recognize him at all?" Mr. Guzman's voice again.

"Naw, I don't see too many kids around here." Then Sharkey added grimly, "But I'll know'm next time I see 'im." Danny shivered.

"What bothers me," Sharkey continued, "is how he got out here. I don't see no boat."

A pause, then Mr. Guzman's voice, ominous. "Perhaps he had a confederate," he said.

"Geez, I hope not," Sharkey said worriedly. "This thing's startin' to get too tricky fer me."

Sharkey played the light more deliberately now, moving from piling to piling. Frightened, Danny watched the bright beam zigzag slowly in his direction, first way out, then closer in, then out, then in; now the brilliant halo of light centered on Danny's piling. Terrified, Danny held his breath.

"There he is," Sharkey announced quietly.

"You've located him?"

"Yeah. I kin see his hands underwater where he's hangin' on to the pilin'. C'mere junior," Sharkey called out, his tone decidedly unaffectionate. "Yer Uncle Sharkey wants to talk to ya."

Danny's heart sank. He shot a glance through the maze of pilings heading toward the shore. Then he turned his face toward the dark river. Where was Homer? Why, the only logical place to be, if you're in a boat! Taking a deep breath, he ducked under the water and kicked off from the piling, but the weight of his wet clothing slowed him drastically. After barely clearing the end of the pier, he was forced to surface for air.

Gasping and choking as he broke the water, Danny turned his head to look back. The bright flashlight beam snaked back and forth across the water; suddenly it was right in his eyes. A sharp sound split the stillness, accompanied by a peculiar "zip!" past his ear.

"Good gravy!" Frantically Danny plunged back underwater even as the sound effects were repeated.

When he finally surfaced again, he was farther downstream than out into the river, having decided to take advantage of the current to offset the drag of his clothes. He saw that his manuever had paid an unexpected dividend; the probing of the light beam was being concentrated toward midstream.

Panting, weary to the point of exhaustion, Danny was content to drift with the current for the moment as he regained his breath. He considered shucking the weight of his water-logged jacket in order to ease the effort of staying afloat.

"Mom would die if I lost this jacket," he reconsidered, "And Pop would kill me!" He discarded the idea completely.

Now the flashlight beam was swinging in wider and wider arcs. Danny quaked at the thought of being rediscovered by Sharkey Bates, anxious marksman.

As noiselessly as he could, he began to stroke for the near shore.

Swimming sidestroke enabled him to keep the light beam constantly in view. The searching shaft of light arced back toward Danny now, and kept coming. Agitating the water as little as possible, he took a deep breath and submerged. He watched the surface above him brighten, darken, and then turn bright again. His lungs felt as though they would burst, but he was afraid to exhale even a bubble of air.

At long last the welcome blackness returned. The grateful lad resurfaced, his tortured lungs sucking in the sweet night air. A quick glance upstream showed him that the accursed light beam was now working the far side of the Snug Harbor pier. Danny resumed his swim to shore, stroking more rapidly now.

"Danny?" came Homer's tremulous whisper. "Is dat you, Danny?"

"Homer!" the exhausted swimmer was barely able to reply. "For Pete's sake, where are you?"

"Down here. Jist drift some."

Danny drifted. An indistinct shape loomed high and black against the faint starlight. Something brushed the boy's face. Danny pulled his hand out of the water and used it to identify a cluster of drooping willow branches.

"Here." Homer's whisper seemed practically in Danny's ear. He bobbed under the branches, felt his feet touch the river bottom, and came up against the boat. As he clutched at it, he felt Homer's warm, dry hand grasp his wrist.

"Not up over duh side, ya ninny," admonished the young boatman. "Yuh'll tip us over." Homer guided his soggy companion to the stern of the boat and dragged him aboard. For a long moment Danny lay draped over the stern seat board, panting, trembling, draining. The dry wood felt warm and comforting to his benumbed face and hands.

"Here comes dat blasted light again," Homer warned. "Don't move."

Don't worry, Danny thought, feeling incapable of raising a finger. Nevertheless, he felt himself grow tense as the sudden brightness bloomed about them. Out of the corner of his eye, he could see the thick spread of branches hanging down from the giant willow looming overhead. Most of the yellow leaves had already fallen, but enough remained to form an effective camouflage. If nobody moved.

Suddenly the probing light winked out, and darkness reigned over the quiet river. Danny raised his wet head and peered toward the Snug Harbor. Still visible was the yellow light falling through the trap door. But all at once it, too, went out.

"Time tuh blow dis place," announced Homer, shoving the boat away from the steep bank. Danny felt the brush of a droopy willow bough as the boat cleared the sheltering tree.

"Think we might be better off walkin' home?" the still prone Danny suggested.

"Are yuh kiddin'?" Homer choked. "If dis boat's missin' in duh mornin', my ol' man'll skin somebody. Mos' likely me." And then he asked, "Are yuh okay, Danny?"

"Yeah, I guess so," the other boy replied, too numb to be certain and too tired to care. "What happened to you?"

"Nuttin' much," Homer talked as he rowed. "When dat trap door opened, I backed off, an' when I seed you jump inna river, I cut out an' made fer dem willa trees. I figgered if ya din't get caught er make fer shore, yuh'd cum by me sooner er later. An' den…" Homer's voice filled with awe, "I seed Sharkey spotcha off da pier. An' he *shot* atcha, din't he?"

Danny nodded, a rather useless gesture in the dark. "I think so," he replied.

"Twice yet! Geez, I tol' ya not tuh go up dat ladder!"

"I had to hear what they said. Didja hear what I heard?"

"No," Homer admitted. "I din't hear much after dey started talkin' serious-like. I jis' heerd it was Sharkey, an' he call dat udder guy Mr. Goozman."

"Well, I heard it all," Danny replied, and his voice and spirits rose as he warmed to his subject. "Ya know what it is? It's a gang war, like on TV! Doggie Blodgett was in a gang, an' he was gonna tell some jury in Chicago, an' these guys from some other gang killed 'im. An' now they're gonna get after that weird duck at Mrs. McClatchy's, 'cause they figure he was in Doggie's gang an' hidin' out here with him, an' now Sharkey's afraid of him."

"Gee!" responded Homer, awe-struck and forgetting to row. Then he snorted. "But den dat don't make no sense, Doggie comin' here tuh hide at Sharkey's place…"

"But Doggie an' Sharkey useta be inna same gang. Sharkey has *changed sides*."

"Duh fink! Duh traitor!" Homer exclaimed indignantly. "I knowed I never liked him."

"Well, it's a good thing he din't see ya, since he knows ya."

"Yeah!" Homer shivered. "But he seed you."

"Yeah."

"Whatcha gonna do?"

"I dunno. Just stay away, I guess."

"But ya can't stay away ferever. Not in dis liddle town. An' he's gonna be lookin' fer ya. Maybe you should call duh cops."

"Oh, sure, an' get my name in the papers, an' have all those crooks lookin' fer me. An' what do I tell my folks? Maybe," Danny said hopefully, "maybe Sharkey'll leave town. An' Doggie Blodgett's friend after him. Maybe they'll all shoot each other someplace else. Nobody will miss 'em. They're all crooks and killers anyhow."

The distant throb of a powerful engine instantly silenced Danny. Both boys stared back up stream. From the approximate locale of the Snug Harbor's pier a searchlight moved into view, its bright beam sweeping back and forth across the water.

"H-Holy Mackerel" Homer chattered. "Sharkey's speedboat. An' wit' a spotlight yet!"

Promptly he angled the rowboat toward the near bank, watching with Danny as the speedboat swung slowly toward the same shore, its searchlight probing the river bank. It seemed to pause near the willows. The boys stared wide-eyed as the brilliant beam picked its way through the jumbled cascade of branches.

"Homer, do ya think they saw us?"

"Dey sure knows where tuh look, don't dey? Duck yer head."

Danny ducked. Homer had rowed them under a piling-supported shed. On the far side, he eased their boat into a covey of rowboats and up to a low-level dock, hopped out of the boat with mooring rope in hand and quickly looped it through an iron ring. In back of them, the approaching speedboat was more readily seen now, catching the reflected glow of its probing light.

"Isn't this Peterson's boatyard?" Danny whispered as he stepped to the dock, his water-logged shoes squishing as he moved.

"Yeah. Quiet, er yuh'll have ol' man Peterson's dog chewin' our tails."

"Then how're we getting' off the dock?"

"We can't, so we ain't. Jis' folla me." Homer padded silently down a catwalk leading under the boatshed. Danny came squishing after. The speedboat was less than fifty yards distant now, the muffled thunder of its engine throttled to a low pitch. The boys ducked under the boatshed.

"Here," Homer had to whisper directly into Danny's ear to be heard. "Dere's room on toppa dese cross-beams if yuh squeeze in. Hurry."

Danny felt for the nearest cross-beam, one of several supporting the floor joists of the boatshed. There was barely space enough between the joists to crawl through, and even then he would have to hold his tired body taut to keep from draping over the beam like a piece of wet laundry. The oncoming searchlight swept toward the boatshed. Danny squeezed.

The speedboat, sleek and powerful, eased up to the boatshed, its searchlight beam dancing amongst the spread of pilings underneath. Danny blinked at the glare reflected off the water. Slowly the speedboat inched past the end of the boatshed, its searchlight sweeping the adjoining dock.

The rumbling motor quit, causing a thick silence to prevail. Terrified, not daring to breathe, the boys held themselves rigid within the cramped confines of their hiding places.

"What's the matter?" Danny recognized Mr. Guzman's voice. "Why did you turn off the engine?"

"That's odd," came the puzzled tone of Sharkey's voice. "See that, Mr. Guzman?"

A pause, and then: "I'm sorry, Sharkey, but I fail to comprehend…"

"That one boat there, the green one wit' the black trim."

"So?"

"So it don't belong there. If I ain't mistaken, them's Josh Peckley's colors. He's a reg'lar at my place." Silently the boys cursed Sharkey Bates' accurate memory.

"Hmmm. Does this Mr. Peckley have a young son?"

"Yeah, but I know the kid. A ugly redhead. He weren't the one on the ladder. I'd a knowed him inna flash."

Homer bit his tongue. His already low opinion of Sharkey Bates reached new depths. But his miff gave way to renewed concern as the probing searchlight again stabbed under the boatshed.

"Now what?" It was Mr. Guzman again.

"I thought I heard sumpthin'."

Drip.

"Hear that?"

"Hear what?"

Drip.

"That." The searchlight beam slid along the catwalk. Danny ground his teeth in silent anguish, hating his soggy shoes. He tried turning up his toes.

Drip!

The searchlight dodged back. A distant howl arose, followed by a fury of barking which rushed up to the end of the dock. The searchlight swung to illuminate the noisy animal, and then blinked out. Sharkey swore.

"Ol' Pete Peterson's hound. We better..." His voice disappeared in the roaring ignition of his craft's powerful engine. The boys listened gratefully as the fast-fading sound of it gave way to the triumphant barks of the dog.

"Fang! Here, Fang!" came a distant call.

"Ol' man Peterson," whispered Homer. The barking subsided, and the boys could hear the heavy animal lope back up the dock.

"Here, Fang. Here, boy." The voice was closer now, and soon mingled with the friendly whimpering of the dog. The boys heard something said about "...midnight joy riders at this time of the year..." as the sounds of man and dog faded away, back toward the Peterson house.

"Whew!" Homer permitted himself to drape over the crossbeam.

Danny was wordless as he eased his chilled, stiff, benumbed self to the catwalk. He eyed the dark river beyond the boatshed. The speedboat was out of sight, but its distant rumble could be plainly heard from the direction of downstream. "We're gonna have to wait fer them to double back," he said finally.

"Yeah, but dey won't be comin' back here, not wit' dat hound raisin' Cain," Homer declared, almost cheerfully. And then a note of pique entered his voice: "Didja hear'm call me ugly? Does dat ol' buzzard t'ink he's beeootiful? I'm gonna fix him!"

"He just recent told on a man, Homer, and it got him killed." Danny's tone was somber. Suddenly, so was Homer's.

"Yeah." A pause. "Danny, What are we gonna do?"

"I dunno. Right now I just wanna go home'n go to bed."

The silence resumed, nearly total except for the faint hum of the speedboat engine. Now it grew louder, but it was soon apparent that the boat was staying to the far side of the river. Occasionally its spotlight showed briefly, searching out a stretch of riverbank. Other than that, the boys had to follow the craft's progress by ear. Sharkey Bates was showing no running lights tonight.

At last it drew well past them, and finally the sound of the engine died. "Dey're back at Snug Harbor," Homer said. "Let's go home."

* * * * * * *

Danny crept down the ladder from the loft of the Van Kuyper's garage, stark naked. He didn't dare take a stitch of his soiled and sodden clothing into the house with him. After they dried, he would sneak them into the family laundry. Except for the jacket, of course; that could be a problem.

Shivering in the nippy night air, his teeth chattering like castanets, Danny was nevertheless grateful for the moonless night. He trotted across the back lawn and quietly let himself in through the basement window, glad he had been prudent enough to leave it unlocked for just such emergencies. Spent as he was, he doubted if he could have managed a rooftop entry tonight.

Carefully he felt his way across the familiar basement and tiptoed up the stairs, avoiding the two well-known squeakers. Stillness reigned in the kitchen, save for the hum of the luminous-dialed stove clock. It was coming up on 3 a.m.

The swinging door leading out of the kitchen had been left propped open, thank goodness. Beyond there – down the hall, up the stairs, right up to his bedroom door – it was carpet all the way. Nevertheless, his anxiety mounted with each step of the stairs. He would be hard pressed for an explanation if he should be discovered totally nude.

Trembling, leaning against the wall for support, he paused at the top of the stairs to listen. He was rewarded with the sounds of slow, even breathing coming from behind closed doors, plus his mother's gentle snore.

Quickly he tiptoed down the hall and eased through his bedroom door, shutting it noiselessly behind him. Again he paused. Silence from the direction of little brother Herbie.

A feeling of gratitude far beyond his ability to express it filled Danny as he crawled under the covers. He was bone tired, but only now, as he tried to settle himself with some degree of comfort, did he become aware of the throb in his left shoulder. He had a vague recollection of striking something when he launched himself from the ladder beneath the Snug Harbor.

A myriad of questions welled and blurred in his mind, but he was too exhausted to try to sort them out, much less attempt to cope with them.

"You sure were in the baf'room a long time," piped the Cute Little One, his quiet soprano breaking the dark stillness. But Danny didn't hear him.

CHAPTER 11

Miss Hecker Has a Heart

The 3:30 p.m. bell rang, signaling the end of the class day at Lincoln School. And the school week, as well, for it was Friday afternoon.

"Class dismissed," announced Miss Hecker in her typical curt fashion, and the eighth grade buzzed with the happy clamor of departing students anticipating the freedom of the week-end.

But Danny Van Kuyper remained seated at his desk. He would wait until the class emptied before he started writing "I must not fall asleep in class" one hundred times.

"Must have been a rough night," Butchie Brockman sneered as he walked by. If you only knew, Randolph, Danny had to smile to himself. Jennifer Markham favored him with a sympathetic look as she filed past, but his downcast eyes failed to meet hers.

"See ya later, pal," Homer clucked sympathetically, patting Danny on the shoulder as he passed by. Danny winced, grimaced in pain. Homer had unintentionally selected the wrong shoulder. But it figured. It had been that kind of day.

Getting up in time for school that morning had been a nearly impossible chore. Danny had considered feigning illness – certainly he felt bad enough to be sick – but he dreaded the questions his mother would surely ask, the hazards of being at her mercy the entire day. Besides, little brother Herbie had already started the day badly for him. He had informed their mother that Danny had again slept without pajamas.

"Haven't I told you a thousand times not to go to bed in your underwear?" Danny's mother greeted him as the sleep-deprived boy groped toward the breakfast table.

"He didn't have *nuthin'* on when he got up this mornin', momma," volunteered Herbie. Danny shuddered, hoping the Cute One's observation would escape their mother. But she had propped back Danny's head and was looking under his chin. "Well, at least you're wearing a clean undershirt this morning," she had observed. "That's something."

And then, as he had prepared for school, there had been the matter of his jacket. More precisely, the lack of his jacket.

"Where's your jacket?" Mrs. Van Kuyper had asked as her shirt-sleeved son had opened the door on the chill, gray November morning. Danny had hoped to slip away unobserved. Now he was forced to think hard and fast.

"I – I musta left it at Henry Rydzik's last night, Mom," he tried.

"Goodness sake, Danny, what's gotten into you lately? Put on your heavy sweater, then, and make sure you get that jacket back right after school. It's supposed to see you through the winter."

So Danny had spent the day struggling in and out of his bulky blue sweater, each turn at it a painful trial for his sore shoulder.

The class was empty now, except for Danny and Miss Hecker, and she was standing over him. "The sooner you get started, young man, the sooner we can both go home," she said.

"Yes Ma'am." He fumbled for a tablet and pencil as Miss Hecker perched herself on the desk in front of him. He could feel her eyes on him.

"What's the matter with you today, Daniel?" she asked. "You don't appear to be your usual self."

"I don't feel so good, Ma'am," he said truthfully. With her hand Miss Hecker gently raised his chin and made him look at her. She studied his face intently.

"You don't look too well, either," she decided. "And I must say, you sneezed convincingly several times today. Perhaps you shouldn't have come to school today."

"Yes, Ma'am. I mean no, Ma'am."

"Well, I'm not about to punish somebody for being ill. You may go now. Take care of yourself over the week-end, and I hope you feel better on Monday."

"Yes, Ma'am. Thank you, Ma'am. Good bye, Ma'am."

The grateful youngster slid out of his desk seat and headed for the cloak room. Despite the thickening chill mist outdoors, he merely draped the heavy sweater over his shoulders and gave the sleeves one loose tie under his chin. The playground was nearly deserted as he popped out of the school door and headed homeward.

He'd have to get into the garage loft without being seen and see if his jacket had dried out yet, and then smuggle the rest of yesterday's clothes into the basement laundry chute. His old shoes would still be wet yet, for sure. He'd try to sneak those in behind the basement furnace.

Inexplicably, his thoughts suddenly reverted back to old Miss Hecker. She had been nearly decent to him. It was getting so a fella couldn't count on anything.

CHAPTER 12

Gruesome Discovery

Friday's thickening mist had given way overnight to light snow, and Saturday morning found the landscape powdered with a thin layer of the white stuff, the season's first snowfall. A dull, ragged sky churned by frigid gusts of wind hinted at more to come.

The snowfall's enchanting transformation of the scenery nearly completed the rejuvenation of Danny Van Kuyper's drooping spirits of yesterday. His clothes smuggling operation had been a success; his jacket had almost completely dried out in the warmth of the back hall.

Now he zipped the jacket up tightly under his chin as he emerged from the Van Kuyper household into the white morning. He noted that the garment still smelled of the river, and hoped that an airing in the day's brisk breezes would take care of that. Good thing that his mother had been content last evening merely to hear that the jacket was back. The smell, the dampness, and the peculiar round hole in the collar would have been difficult to explain.

Broom in hand, he attacked the light accumulation of snow on the front porch with as much vigor as his still tender shoulder would allow. He worked his way down the walk, and finally to the sidewalk in both directions to the property lines.

"Hey, lookit mamma's liddle helper," joshed Homer Peckley as he trudged up behind Danny, just in time to witness the completion of the sweeping operation. Homer tried making a snowball out of the light stuff, but it was too fine and powdery to pack well, and his fragile missile disintegrated in mid-flight as he threw it at his friend.

Danny retaliated by sweeping a broomful at the advancing red-head, succeeding in dusting him liberally from the cap down. Laughing, Danny broke for the back yard, the pursuing Homer vainly kicking up clouds of snow after him. The contest ended when Danny reached the safety of his garage.

"Hey, pal," the puffing Homer switched to a new subject. "Let's go trackin' dis mornin'. Perfeck day fer it."

"Where?"

"How 'bout along da river? Lotta critters go down to duh water."

"Not upstream, I hope?" Danny asked, envisioning a long detour around the Snug Harbor.

"Naw, not t'rough town. Down toward the lake. It's safer, fer sure."

Fine. They needed an opportunity for some serious private talk.

Danny checked out with his mother, and ten minutes later the boys slid down to the narrow, irregular strip of beach which paralleled the Wausupee's last few miles into Lake Michigan. Hornville disappeared behind them at the first bend of the river, and the stillness of the wintry morning closed about them.

There were plenty of tracks to see, all right, from assorted birds, small animals, and what appeared to be some deer. But the boys' interest in them was secondary. They swung their hiking sticks idly as the discussed their man-sized problems.

"Ever'thin' okay wit'chu at home?" Homer inquired.

"Yeah, no problems. But Herbie scared me yesterday mornin' with his big mouth."

Homer chuckled. "Sum-times I t'ink it's purty good, bein' a only chile."

"Well, Doris ain't so bad, fer a girl, but I dunno about Herbie. He don't show much promise."

"So, What we gonna do 'bout Sharkey?"

"Nuthin'. He didn't see you, an' he don't know me, so let's just stay away from him." Danny shivered suddenly. "Twice yesterday I jumped when I seen big guys drive by in cars."

"Was it him?" Homer asked nervously.

"No, but it sure made me nervous. I'm gonna stick to the alleys, comin' home from school. An' another thing – I ain't tailin' that guy at McClatchy's boardin' house no more. I found out more'n I want to know about him, an' if him an' Sharkey's gang are gonna tangle, I don't wanna get caught between."

"But don't it bodder yuh dat we knows who kilt Doggie Blodgett, and da cops don't?"

"Not that much. The cops kin find out all by theirselves. Maybe I'd feel diff'runt if Doggie weren't just another crook."

"But here's a chance to get our names in duh papers. Maybe a ree-ward even."

"Yeah, an' maybe holes in our head. I thought you was the guy who didn't like trouble!"

"Yeah, an' I t'ought you was duh guy what was gonna do big t'ings…"

"Right, an' I wanna stay alive to do 'em."

Homer shrugged. "Well, maybe yer right. Seems we should be able to do sumptin', d'ough. How about a a-non-ee-mus letter?"

"The more we stir things up aroun' Sharkey, the harder he an' that gang are gonna look fer us. Which could still get us the holes in the head, an' no credit in the papers."

"Hmmm."

The boys walked in silence awhile, stopped to poke at a snow-dusted thicket, flushed one frightened cottontail, but didn't bother to chase the rabbit as it bolted up the steep embankment. They resumed their walk, and Homer resumed their discussion.

"Seems a shame, but I s'pose yer right. Maybe jist as well to back off 'n leave things be. 'Sides, I got us anudder projeck."

Danny eyed his grinning friend suspiciously. Homer's last project had turned out to be quite a bit more than they had bargained for. Homer sensed Danny's apprehension.

"Naw, dis ain't like duh last one," the red-head reassured his friend. "Dis one's a snap, a cinch."

"Uh huh. Sure. I'm listenin'."

"You been past Brockman's butcher shop lately?" Danny shook his head. "Well, in da window, dey got dis big bottle," Homer used his arms to describe a sizeable object, "An' its fulla beans."

"So?"

"So itsa guessin' game. Duh customer what guesses closest how many beans in duh bottle wins a turkey bird fer T'anksgivin'!"

"Big deal. Whatchu gonna do with a dead turkey?"

"Dat ain't all," Homer's face registered his annoyance at being interrupted. "First prize also gets a choice – one a dem lean-back rockin' chairs what shakes yuh, or," and the red-head licked his chops, "Or a bran' new offishul-size racin' bike!"

Danny couldn't resist a bit of tongue in cheek. "So whatchu gonna do with a 'justable rockin' chair?' he asked, dead pan.

Homer kicked some snow-sprinkled gravel at him. "Yuh schnook! Duh bike!"

"I got a good bike."

"Well, I ain't! An' wit' duh boat biz'ness lousy an' my ol' lady sick so much, I know I ain't gonna get one fer Christmas. Jis' dumb clothes again, I bet, like last year. Me, I got all duh clothes I want. What I want is a bike."

"So you want I should go stand in fronta Butchie Brockman's house with ya an' help ya count beans in a bottle? Even with his Pa there, Butchie's likely to come out an' start a fight."

"Naw," Homer waved his hand disgustedly. "Jis' lookin' at duh bottle is fer schmoes. I'm in dere buyin' ham hocks las' night, ol' man Brockman sez "Yer fambly's been good customers, Homer; whyn'tcha fill out dis entry blank, stick it in duh box?" I take duh blank an' I sez I'll t'ink on it."

"When's the big drawin'?"

"Nex' Wednesday, just 'fore T'anksgivin'."

"Not much time," Danny mused. "Whatcha gonn do? Try to bribe Butchie at school Monday tuh tell ya how many beans in the bottle? Or maybe threaten to beat him up?" Danny teased.

"Don't be stoopid. I figger Butchie don't even know, 'cause ol' man Brockman ain't so stoopid, eider. Duh t'ing tuh do is take duh beans *outta* duh bottle an' *count 'em!*"

Danny's first impulse was to question the red-head's sanity, but his better judgment prevailed. "You got a plan," he guessed.

"Right!" Homer grinned, his bright blue eyes nearly disappearing in a crinkling of freckles. "An' I need yer help."

"When?"

"T'night. Kin yuh get out?"

"I guess, but what about the Brockmans?"

"Dey'll be gone. When I'm in duh store las' night, li'l Randolph is braggin' about dem goin' tuh Green Bay t'night an' visit relatives an' seein' duh Packers play t'morra. Ol' man Brockman's a big football fan."

"Nice! But how do we get in? They got a mean dog in that back yard."

"Easy. I got dat figgered." Homer's tone was smug. "Duh butcher shop is next by Ortman, duh tailor, right? An' next by dem is duh Majestic T'eater, right? An' backa duh t'eater dey got dat swing-up fire escape ladder yuh kin pull down wit' a long wire."

"And an iron ladder from the landing to roof," Danny recalled.

"Right, pal! Wit' a long board, we get on Ortman's roof, den tippy-toe we take duh board an' gets on Brockman's roof, den easy down tuh dere upstairs sun porch. I figger if duh door ain't unlocked, wunna dem windahs is. After dat, duck soup!"

Danny had to marvel at his friend's ingenuity. "The Ortmans are pretty old," he added thoughtfully. "They don't hear so good."

"Yeah, an' it's a war pitchur at duh Majestic. We ain't gonna stir up nobody," Homer smiled confidently.

So engrossed were the boys in their discussion they had taken little notice of their progress downriver. They had reached a point where the river narrowed and foamed over a stretch of rapids. The river bluffs, nearly a hundred feet high at this point, shot up steeply to the mixture of birch and pine edging their crests. Between the sharp rise of the bluff and the rapids, the beach narrowed to little more than a path. The boys paused to admire the familiar scene, now transformed by the coating of snow.

Overhead, the rumble of a large truck easing around the sharp bend of River Road broke the stillness. "Shouldn't we start back?" Danny suggested.

"It's early yet," countered Homer. "Let's go down t'duh lake an' t'row rocks at seagulls. Den we kin climb up t'duh road an' hitchhike home."

Danny nodded his assent, and took the lead along the narrow path. Soon both river and path turned abruptly to the right, bringing a gray stretch of Lake Michigan into view, framed between the bluffs. White caps on the lake were plainly visible, and the rhythmic sound of surf could be heard.

The beach widened again as the bluff broke away to form a deep, narrow ravine, coursed by a tiny brook splashing down to the Wausupee. It was a favorite camping spot for the boys, strewn with great splits of exposed rock and sheltered by a scattering of trees clinging to the steep sides. The boys studied appreciatively the changes a dusting of snow had wrought on their secret place.

It was Danny who first noticed the unexpected splash of metallic maroon coloring.

"What's that?" He pointed into the shadows of the ravine.

Now Homer saw it, too. "Beats me," he replied. "Let's go see." Danny took the lead up the steep crooked path, made slick by the snow.

It was a car. A big maroon Lincoln. The sleek rear end stuck straight up into the air, its horizontal, surfaces crusted with a light patina of snow. Snow clung to the tops of the wheels. The front end was crushed, partially wedged in a jumble of huge rocks, partially telescoped into the interior of the car.

The boys scrambled over the rocks, approaching the car from the driver's side. The door was badly buckled, but still closed. The window was rolled down.

Apprehensively, Danny peered inside. "There's a man in there!" he gasped.

"Yeah," Homer's voice was scratchy as he peered around Danny. "Anybody else?"

"I don't think so." Hesitantly, Danny poked his head through the open window. The still form of the man, clad in a lustrous tan topcoat, lay grotesquely crumpled over the bulge of the dashboard, wedged against the middle of the front seat. His head hung into the space vacated by the shattered windshield, with only the dark, neatly combed hair visible to Danny.

The motionless left arm, sprinkled with a scattering of powered snow, hung over the twisted steering wheel, the brown gloved hand hanging limply only inches from Danny's nose. Between glove and topcoat sleeve, a bare white patch of wrist. Danny touched it.

The boy yanked his hand back as though seared. "He's dead! I know he's dead!" His voice shook.

"Good gravy! How'dja t'ink he managed tuh get hisself kilt 'way in here?"

The boys looked up the steep wall of the ravine. Torn treetops, now etched with snow, clearly marked the path of the car's swift descent.

Homer answered his own question. "He musta come off dat River Road curve like a bat an' dived in here like a airplane," the red-head concluded aloud. "What'll we do?"

"We gotta tell somebody."

"Yeah."

Danny took the lead again. The boys circled the rock heap clutching the mangled car and continued to climb up the ravine. Soon they stood at the crest, only yards from the tight loop of River Road. Danny looked back and forth from the road to the now-obscured location of the car, trying to gauge where the car would have had to leave the road to end up where it did. He walked a few yards in the direction of Hornville, Homer tagging at his side. Most of the trees had been cleared from this area, but one small sapling lay prone, snapped off at the base. Even under the snow, the matted grass showed the double tire track headed straight for the lip of the ravine.

"He musta been asleep er sump'tin, tuh travel dat far wit'out turnin'," Homer observed.

"Or maybe he had a heart attack. I've heard of that happening," was Danny's suggestion. But then a puzzled look clouded his face.

"Why was his window rolled down?" he voiced quietly, as if to himself. "In this weather?"

"C'mon Homer, let's start hikin'. Maybe we can hitch us a ride."

"Hey, Danny," Homer speculated as the two of them stepped along, "*Now* we kin get our names in duh papers. An' pitchers, too, I bet. Maybe even a ree-ward!" He rubbed his palms in happy anticipation.

"I never heard a' gettin' a reward fer reportin' an accident," Danny scoffed.

"Why not? He looked rich. An' what a boat dat car is! Was," Homer corrected himself.

"I think we'd be smart to settle for one of them a-nonymous phone calls," Danny urged. "Nobody can do that poor guy back there anymore good anyhow."

"Are you nuts, pal?" Homer objected. "Leave all duh glory fer somebody else? An' maybe miss out on duh ree-ward? Nuttin' doin'!"

"Okay, Homer." Danny sounded annoyed. "When you get home, *you* phone the cops. Tell 'em all about it. Say *you* found him, all by yourself. Leave me out of it! I don't want my name in the papers. An' I sure as shootin' don't want my picture in the papers!"

"Okay, okay… any 'tin' yuh say. An' if dere's any ree-ward, I get tuh keep it all!"

"Fine with me."

Homer looked at his friend anxiously. "Yuh ain't mad er anyt'ing, are yuh, Danny?"

"No, I ain't mad."

"Yuh still comin wit' me t'night, aintcha?"

"Sure. What time?"

"'Bout 'leven, backa my place. Yuh'll hafta help me tote duh board."

The sound of a laboring engine behind them caught their attention. They turned to see a loaded hay truck wheel ponderously around the slick curve of River Road. Here was a ride to town, whether the driver chose to stop or not.

CHAPTER 13

Cheaters! Finks! Crooks!

Frigid gusts of night wind buffeted Danny and Homer as they crunched across the graveled, flat rooftop of the Majestic Theater. The long plank stretched between them was getting to be quite a burden. They had toted it more than a mile now, skulking through the darkened alleys of sleepy Hornville like a pair of thieves.

At Danny's urging – and Homer didn't need much – they had avoided the alley behind Miller's Bakery. As it was, the bakery and McClatchy's boarding house were only a block and a half away down Packard Avenue, close enough to make Danny in particular a trifle uneasy.

Getting the plank up the fire escape ladder had been a relatively easy chore; the resourceful Homer had brought along a long length of nylon cord. Peckley's boatyard seemed an inexhaustible source of useful materials. Now as the boys paused at the edge of the theater roof, they listened briefly to the muffled sounds of violent warfare blasting asunder the movie screen housed beneath their feet.

"'Sposed to be a good pitchur," Homer commented.

"Maybe we kin catch the matinee tomorrow – if we ain't in jail," Danny replied.

"Er duh hospital," Homer teased back, staring down into the dark chasm between the theater and Ortman's tailor shop. The brick-lined canyon was less than six feet wide, but the boys crossed it gingerly, each boy holding the plank in turn as the other inched over.

"Kinda gets to ya, the way it droops in the middle," Danny whispered.

"Yeah!" Homer gulped.

No trace of snow remained on the black asphalt rooftop of the tailor shop. The boys' tip-toed soundlessly above the sleeping Ortmans. The roof of Brockman's butcher shop had a gentle pitch to it, and at their closest points, sloped a little lower than the flat top of Ortman's place. The boys braced their board against a chimney protruding from Brockman's roof, and carefully slid down the sloping plank from roof to roof.

Danny gave a small sigh of relief as he grasped the reassuring solidity of Brockman's chimney. "Should we leave the board in place?" he whispered.

"Might as well. We gotta come back dis way." Homer led the way across the sloping shingles to the back of the building. Reaching the edge of the roof, they stretched out on their stomachs and peered over the eave. Despite the deep darkness, they could readily make out the high, white wooden railing enclosing the broad sun porch. The stout railing was anchored to the house wall barely three feet below them.

"I'll go first," volunteered the nimble Homer. "We'll help each udder down."

The boys gained the porch with ease. From the pitch black depths of the yard below came a low, deep-throated growl. Brockman's German shepherd.

"Never mind about him," Danny whispered. "Try the door."

The heavy storm door wouldn't budge. The adjoining window, however, slid open readily. The ecstatic Homer was nearly beside himself in silent glee. Parting the curtains, Danny eased himself into the darkened room, Homer close behind him. Reaching into his jacket pocket, Danny pulled out a large kitchen match and with practiced thumbnail snapped it into life. The sudden flaring flame revealed furnishings which plainly marked the room to be the lair of his perennial nemesis, Randolph Butchie Brockman.

"Where's yer candle?" Danny asked. Homer promptly produced it; the flame was transferred and the match blown out. Danny waved the expired match cool before thrusting it back into his pocket.

Fat candle held high, Homer led the way through the unfamiliar house – out to the hallway, down a steep, straight flight of enclosed stairs to the street floor, along another broad, sawdust-littered hall toward the butcher shop itself. The not unpleasant smell of fresh meat came to them strongly as Homer pushed open a heavy swinging door. He blew out the candle.

"Jist in case anybody's on duh street," he advised unnecessarily, handing the candle to Danny.

The streetlight streaming through the broad plate glass windows gave them all the illumination they needed now; more than they desired, in fact. Staying behind the counter, they moved cautiously toward the front of the store, keeping a wary eye on the deserted thoroughfare.

"Easy," Danny warned. "There'll be people comin' by any time, when the show lets out. I just hope they don't miss the bean bottle."

"Outta sight, outta mind," preached his optimistic friend.

A large, elaborate apothecary jar stood centered in the near window, filled to its elegant glass top with dry speckled beans. Propped flanking the jar were two stiff poster boards, detailing the rules of the contest. Also displayed were large, brightly-colored pictures of a vibrator chair and a racing bike.

Danny studied the jar carefully. The thick, irregular fluting of its sides made it difficult to get a clear view of the jar's contents; the column of beans seemed to widen and narrow as he moved his head.

"They sure ain't makin' it easy," he muttered to himself.

Homer took one last quick glance up and down the empty street before he snatched the jar out of the window and ducked below the level of the counter.

"Steady, pal!" Danny cautioned nervously.

"Hey, it's heavy!" Homer announced. He gingerly tested the jar's lid. "See, I toldja; dey got it taped shut."

"Didja bring some more see-through tape?"

"Yeah; I got a whole roll. Let's set up shop in dat back hall. Duh candle'll be enough light."

Crouching low, Danny led the way back through the store, back to the wide hall beyond the heavy swinging door. There he relit the squat candle, set it on the floor and sat down beside it.

Homer sat with his legs hugging the bean-filled jar and began attacking the transparent tape sealing its lid. His tongue began to wag freely as he peeled off bits of tape. Actually, it was their first real opportunity to chat since they had joined forces for the evening. "Hey, lemme tell ya 'bout my talk wit' duh law when I got home dis afternoon," Homer began.

"Make sure you put all them pieces a' tape in yer pocket," Danny interrupted, watching his friend carefully. Anxious as he was to hear what Homer had to tell, he was even more concerned that there should be no signs of their unauthorized visit to the Brockman residence.

"Yeah, sure," Homer nodded, plucking at the stubborn sticky strips. "Anyways, I gets home, I sez Ma, I took a hike down duh river, an' where dis big gulch is by River Road dere's a car wreck in duh bottom, an' a dead guy inside. An' she sez don't be tellin' sich whoppers er I'll hit ya, an' I sez honest, I found 'm all by myself. I din't say nuttin' aboutcha, Danny, jis' like yuh said I shun't."

"Fine. Then what?"

"Well," Homer turned the jar around, "Den my ol' lady sez how'dja know he's dead, an' I sez 'cause he's been snowed on an' ain't moved since, an' his car's been standin' dere on its ray-dee-ayter gettin' snowed on, too, an' she sez My Gawd. How long's duh poor man dere an' I sez how should I know, an' she swings at me an' sez don't git smart. Kin yuh figger dat?"

Danny ignored the question. "Go on," he urged.

"So den she sez who is it, an' I sez duh car I don't know, an' duh guy's face I can't see, an' I don't wanna anyhow; 'sides, from his fancy coat I don't know anybody who looks like it."

At last Homer succeeded in freeing the jar lid, but he was content to set it aside for the moment as he leaned back against the wall and continued his story by flickering candlelight.

"My ol' lady she's really worked up by now. Didja call duh cops, she sez. I sez no, I came home to; an' she sez whyn'tja stop right away at somebody's house, an I sez like you said, What's duh rush, he's dead; an' she sez yuh numskull an' she grabs duh phone an' hollers "Emergency! Gimme duh po'leece!" She tells 'em what I said, an'gives dem our names an' address an' ev'ryting. Den I get on duh phone an' tell dis cop ev'ryting again.

"Den later on," Homer's manner took on an elegant air, "'bout suppertime, duh phone rings. It's duh reporter from duh Hornville Bugle, no less. He wants tuh talk wit' me, personal. So he asts me tell him all about it again yet, so I does, den he sez kin I cum take yer pitcher? An' I sez sure, an' out he comes, a gen-yewine bony-fied reporter! How yuh like dem apples?"

"Grand. Real grand," enthused Danny, feeling no real envy. "What he have to say 'bout the dead guy?"

"My ol' man ast him. He sez duh cops won't say 'till dey check him out. But he ain't from around here. Car's from outa state."

"Where?"

Homer shrugged. "I dunno. He din't say."

"Well," Danny commented, "At least yer gonna get in the papers, like ya want. But I wouldn't spend no reward yet if I was you."

"Don't knock it," Homer defended. "I gotta feelin' dis guy was a rich bugger, an' I'm gonna get sumptin' outa it yet."

Danny was in no mood to renew their debate. At the moment his anxiety centered on their illegal status in the Brockman house. He was also concerned with staying out so long that little brother Herbie might miss him. "Let's get with countin' them beans," he said. "I can't stay out all night."

Homer used his jacket sleeve to clean a small area of the floor near the candle. Then cupping one hand over the mouth of the jar, he carefully tipped the container toward the floor, seeking to control the expected avalanche of beans. Danny was on his knees now, alert to corral any bouncing strays. The beans had hardly begun to pile up when a large, gleaming cylindrical object slid partially out of the jar.

"What duh - ?" exclaimed the startled Homer. Equally surprised, Danny watched as his friend pulled the object out of the jar and held it up in the dim light.

"A can! A big can fulla peaches," Homer exclaimed, reading the label.

"Must take up half the bottle," Danny calculated. "That oughta throw mosta the guessers off pretty good."

"What cheaters! What finks! What crooks!" Homer exclaimed indignantly. "Itsa good t'ing we cum in here tuh check dis bottle out. Yuh cain't hardly trust nobody no more."

"Well, it's their contest," Danny noted. "Maybe they just got tired a' countin' beans."

"Dey jist cain't count dat high, is all," Homer sneered as he finished emptying the suddenly depleted jar. "Which is okay wit' me. Now dere ain't so many fer us to count."

It took them less than ten minutes to reach and double check their total. The count came to exactly 1,621 speckled beans. Then they carefully reconstructed the previous arrangement inside the jar, making sure that the can of fruit was completely hidden by beans.

Homer gently replaced the lid and began the tedious task of duplicating the Brockmans' cellophane taping job. Danny watched his meticulous friend admiringly. Homer had his faults, to be sure, but he also had some genuine talents.

The re-taping done, Homer set the large jar carefully aside. Then he pulled a crumpled fold of paper out of his pocket, and the stub of a pencil. Flattening the paper on the floor in front of the candle, he began to print laboriously.

"That what I think it is?" Danny asked.

"Yeah. A entry blank," Homer nodded.

"I wouldn't put down the 'xact number if I was you." Danny advised. "Only pretty close."

Homer nodded.

"How much are ya puttin' down?"

"Sixteen hunnert an' twenny."

Now it was Danny's turn to nod. That was pretty close.

The entry blank completed, Homer stood up, taking the large jar tenderly into his arms. Danny retrieved the fat candle, checking the floor for wax drippings. There were none. Then he led the way back to the butcher shop, blowing out the candle as he shoved open the swinging door. Again staying behind the counter, they started for the front of the store.

"Duck!"

A figure swept past the storefront, closely followed by a couple, and then a whole cluster of people.

"Show musta jist let out," Danny concluded.

"Rats! We shoulda started a liddle sooner."

"I think we're all right. I don't see anyone doin' any window shoppin'."

Indeed, the passersby seemed intent on departing the scene as speedily as possible. The cold wind had obviously increased in force, and the scurrying people leaned into it, clutching at their coats and hats. Cold car engines sputtered into life; the muffled sounds of voices filtered into the butcher shop where the boys sat still in the shadow of the meat showcase.

It seemed to end as suddenly as it began. Once again Packard Avenue was still, the street deserted. Danny crept forward to reconnoiter, and then motioned to his friend. The heavy jar was promptly set back in place, centered precisely in the dust ring its presence had created on the display stand. Then the completed entry blank was slipped into the slotted keg conveniently provided for same.

Two minutes later the boys were crawling out of Butchie Brockman's bedroom window. The brisk breeze snatched wildly at the curtains as Danny carefully slid the window shut. Then he boosted Homer up the porch rail and onto the roof, where the red-head stretched out on his stomach and extended a hand to assist his friend.

Danny had just reached the roof when the gusting wind tore lustily at them again, forcing the boys to cling tightly to the sloping expanse of shingles. The wind whistled shrilly in their ears, but suddenly a new sound intruded – a scraping, a thumping, a bumping, then a brief silence ended by a resounding, splintering *crash*! The startled boys shook against the shingles.

"Holy Toledo!" croaked Homer. "What wuz dat?"

"Our board," Danny guessed, his voice quavering. "The wind got ahold of our board!"

Lying prone, they couldn't see any of the tailor shop's windows, but the sudden glow from that direction let them know that lights were blinking on in the Ortman's upstairs living quarters. They heard the harsh scraping of a window being forced open.

"Who's there? Who is it?" came the nervous voice of old Mr. Ortman.

A mere 20 feet away, the boys clutched silently to the roof opposite. For the moment the wind had quit, but Brockman's basso-voiced German shepherd was just reaching a fine crescendo.

"Do you see anything, Sidney?" A nervous woman's voice. Mrs. Ortman.

"No, dear, but that monster hound of Brockman's sure is excited."

"Well, don't be shooting it by accident. Heinie Brockman would have a mad fit, even if you also got a burglar."

"Don't fret, Hannah. I'm not about to waste good birdshot on anything I can't see."

The tailor's pronouncement comforted Danny and Homer, but not much. The unpredictable wind began huffing again, and the boys could hear Mr. Ortman muttering.

"What did you say, Sidney?"

"I said such a wind! Maybe it just blew something over – a garbage can, maybe."

"I hope..."

The boys would never know what Mrs. Ortman hoped. Mr. Ortman had shut the window as abruptly as he had opened it. Nor did they particularly care. They had other problems.

"So what do we do now?" Danny wondered aloud. "We can't go outa the store without leaving it unbolted. An' out the back is that dog…"

"An 'duh board. We can't leave duh board!"

"Let's get back in the house," Danny directed as he began to ease himself over the eave toward the sun porch railing. "We gotta think."

Homer was prompt to follow. The German shepherd began to bark again at the renewed activity, but stopped when the boys disappeared through Butchie Brockman's bedroom window. All was dark again at the Ortmans', and Homer wondered aloud how long before the old couple fell asleep again.

"Never mind about them," Danny said, relighting the fat candle and starting toward the hallway. "That dog down there, he's chained, ain't he?"

"Yeah, udderwise dey needs a twenny-foot high fence. Where ya goin'?"

"Let's go check that back door."

As Danny had hoped, the back door was secured by a spring lock which would snap shut behind them as they left. Shielding the candle, he quietly pointed this out to Homer.

"Big deal," was the red-head's sarcastic reaction. "So how da we gonna git past dat wolf out dere? He's got us covered from duh door ta duh back gate."

Danny parted the door curtains and peered out. The huge dog stood only a few feet from the door, alert and suspicious, silhouetted against the traces of snow. Danny noted that the thin sheet of snow stretching toward the tailor shop was relatively undisturbed.

"See?" He pointed. "His chain keeps him on that side a' the yard. An' the walkway goes straight toward Ortmans'. There's gotta be a gate there, for the walkway to the street."

"Yeah, sure, an' dat's where our board is," Homer whispered impatiently. "But howda we get past *him*?" He pointed toward the dog. "Jist run fer it? He'll tear us apart duh second we open duh door, an' what he don't chew, ol' man Ortman is liable tuh shoot."

"No, we sure don't want any more noise. What we want is a quiet, friendly dog."

"What we gonna do?" Homer sneered. "Go out dere an' hug 'im an' kiss 'im?"

"I don't think you're his type," Danny sneered back. "No. What he loves, we got a whole store full of up front."

The light dawned on Homer. "Yer gonna bribe 'im wit' a pork chop!" he said admiringly.

"No. No bones," he replied, leading the way. "We'll find something else."

Packard Avenue still appeared to be deserted as they again eased through the swinging door back into the store. Danny tried the massive door of the walk-in refrigerator. It swung open quietly on well-greased hinges. He raised the candle aloft, revealing an assortment of beef quarters, pork sides, bacon slabs and poultry hanging from thick steel hooks.

"Man, looka duh meat!" Homer enthused. "Should we t'row 'im half a cow?"

"No, this'll do." A metal tub full of meat scraps, no doubt destined to become hamburger, had caught his eye. "Here, grab a few pieces a' this stuff." The boys each gathered up several chunks of meat and cautiously made their way back through the building to the rear door. Danny blew out the candle and parted the curtain.

"He's still standin' right outside the door," he informed Homer. "Open it just a crack, an' hold against it, make sure he doesn't come bustin' through."

Operating the spring lock knob with one hand and the door knob with the other, Homer eased the door back a few inches, keeping his body braced against it. A low, menacing growl greeted them.

"Pssst! Here, boy! Nice boy," Danny coaxed, tossing a small chunk of meat toward the big dog.

The brute hesitated an instant, sniffed the offering, then quickly gulped it down. Pleased, Danny tossed another meat scrap further back into the yard. The dog quickly retrieved it.

"Open wider, Homer," Danny instructed his friend.

Homer cautiously drew the door back, watching the proceedings carefully. Now Danny arched a meat chunk half way to the back fence and the alert dog bounded after it, his chain whipping along the ground. Snap! The tidbit was consumed, and the dog came bounding back toward the boys.

"Ready, now," Danny alerted Homer. "This time I'm throwing all the rest 'way back. You pull the door shut quiet-like."

Danny flung the last half-dozen meat scraps in a scattering beyond the expectant dog, which gave a delighted "yowp!" and snatched one of the pieces out of the air in mid-flight.

The boys had no time to be impressed. They made straight for the side of the building, found a narrow gate, simply latched, and were through it in no time into the dark passage between the tailor and butcher shops.

Casting anxious glances toward the darkened upper windows of the tailor shop, the boys moved quietly up the passage to where their plank lay. It was badly split through most of its length, but still hung together in one piece. Carefully they picked it up, one boy at each end.

"I'm afraid we're gonna have t' go out to the street," Danny whispered as several plaintive whines sounded behind them.

"Yeah, I t'ink he's run outa goodies," Homer agreed. "Let's not press our luck wit' dat mutt."

The boys moved quietly toward the bright stillness of Packard Avenue. Danny peeked furtively both ways as they reached the sidewalk. Up toward Central Avenue were a number of cars parked under the blinking neon signs marking Hornville's major intersection. But nothing in sight was stirring.

"This way!" Danny instructed.

Trotting together, the boys cut in front of the butcher shop, past the next building and then two houses, clutching their board between them. They turned into a narrow empty lot leading back to the friendly darkness of the alley and paused to catch their breath. Back up the alley Brockmans' dog was at it again, barking loudly.

"Boy, dat sure was slick, how yuh got us outa dere," Homer praised his chum warmly. Another sound mingled with the barking. "Wuz dat ol' man Ortman's windah again?"

"I don't know an' I don't care. He can't spot us here. What we gonna do with this lumber?"

"It ain't much good no more. Let's dump it behind Segall's Garage," Homer pointed toward the near end of the alley.

"Fine."

The jumbled litter amongst the wrecked automobile carcasses behind the repair shop was promptly graced by the addition of a length of kindling. Now the boys found themselves directly across the street from the alley leading behind Miller's bakery. This was the direct route home, the darkness favoring them. Still, the boys hesitated.

"Aw, c'mon," Homer finally urged. "Dat guy don't live in dat alley. 'Sides, its' put-near one a'clock in duh mornin'."

"You'd think he did, the way he's always hangin' around," Danny muttered. "Okay," he agreed reluctantly. "But let's get through fast."

They waited for a slow-moving car to clear the nearby intersection, then darted across the street into the gloom of the alley. Striding swiftly in the darkness, they moved along wordlessly. As they passed the back of the bakery, they both focused on the black rectangle denoting the recessed rear entrance, but could see nothing. Danny gave a fleeting thought to Jennifer Markham, no doubt sleeping peacefully upstairs.

A high board fence cornered at the end of the alley. As they drew up to it, they paused to check the street. Then Danny peeked around the fence, looking toward Packard Avenue. He could feel his hair rise stiffly on his head.

He whirled swiftly in his tracks, grabbed Homer by the sleeve and began pulling him up the alley. Homer knew better than to delay for the purpose of making inquiries. Almost instantly he was matching Danny stride for stride through the darkness.

"Wh-what is it?" He managed to gasp between breaths.

"It's him!"

Homer looked back. Silhouetted at the end of the alley was the tall figure of a man dressed in a hat and topcoat. The tall figure seemed suddenly to plunge into the gloom behind them.

"He's comin'!" the freckle-faced boy blurted, terrified.

In seconds they reached the far end of the alley. Across the street lay the alley they had only so recently been happy to vacate. Now several dogs were barking, the basso of Brockman's shepherd easily distinguishable among them. As if directed by a single mind, the boys' feet voted against re-entering the far alley, electing to turn down the street instead.

Together they dashed pell-mell down the quiet residential avenue, staying on the snow-streaked lawns of the darkened houses to deaden the sound of their charging footsteps. Near the corner, they paused in the shadow of a thick fir tree for a hasty look back.

There was that man again, standing at the mouth of the alley, plainly outlined against the lights of Packard Avenue. He appeared to be looking in their direction, but no longer moving in pursuit of them.

"Looks like he quit chasin' us," Homer puffed hopefully. "Maybe he's outa shape."

"Maybe so," Danny huffed. "But he musta come up that alley pretty good."

"Yeah he did. So let's go while duh goin's good."

"No. Let's wait an' see. We got a pretty good lead, if he start's comin' again."

Homer eyed his friend questioningly, but made no further comment. Together they stood watching the distant figure, at the same time trying to ease their intake of the chill night air which rasped at their aching throats.

For a long moment none of the trio moved. The boys felt the resurgence of the erratic wind; saw it tugging at the topcoat of the man up the street. Finally he clutched at his hat, turn his back upon them, and began walking toward Packard Avenue. They watched him until he rounded the corner, out of their view.

"Let's go," Danny directed, turning in the opposite direction and breaking into a dog trot. The boys jogged on for several blocks, angling through a series of deserted side streets and alleys.

"I can't figure that bird out," Danny wondered aloud as they hiked down a long, gloomy alley. "For a guy what's supposed to be hidin' out, he sure walks around a lot."

"An' sich hours he keeps," Homer noted. "If Sharkey's friends plan on catchin' dat bird nappin', maybe dey better try lunch-time."

Danny rewarded Homer with a chuckle. "Y'know, Homer, I don't check up on him any lunch hours. Could be that's when he does sleep. But I ain't so curious as to get 'tween him an' yer friend Sharkey to find out." Danny shuddered at the thought. "It's terrible to know what we know, an' not be able to do somethin' about it."

"Well, like yuh said before, why stick our necks out fer a buncha crooks? We could end up deader'n all of 'em. Leave 'em have dere private war, long as dey ain't bodderin' nobody else.'

"But what if they were after somebody else here in town?"

"Like who? 'Sides us, I mean," Homer added wryly.

"I dunno who. Just pretend."

"Well, I'd say dat'd be duh time fer a a-non-eemus letter, but sich ain't duh case, so right now we don't do nuttin' an' keep our nose clean, right, pal?"

"Right." They had come to the point of parting. "Still wanna see the movie t'morrow?" Danny asked.

"Sure," Homer agreed. "I'll come holler fer ya right after lunch."

They exchanged quick waves of farewell, and Danny silently trotted the last block and a half to his back yard. Tonight he had to re-enter via the roof route, not having had an opportunity to slip out the back door and leave it unbolted. And his favorite cellar window was locked; he had decided to leave it alone for awhile after playing dumb to several inquiries about its frequent unfastened state.

Parents ought to go to bed earlier on Saturday nights, Danny reasoned as he teetered on the back porch rail and reached for the sun porch buttress overhead; their staying up late sure can cramp a young man's style. Now he was on the sundeck, but he had no interest in the door which opened into the upstairs hall, a door which he knew to be unlocked. Trouble was, it stuck like glue, and squealed like chalk on a black board when it came unstuck.

Instead, Danny quickly mounted the porch rail and hoisted himself to the shingle roof. Silently he padded over it, coming down to the gable housing the window between his and Herbie's beds. Danny pulled back the recently hung storm window he had prudently left unlocked. The inside window slid open with silent ease, the result of much usage. Danny slipped through the opening quietly, ducking under the shade, and just as quietly closed both windows.

"Whatcha doin' out there?" came the whispered words of little Herbie through the darkness, startling his big brother no end.

"I wasn't out there," the shaken big brother lied. "I was just lookin' out!"

"What for?" pressed the Cute Little One.

"Santa Claus!" came the annoyed reply.

"Ninny. It's way too early!" Danny could hear Herbie snickering to himself as the little boy settled back into bed.

Danny slipped out of his sneakers and slid into bed fully clothed, filled with a silent mixture of panic and anger at so nearly being exposed. Now he would have to lie awake until his little brother lapsed back into sleep before he could risk undressing. It was apparent that, as Herbie grew older, slipping out after bedtime would become more and more risky for Danny. He debated the possible consequences of taking Herbie into his confidence. Could he trust the little blabbermouth?

Outside, a sudden gust of wind buffeted the house vigorously. Little Herbie tossed and muttered dreamily, and Danny sat up silently and began disrobing for bed.

Well, there was at least one tactical error he wouldn't be guilty of this time, he thought to himself ruefully. His pajamas were conveniently bunched under his pillow.

CHAPTER 14

Another Gangland Slaying

Sunday morning found most of the previous morning's thin layer of snow melted away, but the ragged skies continued threatening. The night winds had diminished somewhat; still, an occasional gust slammed the house with window rattling intensity.

The general effect of the weather outdoors made the atmosphere in the Van Kuyper kitchen seem that much more warm and cozy. The chatter was lighthearted and amiable, the waffles, bacon and hot chocolate all seemed extra tasty. The sleepiness in the hard-to-awaken Danny had given way to a ravenous appetite. Munching wordlessly, he was doing more than his share in disposing of the ample breakfast.

A thump on the front porch announced the arrival of the Sunday morning edition of the Milwaukee daily newspaper.

"I get the funnies!" little Herbie staked his claim as he bolted from the table. In a moment he was back, parting the comic section from the thick fold of papers.

"Here, son, I'll have the rest of that," spoke Ray Van Kuyper, setting aside his coffee cup.

"How about the women's section, Dad?" asked Doris, rising from the table. But her father seemed not to hear her. "Dad?"

A low whistle escaped from the senior Van Kuyper's lips. "Well, whaddaya know, li'l ol' Hornville is making national headlines again," he announced to nobody in particular.

"What are you mumbling about, Ray?" inquired his wife. Elsie Van Kuyper left the steaming waffle maker and strode briskly to the side of her husband.

"Listen to this," he replied, and began to read aloud. "Gangster Found Murdered in Remote Upstate Area." Then he read the sub-headline: "Hornville is Again Site of Gangland Slaying."

The whole family was listening intently now, even the Cute Little One. Danny continued chewing, but slowly, his fading appetite giving way to a rising tide of apprehension. Ray Van Kuyper read on, plunging into the story.

"A prominent member of a Chicago-based crime syndicate was found slain yesterday near the small lumbering community of Hornville, scene of the recent slaying of Douglas "Doggie" Blodgett, a small-time Chicago hoodlum. The latest victim was identified by police as Max Guzman, age 45, reputed to be a front man and treasurer for – Danny, what's the matter with you?"

The boy seemed on the verge of choking to death. Doris thumped his back vigorously.

"Waffle," Danny squeaked lamely, pointing at his throat.

"Then don't eat like such a pig," his mother admonished him. "What else does it say, Ray?"

"Let's see," Ray Van Kuyper began again. "The body was found in the victim's wrecked auto, which was wedged in a rock formation well down in a deep ravine. Authorities say it was evident that the death was made to appear as an accident. But an autopsy conducted by the state crime laboratory late yesterday revealed the cause of death to be a small puncture wound through the heart, possibly administered by an ice pick."

"Ugh!" Doris reacted. "How awful."

Her father read on: "The autopsy was ordered when fingerprint records confirmed the identification found on Guzman's body. Time of death was fixed at 24 to 36 hours prior to the autopsy."

"Holy moley! Listen to this!" a new note of excitement sounded in Ray Van Kuyper's voice.

"Guzman's body was discovered yesterday morning by Homer Peckley, thirteen-year-old son of a Hornville boatyard operator." He turned to Danny. "How about that, son? Your little pal is makin' the big city papers."

Elsie Van Kuyper fixed a quizzical eye on her older son. He wasn't eating now. "Didn't you go hiking with Homer yesterday?" she asked.

"Yeah, but he wanted to go clear down to the lake. I didn't."

"You didn't get home until lunchtime."

"I went to the park. A lotta kids were there, messin' up the snow."

"Sled-ridin', I bet," Herbie chimed.

"Yeah. Some."

"Too bad you didn't stick with Homer," Doris clucked. "This morning you'd be in the papers."

"I'm just as glad he isn't," Mrs. Van Kuyper put in as she bustled back toward the stove. "I wouldn't want to have even that little to do with those terrible gangsters. For the life of me, I can't imagine what's bringing them here to Hornville in the first place."

"That's about what it says in the papers," her husband spoke up. "It says here: Authorities are puzzled by the fact that both the recent slayings apparently took place in or near Hornville, an isolated town of modest homes with a population of approximately two thousand persons. They claim to be unaware of any direct connection between Hornville and organized crime, or for that matter, between the victims themselves.

"Thus far, none of the legal agencies investigating the crimes have indicated any strong leads as to the possible identity of the killer or killers involved. However, some speculation hints at possible gang warfare."

"Heavens!" Elsie Van Kuyper fussed. "That's all this town needs is a gang war!" She took a deep breath then untied her apron and hung it on a hook by the door. "Come, come," she hustled her brood. "Let's cut out the nonsense and get a move on. We just have time to get ready for church."

Ray Van Kuyper turned to son Danny, who was idly poking a fork at some bacon remnants on his plate. "Why such a long face, boy? Could it be that you're jealous of your buddy Homer for getting his name in the paper, and you didn't?"

"Yeah," replied Danny, sadly sardonic. "Just thinka the reward."

"Don't be silly," Doris laughed, jumping to her feet. "People don't get rewards for finding dead bodies."

Danny made no further comment as he rose slowly from the table. Inwardly, he was terrified at the thought of what form the reward for finding Mr. Guzman's body might take.

CHAPTER 15

Smoking Out the Bad Guys

Danny didn't wait. Matinee date or no, right after church he changed his clothes and went to call for Homer.

As he approached the river, he could see several people standing on the Peckley's front porch, talking to Homer's father. He went around to the back door and knocked.

"He ain't home, Daniel," the portly Mrs. Peckley answered his inquiry, wringing her hands. "All dese people comin' dis mornin' tuh ast questions 'bout dat dead crook he found has got duh poor boy flustered, I'm afraid. Said he wuz goin' for a walk."

"I hope he doesn't find any more dead people," Danny found himself mumbling.

"What's dat yuh say?"

"Nuthin'. Thanks, Mrs. Peckley." Danny turned to depart.

"Yuh find'm, tell'm get home 'fore dark," Mrs. Peckley called after him.

The boy nodded and disappeared from her view. With his jacked zipped against the chilliness of the overcast day, Danny broke into a trot, headed toward Hickory Hill. There was sanctuary. There he would find Homer.

A short time later he crested the hill and started down through the thick woods on the far side. Yesterday's light snow was largely undisturbed here, and a single set of footprints along a fragmentary path were easily discerned. Definitely Homer.

A thin wisp of smoke curled up from below. It marked the location of "the hut", a crude structure built of scraps by Danny and Homer last summer to enclose the "cave" they had found, a minor indentation in the rocky hillside. Danny gave a low whistle as he approached the thicket concealing the hut.

"Who's dat?" Homer called out nervously. "'Dat you, Danny?"

"Yeah, Homer," Danny called back reassuringly as he half-crawled through the maze of snow-dusted branches toward the hut. Reaching it, he ducked through the open doorway, exchanging the gloomy outdoors for the even gloomier atmosphere prevailing within.

Homer was seated on a flat rock, feeding a fitful fire in a 10-gallon can by tossing bits of dead twigs and branches into it. Danny straddled the remains of an old wooden chair and leaned back against the dirt wall. He coughed as an acrid curl of smoke reached his nose. There was no chimney as such on the hut; the several holes in the corrugated metal sheet comprising most of the roof had to suffice.

For several moments neither boy spoke. Then Danny broke the gloomy silence. "I guess you got in okay last night."

"Yeah. Some people come by dis mornin' even before duh paper come. Said dey heard it on duh radio. Boy, did dat get my folks excited. My ol' man even shaved!"

"Still think ya might get a reward?"

Homer was too disconsolate to care about being needled. "Boy, dat's one guy's fambly I don't ever wanna hear from! An' I'll bet his friends is worse. Man oh man, we got troubles."

Danny nodded. "Yeah, troubles we got, but I'm havin' trouble just tryin' to get it straight in my head 'xactly what kinda troubles we got."

"Yeah, I know whatcha mean. You'n me bot'. I'm gettin' a sore head jis' from t'inkin'."

"Now, we know what guys killed Doggie Blodgett, an' why. But who'd kill Mr. Guzman, an' why? From what the papers said, he was killed that same mornin' after he an' Sharkey were chasin' us in the speedboat. All the way up here I've been wonderin' if whoever got Mr. Guzman also got Sharkey, only they ain't found his body yet."

"My ol' man wuz at duh Snug Harbor last night. Bizniss like usu'l, Sharkey 'n all."

"Hmmm. Well, maybe last night Sharkey didn't know about what happened to his friend Guzman. Maybe when he does, he'll get outa town fast an' stay lost, an' our troubles will be over."

"Could be, but what if he don't? In dis liddle town, sooner or later he's gonna see yuh, an' recanize yuh."

Danny winced at the thought. Besides, he was getting tired of jumping every time a strange car passed him on the street. "If this Guzman thing doesn't scare Sharkey outa town, an' quick, then maybe we should do somethin' to let the cops know what we know about him gettin' Doggie Blodgett killed. Maybe one of your a-nonymous letters."

Homer nodded. "I wisht now I'da settled for a a-non-ee-muss phone call to duh cops yesterday. I don't like duh idea a' Sharkey t'inkin' 'bout me an' Mr. Guzman an' my boat at Peterson's dock dat night all at once at duh same time."

Danny understood. "Ya know, when Sharkey finds out about Mr. Guzman, he's gotta be thinkin' 'bout that guy at McClatchy's boardin' house, the one he figures is Doggie Blodgett's pal. I wonder if he might try to get him 'steada leavin' town."

"Yuh figger dat guy kilt Mr. Goozman?"

"I dunno; but if he didn't, who did? An' if he did, he's a mighty cool customer, hangin' around town, chasin' kids up dark alleys…"

"Yeah, but when he was chasin' us, maybe he din't know 'bout Mr. Goozman bein' found yet."

Danny nodded. "Good thinkin', Homer; could be now he's got good reason to leave town, too. That's what we gotta do. Watch an' see if either or both those guys leave town. Sure, they know a little 'bout us. But we know more about them! An' we can't hide forever. Agreed?"

"Agreed. How do we do it?"

"Well, keepin' tabs on Sharkey oughta be simple. 'Bout all you hafta do there is keep in touch with yer Dad."

Homer laughed. "Okay. But how 'bout ol' lady McClatchy's star boarder?"

"Well, I suppose if he moves, she'll start running ads in the Hornville Bugle again, but we oughta do better'n that. We'll have to give it some thought."

Homer broke up several small, dry branches and began tossing the pieces into the fire bucket. The heat generated by the improvised stove made the hut's interior fairly comfortable, provided one had a fair tolerance for smoke.

"I got a idee, a dee-lishus idee," Homer chortled. "Why not let's get us a job at Miller's bakery? Dat way we keep a eye on McClatchy's, an' be right in dere wit' all dem goodies."

"Like Jennifer Markham," Danny teased.

"Dat ain't 'xactly what I had in mind," Homer retorted. "Be-sides, <u>you</u> is her hero," he jeered.

Danny didn't like the barb, but he'd asked for it. "No," he returned to business. "If we're around there all the time, that guy'll see more of us than I'd like. But you gave me an idea."

"Like what?"

"Like who do we know lives practic'ly across the street from McClatchy's boardin' house?"

"Like I said, duh bakery. Jennie Markham?"

"Right! An' she lives upstairs over the bakery, an' can see right over t'where that guy lives, and who'd ever 'spect a girl livin' there of spyin' on him?"

Homer scratched his freckled nose thoughtfully. "Hmmm. I dunno. I ain't never trusted girls much. Dey're blabbermout's."

"True, but I don't think Jennifer's as bad as most. 'Sides, we won't tell her the truth. Most prob'ly she'd die a' fright."

"No doubt. But what'll we tell her?"

"I dunno. We gotta thinka somethin'. Make somethin' up."

Silence and smoke filled the hut as the boys consulted with their respective muses. Danny teetered on his chair and Homer snapped twigs. Danny hatched the first idea.

"Yer Uncle Herman is still with the state highway patrol at Madison, ain't he?"

"Yeah. So?"

"So let's tell Jennifer that he's hired us to keep an eye on the guy fer bein' a suspected car thief, er shop-lifter, er somethin' what ain't so scary as killin'."

"I dunno. Hirin' sounds like money. Maybe she'll wanna get paid. 'Sides, cops don't hire kids fer spyin'."

"So how would she know? An' we don't hafta say hired. We can just say yer Uncle Herman asked us to keep an eye out, real casual like, an' every mornin' she can report to us at school. It'll be like playin' cops an' robbers. She'll like it."

"Well, maybe. But one time at least we'll hafta show 'im to 'er."

"Naw, we'll just describe him, an' where he lives. She's prob'ly seen him around there a hunnert times already."

"Prob'ly. Okay, it sounds like a good plan. Yuh gonna ast her t'morra at school?"

"Might as well - the sooner the better."

"Boy, I feel better now," Homer enthused. "It's good to talk, an' have a plan. Now what'll we do? Go to the show?"

"Naw, too late. Let's go chase rabbits."

A mixture of snow and dirt quickly doused the fire, but not without first creating considerably more smoke. The boys ran into the fresh air, coughing to clear their lungs as they snaked their way through the surrounding thicket. Once free of the thicket, they spent the rest of the afternoon harassing the hillside's cottontail population. Smelling like a pair of burnt chestnuts.

CHAPTER 16

Agent Markham, Girl Spy

It was the Monday before Thanksgiving, and already a holiday atmosphere prevailed at Lincoln School. Many of the windows were decorated with paper turkeys which showed their young creators more inclined toward a liberality of form and color rather than slavish accuracy.

It was to be a short, three-day school week capped by a Thanksgiving play in the school auditorium on Wednesday afternoon, courtesy of the fifth and sixth grades, and the restlessness showed. Even the teachers were eyeing the classroom clocks with increasing frequency.

Homer Peckley found himself the object of much curiosity and the target of endless questions. It was a rare day when any citizen of Hornville merited mention in the big city papers, and usually such momentary celebrities were well past the eighth grade.

A touch of envy for all the attention paid Homer could also be noted, particularly in the unfriendly countenance of Butchie Brockman. He had come prepared to boast at length about attending the professional football game at Green Bay the previous day, only to find himself almost totally ignored. Obviously, the managed mayhem of the gridiron couldn't hold a candle to a genuine murder, complete with notorious corpse.

But Homer was not enjoying his new prominence. The silent hostility evident in Butchie's face was cause for discomfort, to be sure. But more than that, he found himself near gagging on the constant repetition of the lie that he alone had found the murder victim.

Further, there was the nagging fear of blurting out more than he was supposed to know. When harassed by questioners, Homer found himself casting glances toward Danny, sometimes guilty, sometimes beseeching, but his friend seemed to pay him little heed.

In truth, Danny did not at all begrudge Homer his new-found notoriety. He was glad to have the burden of it off him. His problem was to find some means, some excuse for talking to Jennifer, alone, at length, and preferably unobserved.

In class, it was impossible, of course. At recess time he tagged along after her at a safe distance. She was part of the jump rope set, a good way to stay warm on a raw day. Once she eyed him questioningly as she caught him watching her, but he felt uncomfortable among so many girls and quickly moved away. He was sure his brief presence had provoked the tittering which now followed after him, red-eared, toward the rowdier action of a touch football game.

Lunchtime. Both he and Jennifer went home for lunch. He would hurry through his soup and sandwich and intercept her on the way back. But as the noon bell sounded, he noticed that she was suddenly in possession of a bagged lunch and was lining up with the school lunch room crowd. The raw weather, no doubt. Foiled again!

Back in class after lunch, Danny weighed the advisability of slipping Jennifer a note asking to see her, but he dreaded the consequences of the note falling into other hands.

After school? Although he had never paid any particular attention, he seemed to recall that she usually left school in the company of a couple of girl friends, a pair of real gabbies. He was beginning to despair of ever reaching her, short of dropping by Miller's bakery, when a wholly unexpected opportunity materialized.

"May I have your attention, please." Miss Hecker's firm tone made the worded request a command.

"Following the afternoon recess, the fifth and sixth grade classes are holding a dress rehearsal of their Thanksgiving program for the school. Miss Jones and Mrs. Gurney have requested some help with costumes, make-up, stage props and curtains.

They need three girls and three boys. First, are there any girls who would like to volunteer?"

A number of hands shot up, several waving excitedly. The wild wavers were ignored. "Mary Lou, Jennifer, and Shirley. Thank you. And now the boys."

There was less enthusiasm from that group, but a few hands were slowly elevated. Miss Hecker visibly flinched. Was that Danny Van Kuyper's hand in the air, or was he preparing to scratch his ear? She had never known him to volunteer for anything in his entire school career!

Homer, too, was momentarily stupefied at the sight, but then he guessed Danny's motive, and raised his own hand. Miss Hecker began her selection. "Randolph, there's a sturdy fellow, and Roger . . ."

Miss Hecker looked again, unbelieving. No doubt about it, Daniel's hand was indeed raised. There were a couple of other more deserving volunteers who could better afford missing some class time, but Miss Hecker found it impossible to permit this rare display of initiative to go unheeded. "… and Daniel," she concluded the selections. "Report to Mrs. Gurney in the school auditorium right after recess."

Danny ignored the puzzled glances of those about him, and tried to do likewise to the idiot grin and big wink Homer Peckley gave him from across the room. He wished Homer wouldn't do that. But Homer persisted, and Danny finally felt compelled to quiet Homer with a sly wink in return. Miss Hecker wondered what sort of blunder she had committed.

****

The auditorium after recess was a lively place. It seemed all of the fifth and sixth graders would be on stage performing in one role or another, and the bustling Mrs. Gurney and the harried Miss Jones had their hands full getting things organized.

Miss Jones finally collared all of her choral reading group and assembled them to one side of the auditorium, where they commenced the mechanical chorusing of their lines. Backstage, the three eighth grade girls were busy helping Mrs. Gurney dress a small tribe of burlap-clad and feathered Indians plus a colony of big-buckled, wide-collared Pilgrims.

Between times, Mrs. Gurney instructed Butchie and Roger on the moving and placement of various props. Danny was stationed at the ropes operating the stage curtains.

Soon the preparations were complete, and Mrs. Gurney took up her station down front. Miss Jones's choral readers launched into their role, setting the scene, and the action commenced. All five of the other eighth graders had gathered at Danny's end of the stage to watch, even though it was the same play all but Jennifer had participated in two years earlier.

Peering through a break in the fixed drapes marking the ends of the stage, Danny opened and closed the curtains on cue from Mrs. Gurney. The job required some effort, and Danny tugged and hauled at the ropes lustily as the scenes came and went. Except for an occasional prop change or costume adjustment, his classmates were largely idle. They watched the proceedings on stage with detached amusement, making comments befitting the superior status of eighth graders.

Most of the comments were made by Butchie Brockman, and were intended for the amusement of the girls. Both Mary Lou and Shirley were flattered by the attentions of the budding he-man, but Butchie kept casting glances toward Jennifer, who stood apart and watched the stage play with quiet interest.

It became more and more obvious to Danny that Butchie was intent on impressing Jennifer, and equally obvious that the girl was having no part of it. Then Butchie thought he saw Jennifer and Danny exchanging quiet smiles, and, infuriated that he might be the object of their amusement, he decided to take forceful action. Danny was just starting to close the curtains at the time.

"Here, Skinny… let a man show ya how," the Butcher Boy snarled as he roughly shouldered Danny aside. Grabbing the rope, he closed the curtains with a grand sweep.

"Very good, Daniel!" exclaimed Mrs. Gurney from her post out front. "Let's have it that way every time."

"That was me doin' it, Mrs. Gurney," Butchie announced loudly.

"Just fine, Randolph. We'll have to make you the permanent curtain engineer. Just watch for my signals."

Butchie turned and beamed on his classmates, eyeing Danny with spiteful triumph. Danny stared back impassively. A flock of sixth graders scurried back and forth amongst them as a new grouping of actors assembled on stage.

Danny began to move back toward the stage door leading to the hall. Then he turned his head, and catching Jennifer's sympathetic eye, beckoned with his head almost imperceptibly toward the door. Jennifer cocked her head questioningly, poised on hesitation, and then began to follow him. Butchie's gaze swiveled back and forth between them like an owl, and the sneer on his face gave way to a look of bewilderment. He came stalking after them.

"Curtain! Curtain!" The excited voice of Mrs. Gurney stopped Butchie short. "Randolph, can't you see my signal?"

At the door, Danny turned and waved bye-bye at the flustered butcher boy. Infuriated, Butchie waved a fist in return, then stomped back to the curtain ropes. The next scene opened with a remarkable flourish.

Danny closed the stage door behind him and Jennifer, and sat down in the shelter of the short stairwell leading to the hall. The girl sat down beside him. The hall was deserted and almost silent, save for the muffled buzz of reciting scholars filtering through closed classroom doors.

"They can get along alright without us for a few minutes in there," Danny began. "I've been wantin' to talk to you anyhow.

"Is that so?" Jennifer replied. "I thought you must have something on your mind. Why, I've received more attention from you today than I generally get in weeks. Usually I have the feeling that you don't know I exist."

Danny pondered her comment for a moment, then decided not to try to understand it. "Homer 'n I have a secret project we'd like to have you help us with."

"I refuse to climb the front of the school and hang any banners," Jennifer interrupted, smiling at him knowingly. Danny hunched his head and stared at his shoes, trying to hide the color rising into his face. "This is a serious project," he said evenly.

"I'm sorry," the girl said. "Tell me about it. But I won't say yes or no until I know what it is."

"Sure," Danny nodded, and then proceeded to spin an involved tale about Homer's Uncle Herman, the state highway patrolman, and Jennifer's mysterious neighbor, the boarder at Mrs. McClatchy's. Danny hinted that their quarry was the suspected leader of a car theft ring. As best he could, he described the man's appearance to the astounded but still dubious girl.

"Him?" she exclaimed. "I've seen him walk past the shop lots of times. He has a nice smile. Certainly doesn't look like a crook to me."

"You ever see him *drive* by?" Danny challenged.

"Mmmm, no," came the girl's puzzled reply. "No car thief owns a car," Danny answered knowingly. "Just ask Homer's uncle."

"Answer me this," Jennifer fixed his eyes with her steady gaze. "Is this why you and Homer came by the shop that one morning?"

Danny nodded. "Sort of," he said honestly.

The girl smiled first, then laughed. "I wondered what you two were up to. That Homer's such a poor liar. I didn't think you'd stoop to visiting me just to steal a pie."

Now Danny's face reddened right up past his eyebrows, and the girl laughed again. "Oh, Homer's not as sly as he thinks. My uncle saw him take it, and later told me; and when I asked him why he didn't make Homer put it back, he said that someday you boys would think about it, feel ashamed, and be the better men for it."

Danny found himself unable to make any further comment. He simply stared at his shoes.

"Cheer up," the girl said, sorry that she had chattered so freely. "I'll be your spy, and report to you every day, although I think Homer's uncle is probably wrong about that nice-looking man."

"Fine," Danny mumbled. He stood up, looking away.

"And I'll tell you one more thing," the girl said solemnly, getting up with him. "I'm glad it wasn't you who took the pie."

Those words did nothing to assuage Danny's feelings of humiliation. He simply hadn't had the opportunity, that's all.

CHAPTER 17

Butchie Seeks Revenge

Wednesday, the day before Thanksgiving, Lincoln School was all abuzz about a new cause célèbre. But it was the same old celebrity, Homer Peckley.

Heinie Brockman had posted the list of contest winners in the window of his butcher shop that morning, and right on top of the list was Homer's name.

It appeared that the celebrated red-head had come within an eyelash of guessing the exact number of beans in the jar on display at Brockman's, while the second and third place winners weren't even close. No doubt about it; this week's edition of the Hornville Bugle would be full of nothing but Homer Peckley, corpse finder and bean estimator extraordinaire, plus the classified ads.

Lincoln School's most heralded eighth grader accepted the congratulations of his classmates with subdued modesty. Even the undemonstrative Miss Hecker was moved to make mention in class of Homer's success.

"Since Mr. Brockman's son is a classmate of Homer's, perhaps Randolph will be awarding the prize to the contest winner," commented the Grand Dame of Lincoln School. The sullen Butchie managed a grimacing smile, and Homer likewise showed his teeth.

Miss Hecker couldn't resist a further comment. "Perhaps this new-found ability of Homer's augers well for a much-needed improvement in his school work," she said, arching an eyebrow in Homer's direction.

"Oh, it's duh new mat' yuh been teachin' us what done it, Ma'am," the Big Winner lied flatteringly.

That was almost too much for Miss Hecker. She hastily opened the text in her hand and launched the day's geography lesson, grateful that she had such a sizeable book to hide behind.

This last restless school day before the holiday wore on; the afternoon recess came and went, and the six volunteers from the eighth grade reported to Mrs. Gurney to aid in the preparations for the annual Thanksgiving program which would conclude the school day. Soon the rest of the Lincoln School's student body would troop into the auditorium to watch the fifth and sixth graders perform.

Miss Jones, looking more harried than ever, was frantically trying to establish some order in her choral reading group. Watching her, Danny concluded that she might need a vacation more than the students did.

Mrs. Gurney, operating with her usual energetic bustle, barked unmistakable orders in no-nonsense tones. She collared two scuffling "pilgrims" and nearly jerked them out of their buckled shoes. Recalling his own tough year with Mrs. Gurney, Danny observed the lady with grudging admiration. "She should have been a man," he concluded silently.

His proficiency with the curtains having been amply demonstrated the previous Monday, Butchie was promptly reassigned by Mrs. Gurney to that operation. The butcher boy silently fretted and fumed over his assignment, for the job he had usurped from Danny on Monday kept him largely isolated and immobile, definitely cramping his style. Even though curtain time was still twenty minutes off, Mrs. Gurney kept him busy with last-minute placement drills for the various groups of performers.

Danny assisted Roger in setting the stage for the first scene and arranging the rest of the props in proper sequence for their eventual use. Then the two of them wandered to a room offstage where Jennifer, Shirley and Mary Lou were busy preparing a small horde of Pilgrims and Indians. The babble was deafening, but the boys enjoyed watching as the application of grease pencil and lipstick transformed the young actors.

Finally the last face was painted and the last costume pinned in place, and the group moved out en masse under the firm guidance of Mrs. Gurney. Shirley, Mary Lou and Roger tagged after, while Jennifer and Danny lagged behind. The room still seemed to ring with the noise of the departed mob.

"Secret Agent X-21 reporting, sir," Jennifer snapped off a comic salute while her small face lit up with a pixie grin. "As of this morning, our suspect was still living at McClatchy's, with no noticeable change in his routine."

Danny cast a worried glance toward the unoccupied doorway. "Careful," he cautioned. "We've *got* to keep this a secret."

Jennifer's expression sobered. "You're really serious about this business, aren't you?"

"You bet. You're sure he hasn't done anythin' that looks like he's movin' out?"

"No, not as far as I can tell," the girl replied. "I've been sort of expecting to see him jump into somebody's parked car and drive off with it. Isn't that what car thieves do?"

"Not 'xactly," the boy smiled wryly. "Leastwise, I don't think so."

Danny's brow was puckered in deep thought as Jennifer studied him intently. "I gather it would mean something if this man moved out," she said. "But what good would it do Homer's Uncle Herman if the man were gone?"

"Well, it's sort of hard to explain," Danny answered slowly, not paying her much heed. Then mumbling to himself, he continued, "He doesn't move, an' Sharkey doesn't move. I don't get it," he said, shaking his head in perplexity.

Jennifer was on him like a cat. "Who else doesn't move?" she demanded, tilting her head to stare him full in the face.

Danny literally bit his tongue. "Nobody," he said, waving her off. "Forget what I said."

"You've got another suspect," she bore in. "And another secret agent, I'll bet! Who is it? Is it a girl?"

"No! No!" Danny protested, figuring he already had one girl too many on his staff. "No other agent, no other girl."

"But another suspect," Jennifer's eyes narrowed.

"Well, maybe," Danny admitted reluctantly. "But never mind right now. You just keep an eye on yours. Can you meet me at the dime store Friday mornin', say 'bout ten o'clock, to let me know what's cookin'?"

"Sure," the girl smiled. "I'll even bring some…" A noise at the doorway snatched their attention. It was Randolph "Butchie" Brockman. He was leaning casually against the door frame, a sinister leer distorting his broad features.

"My, my, ain't this cozy," he sneered. "Whatsa matter, don't you guys like the play?"

Fear welled up in Danny. Ever since their brush backstage on Monday, he had had the distinct feeling Butchie was angling to get him alone. And now, although Jennifer was present, he knew his hunch was confirmed. And he was trapped.

"Oh, it's started already, huh?" Danny tried a pleasant smile. "Isn't Mrs. Gurney gonna be needin' yuh?"

"This first scene is a long one," replied the butcher boy with malevolent reassurance. "An' just in case I'm late getting' back, I got Roger standin' by."

Butchie swaggered into the room, hooked the open door with his heel and slammed it shut. He glanced from boy to girl as he moved slowly across the room, his cruel squint finally settling on Danny.

"You wave bye-bye purty good, Skinny," he said, pausing beside one of the tables littered with leftovers of costuming the troupe. "So why don'tcha wave bye-bye to yer girlfriend here so's we can have a little chat?"

Jennifer looked at Danny, who was nodding in agreement with Butchie. "I think you'd better go," he said quietly.

The girl was indignant; her eyes flamed and her voice seethed as she turned on the advancing butcher boy. "Randolph Brockman, you behave yourself. If you don't, I'll go straight to Miss Hecker. And I'll tell her about last time, too!"

"Naw yuh won't," Butchie smiled confidently, never taking his eyes off Danny. "If yuh do, yer skinny friend here will say yuh lied. Why, he'd die if the kids heard he was hidin' behind ol' Hecker's skirt, right, Skinny?"

Jennifer looked back to Danny and met his troubled gaze. She couldn't read his face, but his words were plain enough. "Why don't you go watch the play, and don't say anythin' to anybody. I'll be okay."

"Sure he will," the butcher boy leered. Furious, frustrated, the girl stamped her foot. "Oh, how foolish you are!" she cried, nearly as angry with Danny as she was with his tormentor. "Very well then, I refuse to go. I won't go, and nobody can make me."

"Stick around then," the butcher boy replied, never taking his eyes off Danny. "Yuh can watch me teach this bag a' bones here he's not tough enough to get smart with me."

Danny had retreated as far as the room would allow. Now he was boxed into a corner, next to a long littered table restricting his room to manuever. Butchie was closing the gap on him, his formidable fists cocked for action.

The trapped boy considered going either under or over the table, but the accumulated jumble both on top and beneath it guaranteed to impede his progress. Besides, with the stubborn Jennifer standing there, he simply could not turn tail and run. There was only one thing left to do. He charged.

Danny's sudden onslaught bowled the surprised butcher boy half way across the room. The immediate success of his tactic astounded even Danny, who suddenly found himself astride his opponent and flailing away with might and main.

But the situation could only be temporary; superior size, weight and strength had to tell. The aroused Butchie tore himself free and leaped to his feet. Danny staggered to his feet and braced to meet the charge.

The two boys slammed together, and for a brief moment rocked like a wind-whipped tree, clutched in silent struggle. Then Danny, game but over-matched, slowly collapsed under the mounting pressure as his heavier opponent rode him to the floor. Their previous position was reversed, with the red-faced Butchie now astride the object of his wrath. The butcher boy began to methodically thump away at his frantically struggling prey.

Jennifer had watched the proceedings with horrified fascination, standing as though petrified. But now the plight of the boy she favored galvanized her into action. She rushed forward and grasped Butchie's hair.

"Why you ____!" the surprised butcher boy swore. He swung his stout arm and slammed the girl across the mid-section, sending her sprawling. He laughed as she raised her head and blinked back at him, dazed. Then he returned to the pleasures of pummeling the already well-battered Danny Van Kuyper.

The aroused Jennifer Markham was not through, however. She sat up and considered leaping on Randolph Brockman with tooth and nail. Then her eye fell on a large burlap bag draped over part of the accumulation on the nearest table, a bag that had been spared the noble fate of being turned into an Indian costume. She rolled over onto her hands and knees and began to crawl toward it.

Butchie Brockman turned his head briefly and leered triumphantly as he watched the apparently beaten girl crawl away. Then he returned to the pleasant task of subduing his wretched victim, who was struggling with renewed fury. Butchie didn't give Jennifer another thought until suddenly everything looked like burlap. Now he again hurled epithets at her as he struggled to his feet, fighting the enveloping bag.

With the bag, Jennifer had straight-jacketed the butcher boy to the hips, and now began thumping her little fists hammer-fashion on his enclosed head. As Butchie stood up, Danny, ever the opportunist, seized the open end of the bag and yanked downward; now Butchie was bagged to below his knees. He toppled heavily to the floor, struggling against the confining threads.

"Let's go!" Jennifer urged as she grasped Danny's hand and pulled him to his feet.

"Not yet." Again Danny seized the open end of the bag encasing the thrashing butcher boy and lifted him partially off the floor. The bag wasn't quite big enough to hold all of Butchie, but Danny now had him like a fish in a net.

"What are you going to do?" the nearly breathless girl panted.

"Get some a' that string over there," Danny indicated with a toss of his head. Butchie heard, and cursed and threatened horrible vengeance and kicked violently. But Danny held him fast.

"Somebody's going to hear him," Jennifer glanced toward the door worriedly.

"No, I don't think so," Danny replied, and the laughter rolling in from the auditorium did make it seem unlikely. Jennifer fetched the string, stout baling cord, and soon Butchie was thoroughly trussed up in the burlap bag, his well-secured feet thrusting out of the end of it.

"You know," Jennifer smiled as she viewed their handiwork. "He looks a little like a turkey just before you put it in the oven."

Butchie's vile threats had given way to frustrated sobs. "You just wait! You just wait! I'll get even," he ranted. Danny was tempted to apply the verbal needle to the sniffling Butchie, but he knew that every jibe was likely to be repaid with another punch, sooner or later. He was content merely to dispose of his nemesis for the time being.

Danny grabbed Butchie by his exposed ankles and began dragging him across the polished floor. "Open the closet for me, will ya, Jennifer?" he asked the girl as he tugged at his feebly resisting load. Jennifer obliged, and Butchie was promptly deposited on the floor of the costume-crammed closet.

"Hey, yer not gonna leave me here, are yuh?" The butcher boy wailed in disbelief. He tried to get up, but the mass of hanging costumes he could not see foiled his clumsy efforts. Finally he laid still, a burlap-bundled lump of helpless futility.

"Just holler when the fifth and sixth graders come back," Danny advised his trussed-up tormentor. "Maybe you've got a friend in that bunch."

"Naw, wait, don't let them see me like this, Danny! I'll make a deal with ya…"

Danny closed the door on the pleading Butchie, reducing that unhappy lad's muffled entreaties to intermittent thumps and sobs. Then he followed Jennifer to a tiny corner wash basin where a stack of wash cloths awaited the return of the painted performers. The girl wet a cloth under the faucet and turned to administer to Danny's bloodied face.

"Seems like this is getting to be a habit." Her eyes were sympathetic as she studied Danny's battered features.

"Then maybe next time you shouldn't butt in," he said, snatching the cloth from her hand and stepping to the mirror, where he proceeded to rectify the damage as best he could.

At the moment Danny could feel the budding bruises better than he could see them, but he knew that by tomorrow they would be very much in evidence and impossible to conceal. He was grateful that the long holiday weekend would give him additional time to heal before he'd have to return to school.

From some mysterious place Jennifer had produced a comb, and was putting herself back in order. "I was only trying to help," she said finally, her subdued words breaking the awkward silence. "It seemed like he would never stop hitting you."

"I'da lived." Danny was pleased to see that most of the blood was from inside his mouth, where his teeth had cut his lips and cheeks under the force of Butchie's blows. His teeth felt numb, but apparently all that he had were still in place. He caught sight of Jennifer's reflection in the mirror and saw the confused look on her face. He knew he had hurt her.

"I guess I just don't understand boys," she said, fighting a tear as she applied the comb vigorously to her hair.

Obviously she didn't understand, Danny thought. But after all, she was a girl. He turned to her and smiled warmly through blood-flecked teeth. "Well, maybe you can't understand boys, Jennifer," he told her, "But you sure can fight like one!"

Instantly she felt better, and returned his smile. "I'm not sure that's supposed to be a compliment, but I'll take it as such," she beamed.

Jennifer turned her head as another muffled thump came from the closet. "Danny, we can't leave Randolph in there," she added earnestly. "When he's found, the teachers will ask a million questions."

"Yer prob'ly right," Danny agreed as he headed for the room's exit, brushing himself off as he went. "C'mon, I know what to do."

He led the way around the backstage to where Roger stood by the curtain ropes. On stage, the undersized pilgrims and Indians seemed to be getting along famously.

"How's it goin', Roger?" Danny asked casually.

"Okay, I guess, 'cept I wish Butchie would – say, what happened to you?" he peered at Danny's damp and reddened face. Then he shot a glance at Jennifer, a picture of wide-eyed innocence, studiously attentive to the action on the stage.

"Nuthin' much," Danny shrugged. "But Butchie's got a surprise for ya. He wants ya to meet him in the dressin' room closet after you've opened the curtain for the next scene."

"I dunno about Butchie's surprises," Roger said dubiously.

"Oh, you'll enjoy this one, won't he, Jennifer?" Danny replied, and the girl, still apparently concentrating on the play, nodded vigorously. "Sumpthin' funny goin' on around here," Roger sniffed suspiciously. "Why can't I go now?"

"Why, that'd spoil things," Danny said honestly. "Besides, Mrs. Gurney needs you here on these curtain ropes."

"This is 'sposed to be Butchie's job," Roger protested. "He promised me he wouldn't be gone long. Where is he?"

"Oh, he's tied up right now," Jennifer couldn't resist commenting as she turned to join the conversation, her eyes twinkling with mischief.

"Yeah," Danny nearly gagged. "An' get Shirley an' Mary Lou to help you with the props. We got somethin' else to do. C'mon, Jennifer," he motioned to the girl as he started toward the stage door. At the door he stopped to address the perplexed Roger. "Don't forget when yer 'sposed to meet Butchie at that closet," he reminded the unwilling curtain engineer. Then he led Jennifer out into the hallway.

The rest of the school was deserted as the pair strode swiftly but silently toward the eighth grade classroom.

"I take it we're going to be leaving a little early," Jennifer guessed.

"I think we better, 'specially after that awful gag you told Roger," he looked at her reprovingly. "Oh, I think he's tied up right now," he mimicked her voice.

Jennifer laughed. "I'm sorry," she said, not meaning it a bit.

They had reached their classroom. Danny snatched his jacket off the cloakroom wall. Jennifer slipped into her coat and a colorful head scarf, then went to her desk to gather up her purse and several textbooks. The impatient Danny shook his head in silent wonder. What a way to spend the holiday weekend!

Again Danny led the way, down the short flight of stairs to the nearest exit. In back of them the ring of applause and laughter sounded from the auditorium. Danny held open the door for Jennifer then closed it quietly behind them.

The blustery wind tugged at them as they made their way swiftly across the school grounds. The dark sky hung ominously low, and a scattering of fat snowflakes spun dizzily in the air. It appeared that the long delayed promise of a heavy snowfall was about to be made good.

Nothing was said until they rounded the nearest corner and were out of sight of the school. Jennifer's face was tinged bright pink with the exertion. Danny's thoroughly thumped features were red anyhow.

"I just had a thought," Jennifer spoke up worriedly as they slowed their walk. "After the program, isn't Mrs. Gurney going to miss us?"

"Naw," Danny scoffed. "That stage an' dressin' room is always a mob scene after one of these things. All the actors' mammas all over the place. Takin' pictures, even."

"Oh? Well, I hope Roger has turned Randolph loose before then," the girl's voice reflected her concern. "If not, there's bound to be a lot of questions asked, and I'm afraid I'm not a very good liar."

"Don't worry. Roger will turn 'm loose. Ol' Rog is very dependable."

"I hope so."

Soon they reached the point of parting. "If yer scared a' Butch, I can walk ya a ways yet," Danny offered awkwardly.

"Oh, I don't think that'll be necessary," Jennifer glanced down the deserted street behind them. "Even if he ran all the way home, I don't think he'd catch up with me. Besides," and her forced smile could not mask the concern in her eyes, "It's not me he's likely to be looking for."

Danny shrugged. Dodging the pugnacious Butchie Brockman had long been a way of life for him.

Jennifer eyed Danny's abused features. "How does your face feel now?" she asked.

"Prob'ly looks worse'n it feels," Danny lied with a smile. The initial numbness was giving way to throbbing pain, and the cuts inside his mouth stung like fury.

"Better get doctored up just as soon as you get home," Jennifer advised. "Do you still want to meet at the dime store Friday morning?"

"Sure. But fer Pete's sake, don't let onto anybody what we're doin'," he again cautioned her. "Not anybody."

The distant sound of the school bell spurred them into parting.

"See ya Friday," Danny waved as he crossed the street. Jennifer waved in reply as she resumed her way down the sidewalk.

"Have a nice Thanksgiving," she called after him.

"Prob'bly sippin' soup," Danny said to himself as he gingerly explored the cuts inside his mouth with his tongue.

Anxious as he was to look back, he didn't want to do so until he was certain that Jennifer was out of sight. So he hurried on, wondering just how close behind him an outraged and absolutely furious Butchie Brockman might be.

CHAPTER 18

Homer Brings Big News

The nicest thing about Thanksgiving Day, as far as Daniel Van Kuyper was concerned, was the sea of snow in which all of Hornville seemed to be adrift, the result of an overnight blizzard. This was not the thin layer of decorative frosting the first snowfall had been – not by a long shot!

This one was thicker than lard and twice as white. The shrubs and trees drooped under the weight of the sticky, clinging mass, and large lumps in the streets were the only clues to the disappearance of several automobiles. The drift on the porch was so high it was impossible to open the front door.

Looking out from the windows of his bedroom, where he had spent most of the day in self-imposed exile, Danny was able for brief moments to forget the soreness of his swollen face as he marveled at the transformation the snow had wrought, at the strange feeling the vast whiteness gave him. Last night the cascading snow had almost obliterated the haloed streetlamp, but the storm had ceased now, and here and there slanting shafts of sunlight seeped through ragged clouds to add dazzling touches to the scene.

The new peace without provided a much-needed balm for the sore and sorely-tried Danny. Arriving home after school yesterday, he had managed to avoid close scrutiny by anybody until the dinner hour. Even then he considered the "I don't feel good; I'm going to bed early" dodge, but at last decided that he couldn't hide his face forever. He would have to get it over with.

As it was, he had slipped into his place so quietly amidst all the chatter that nobody noticed his condition until the bowl of mashed potatoes had nearly completed its circuit around the table. Then Mrs. Van Kuyper looked at him and dropped the bowl.

"Good heavens, Danny! What happened to you?" she said, shocked, never noticing that the falling bowl had fractured her dinner plate.

The rest of the suddenly silent family snapped their heads from a quick glance at the broken china to a hard look at the cause of it all, Danny's face. They remained speechless.

Danny looked down at his small scoop of mashed potatoes, all he had planned to have for dinner.

"Daniel!" his father's stern voice commanded. "Look at me."

Danny raised his head slightly, and out of the corner of his eye looked at his father's nose.

"Your mother asked you what happened," Ray Van Kuyper continued quietly.

Danny shrugged. "Had a fight," he mumbled.

"Who with?"

"Butchie Brockman."

"Why?"

"Dunno."

"Whaddaya mean you don't know?"

Danny shrugged again. "Dunno, is all. He started it."

"Daddy, why does he talk so funny?" Herbie chimed in.

"Mouth chopped up inside?" Mr. Van Kuyper continued.

Danny nodded.

"Teeth all there?"

Danny nodded again.

"Oh, Danny," Mrs. Van Kuyper wailed, wringing her hands. "Are you and that Brockman boy ever going to learn to get along?"

Again Danny shrugged.

"Eat whatever you can," his father advised. "Then you'd better try some warm salt water rinse, or maybe the mouthwash."

"Yethir," Danny replied, only it was more of a whistle. Then he mouthed a small forkful of mashed potatoes and tried swallowing without chewing.

Doris had quietly replaced her mother's broken dinner plate, but Mrs. Van Kuyper was still too distraught to eat. Not so little Herbie, who was munching happily on a piece of flank steak. Even Mr. Van Kuyper had returned to the task at hand.

"Ray, don't you think we ought to take him to the doctor?" Elsie Van Kuyper asked her husband.

"Naw," he replied, looking at his son. "No broken bones, no cuts to speak of, just a few bruises. And he says his teeth are okay, so why bug the dentist on Thanksgiving Eve?"

"Did you put disinfectant on those scratches?" Doris asked her brother. Danny swallowed a lump of mashed potatoes and nodded.

"See, he's all set," Ray Van Kuyper reassured his wife. "He'll heal in a few days."

"Then probably he'll get into another fight," she said. "Ray, why don't you speak to Mr. Brockman about his son?"

"Oh, I 'spose I could," her husband replied, not sounding overly enthusiastic. "Heinie Brockman bowls in my bowling league. A real nice guy. The boys just haven't learned to get along yet, that's all."

Thus had gone last night's dinner hour. Danny had spent most of last evening in the kitchen, rinsing his mouth with warm salt water. It felt good. His sleep had been fitful, but the blizzard had kept the waking moments interesting. And the breakfast oatmeal had gone down fairly easily.

Despite his aches, the aroma of roast turkey drifting up from the lower reaches of the house tantalized Danny. He resolved that he would have some, even if he had to grind it up like hamburger.

Far up the street Danny saw a couple of hardy souls venture forth with snow shovels in hand. Then his gaze reverted to the near corner, where a familiar figure had just slogged into view. It was Homer Peckley, tramping along on a pair of show shoes.

Homer was evidently a believer in the straight line – shortest distance theory. He tromped right over a couple of drifted mounds that had to be parked cars as he headed straight toward the Van Kuyper house.

Danny raised the inside window and pushed out the storm window. Several crusts of snow plopped noiselessly into the mass of the stuff already on the roof beneath the gable.

Seeing his friend, Homer stopped between the snow-laden spruces in front of the house. He looked taller; no doubt because he was standing atop about two feet of snow. Danny was glad to see him.

"Where's yer new bike?" Danny started right in ribbing his visitor.

"Ain't got it yet," the freckle-face replied matter-of-factly. "But I had tuh see yuh. Kin yuh cum out?"

"Nope, an' I don't think my mom'll letcha in, either. I'm kinda in the doghouse."

"Yeah, an' yuh don't hafta tell me why, eider. I kin see dat plain enough from here," Homer replied, eyeing Danny's puffed face. "Boy, it musta bin a real knock-down, drag-out doozer."

"Yer pretty sharp!" Danny complimented his friend.

"It don't take no brains tuh see," observed the redhead. "What I wanna know is, howdja get Butchie in dat shape in duh closet yet?"

Danny startled. "Whaddaya mean? You been talkin' to Roger?"

"Naw, I ain't seen Roger, an' yuh know doggone well what I mean. Why, everybody knows what I mean. Man oh man, when dem kids opened dat closet, an' dey screamed fer dere mammas an' teechurs, an' Missus Gurney unwrapped Butchie in fronta everybody..."

"Oh, Lordy," Danny moaned, holding his sore head. Now it *really* hurt.

"Boy, yuh shoulda seed ol' Randy-baby tear outa dere, bawlin' his head off. Why, he din't stop fer nuttin'. Tore right outa school an' disapeart. Yuh shoulda seen ol' lady Hecker when he come zoomin' by. I wuz sure her teet' an' her eyeballs wuz gonna pop out."

"Oh, Lordy," Danny moaned again.

"Yuh ain't sayin' much," Homer commented, shuffling around atop the snow. His feet had to be cold. "Is dat who helped yuh? Roger?"

Danny was holding his head in his hands, his elbows propped on the windowsill. "No," he finally replied, then briefly outlined the details of his battle with the butcher boy.

"Hey, you and dat Jenny make quite a team," Homer teased. "Better'n Batman an' Robin."

But Danny was feeling too miserable to mind. "Roger was supposed to turn 'm loose," he groaned. "What happened?"

"I dunno," Homer chipped in. "But after Butchie took off, ol' Miz Hecker went lookin' fer her volunteers. She only found Mary Lou an' Shirley."

"Good grief, that's all I need, trouble with Miss Hecker," Danny commiserated aloud. "An' I get Jennifer in trouble to boot."

"Well, I got sumptin else fer yuh, maybe make yuh feel better, maybe worser. I dunno."

"Like what?" Danny asked automatically. It seemed he could hardly care.

Homer looked around carefully, ensuring Danny was his only listener. "Like I tippy-toed past Sharkey's Snug Harbor comin' home yestidday," he whispered. "Dere's dis big car parked 'roun' duh side, got dem Illy-noise license plates on it."

Suddenly Danny cared. "What else?"

"Nuttin'. But maybe it means Sharkey's blowin' town."

"An' maybe it means more trouble 'round here."

"Could be. I dunno." Homer was agreeable.

"Just don't go findin' any more dead bodies," Danny advised his friend.

"Don't worry 'bout dat, pal. Right now I'd step right over me own mudder's dead body, an' not notice," Homer reassured him.

"For heaven's sake, Danny," his mother's voice rang up the stairs. "Are you talking to yourself up there?"

"No, Mom. Homer's out front."

"And I'll wager you're hanging out the window in this weather with only your t-shirt on!" Mrs. Van Kuyper's voice was critical, and her guess correct. "You close that window and get ready to come down and *try* to eat some dinner." Her sarcasm was most obvious.

"I gotta see Jennifer in the mornin'," Danny bade his friend farewell. "I'll come out to yer place 'bout noon."

"Sure t'ing," Homer waved a red, chilled hand and began to tromp off into the early dusk. "Don't eat too many sour pickles."

Homer needn't have worried. Danny had already tried sucking on one for lunch. Ooooh, how that vinegar had stung!

CHAPTER 19

Vanished!

Danny marched down the middle of the freshly plowed street, his rubber galoshes swishing together as he headed toward Central Avenue and his dime store rendezvous with Jennifer. Overhead the sky was bright blue, and all the vast tonnages of snow were radiant in the mid-morning sun.

Hornville was busy digging out this Friday after Thanksgiving. The snow plow crews had evidently been busy all night, for most of the streets had at least one lane cleared through them.

Few cars were in evidence. Most of them were still buried, or marooned in snowbound garages. Those few that were free to move rolled along slowly on chained tires through the glazed crust left by the snow plows.

As Danny approached Central Avenue, an unfamiliar whirring, chopping noise brought him to a startled halt. A helicopter, something rarely seen in the Hornville area, rose up from somewhere in the business district and sloped off in a northerly direction toward the river, its spinning rotor glinting as it climbed into the sky. Danny wondered what snowbound farmer might have an emergency warranting this kind of attention.

"I guess everybody's got problems," he philosophized as he reached Hornville's main thoroughfare.

The motor traffic on Central Avenue was sufficient to make him pause. Already the flattened crust left by the snow plows had been worked into a frozen brown slush which plopped in heavy sprays as the passing vehicles lumbered through it. A break in the traffic gave Danny the opportunity to make his way across the street, the slush squirting out from beneath his galoshes as he slogged along.

Jennifer Markham was already inside the nearly deserted dime store, sitting in a booth opposite the lunch counter, absentmindedly stirring a cup of hot chocolate. Danny noted her troubled expression as he entered the store. As he sat down opposite her, he could have sworn by the looks of her that she had been crying.

"Butchie Brockman's gotten hold of you, I bet," were his first words, and his tone was angry.

"No, of course not," she answered, shaking her head, a question rising in her voice. "Don't you know? Haven't they called your house yet?"

"What about?"

"About Randolph. Nobody's seen him since he ran out of school Wednesday afternoon."

"Butchie's run off? I can't believe it!" Danny gaped, propping up his disbelieving head.

"Apparently he has," the girl assured him. "Mr. and Mrs. Brockman are frantic, and this blizzard we had didn't help a bit. The police are phoning everybody who knows Randolph, and they've even brought in a helicopter to search the countryside…"

"Is that why it's here? I just saw it take off," Danny interjected.

"Yes. They land it on the parking lot next to the police station," Jennifer continued. "Also, the volunteer firemen are forming search parties to look for him."

"In all that snow? Boy, he'd better found a warm place to hole up before that blizzard hit."

"Oh, Danny," Jennifer was near tears. "I feel just terrible! What if he's lying somewhere under all that snow?"

"Geez, they mightn't find 'm 'til spring." Danny's comment didn't help Jennifer a bit. "I just can't believe he'd take it so hard."

"I guess the humiliation of being found as he was by all those people was too much for him. What happened to your little plan? Why didn't Roger turn him loose?"

"I dunno," Danny shook his head. "But it really don't matter much now."

The waitress finally came over and Danny ordered a hot chocolate for himself. Soon both young people were glumly stirring their cups. Jennifer's marshmallow was already melted, and Danny used his spoon to submerge his in the steaming liquid. But neither one had much appetite for the treat set before them.

"I meant to bring some doughnuts from home," Jennifer apologized. "But I was so upset I forgot."

"That's okay; I'm not chewin' too good lately anyhow."

"How do you feel? You look much better than you did the other day."

Physically, at least, Danny was feeling much improved, and he said so. Most of the swelling had receded, and the redness replaced by a few dull-colored bruises. Outside of the cuts in his mouth, which bothered particularly at mealtimes, he felt no particular discomfort.

"If something... awful has happened to Randolph, we're sure to be blamed." Jennifer finally took a tentative sip of her chocolate.

"Not we, just me," Danny corrected her. "There's no point in both of us takin' the blame. When Miss Hecker calls us on the carpet, I'll tell her I did it, an' I asked ya to walk me home 'cause I wasn't feelin' so good."

The girl shook her head. "No, it won't work. Roger knows we were both involved."

"I'll talk to Roger first."

"No," Jennifer was emphatic. "I won't shirk my responsibility in the matter. Besides, some people might find it a little hard to believe that you bundled up Randolph all by yourself."

Danny hated to admit it, but the girl was right. "Okay. But we tell 'em I made ya help me."

Now Jennifer was actually smiling. "Danny, why don't we just tell the truth? It'll be a whole lot easier."

Danny shrugged. "You haven't told anybody yet, have ya?"

"No. When the police called this morning, they spoke mostly to my Aunt. About all they asked me was if I had any idea where Randolph might be. And I certainly didn't – I was so flabbergasted I could hardly talk."

"Hope that didn't make yer aunt or uncle suspicious. No point in gettin' 'em riled up any sooner'n necessary. Before Butchie shows up," Danny added hopefully. He gave up trying to drown the remainder of his marshmallow, and began to sip his chocolate.

"No, they were already too upset, which brings up the other thing we have to talk about. I almost phoned you yesterday, but I don't imagine your mother approves of girls calling boys any more than my mother does…" Jennifer almost bit her tongue, but Danny pretended not to notice. "Anyway, "she concluded, "I didn't want to cause any more problems for you at your house."

Danny smiled. "I don't get many phone calls," he said, not bothering to add that such few he had were never from girls. "There'da been a few questions asked, fer sure."

"Well, I've got a few questions of my own," Jennifer replied. "About your suspected auto thief. He's gone, too."

Danny perked up. "That's the first good news I've had in awhile! I'll hafta tell Homer, so's he can tell his Uncle Herman."

"Maybe you ought to hear the rest before you rush off to Uncle Herman." The girl eyed Danny skeptically, causing him to shift uneasily. "Wednesday evening, before it started to snow so hard, I looked out my window upstairs. There were two police cars parked in front of Mrs. McClatchy's. I could see straight into the man's room, and two policemen were looking all around in there, and Mrs. McClatchy was standing there, waving her hands in the air. Then one of the policemen came directly across to the bakery and talked to my aunt and uncle."

"Did they talk to anybody else on the street?" Danny asked. His earlier elation about the matter was giving way to a growing unease.

"Not as far as I could tell. When I came downstairs, they had finished talking, or at least they quit, and the policeman left. My uncle tried not to act upset, but my aunt was crying. And when I asked what the matter was, they said it was none of my concern, and I shouldn't worry about it. Later I heard him say to her, "Don't carry on so, Hilda. Jennifer has noticed the man, and she will know something is wrong." And I haven't seen the man or a light in his room since."

Danny was lost in a confusion of thoughts. He sipped his chocolate without tasting it. "Yer sure the cop didn't come askin' about Butch maybe bein' at the bakery?"

"This was Wednesday evening," Jennifer reminded him. "I don't think they even knew yet that Randolph was missing. They didn't call me about him until this morning."

Danny continued to ponder the significance of Jennifer's story. Some it seemed to make sense and some of it didn't.

"Danny," the girl broke quietly into his thoughts. "Was that man really a car thief?"

Danny shrugged. "No," he finally admitted. "Least, not as far as I know."

"What *do* you know about him?"

"I'm not sure what I think I know anymore," Danny admitted candidly. Then he looked the girl straight in the eye, hard. "Jennifer, I ain't never heard, an' as far as I know, you ain't never said, but where'dja live before you 'n yer little brother came to Hornville?"

Now it was the girl's turn to shift about uneasily. She looked down into her nearly empty cup. "Down state," she said. "Racine."

"I went through there once, when we drove down to Chicago."

Jennifer continued to stare into her cup.

"I don't mean to pry, but how come yer Mom 'n Dad didn't move up here with you?"

Jennifer looked up, trying to appear nonchalant. "Oh, um, they're... they're on a long trip. Couldn't take us along."

The girl lied so poorly it embarrassed Danny, but he wasn't about to embarrass her unduly. "Just answer me yes or no on this one thing," he said quietly. "There's been some kinda trouble in yer fam'ly that the cops know about, ain't so?"

Jennifer's eyes dropped again. She trembled, then nodded her head ever so slightly.

Danny proceeded to drain the residue of his hot chocolate. Now some things are beginning to make sense, he thought. "C'mon," the boy said cheerily, picking up both checks as he slid out of the booth. "We've got lots of work to do."

"Danny, I can pay for my own," Jennifer protested, making a futile grab at her check.

"I owe you just this one," Danny replied, leading the way toward the cash register. "You earned it."

The two checks wiped out most of a fifty-cent piece. It was the first time Danny had ever bought anything for a girl. And it was the same coin he had recently saved on the non- purchase of a pumpkin.

CHAPTER 20

Doughnuts, Detectives, and… Danger!

"What's all this work we have to do?" Jennifer prodded Danny as she hurried to keep up with the long-striding lad.

They were marching down the newly cleared sidewalks of Central Avenue, away from the dime store. Much of the sidewalk was sprinkled with rock salt, spread by Hornville's more provident merchants, intended to melt the residue ice and prevent any disastrous falls in front of their business establishments.

There was plenty of work to do all right, Danny thought, but he really hadn't intended to include the girl. His remark back in the dime store was primarily intended to soothe her feelings, not invite her along. Now he was trying to think of some way to abandon her gracefully.

"Well, first we gotta find Homer," Danny stalled, "An' then we might hafta do some serious hikin', which you ain't 'xactly dressed for." He eyed the stretches of goose-pimpled leg extending from her skirt hem to her tiny transparent plastic shoe covers.

"My place is right on the way to Homer's, isn't it?" Jennifer asked, and the boy nodded reluctantly. "Fine! We can stop in the bakery shop and I'll ask my Aunt if I may go along."

Danny grumbled inaudibly. He lengthened his stride, hoping his pace might discourage her, but she moved along with short, quick steps, apparently having no trouble keeping abreast of him.

They reached the corner of Packard Avenue and turned north, Danny's rubber galoshes fairly whistling as they brushed together with his every step. The sound blended with the clank and scrape of snow shovels heard in all directions, and together with the sun-brightened spectacle which met the eye, the total effect was not unpleasant.

But the mood changed as they passed Brockman's butcher shop. The bean-filled apothecary jar still stood in the window, and posted alongside was the list of the contest winners, Homer Peckley's name very prominent at the top. Stuck to the window of the shop door was another sign, hastily printed, that read "Closed Until Further Notice". The inside of the shop was dark and still.

"Oh, those poor people," Jennifer said. "Really, kids ought to think more of their parents when they do foolish things like run away."

Danny had to think about that one. He had long held the notion that some parents, at least, might be grateful.

Miller's Bakery was on the next block, and the young people edged their way around an emerging customer as they entered the shop. Mrs. Miller greeted them cheerily, but her smile failed to mask the strain of worry showing in her face. Jennifer asked if she could go hiking with Danny and Homer, and much to the boy's surprise, and dismay, the old Aunt agreed.

"I'll be down as soon as I change," Jennifer piped as she disappeared through the swinging doors into the back of the shop.

"Here, mine boy, haff ein chuklid doughnut," urged the old lady, and Danny was happy to oblige, hooking his finger through a big one.

"My, vot heppin mit yer face?" Mrs. Miller asked, looking at him with concern.

"I hurt it," Danny answered. "It's all right now."

He stepped to the front window and munched the doughnut slowly, mindful of his sore cheeks. Down and across the street a sludge-streaked police car was now parked in front of Mrs. McClatchy's boarding house, and Danny thought he could see some activity in the front room, upstairs. He wondered if this could be why Mrs. Miller was so agreeable to Jennifer's leaving for awhile.

"Let's go!" Jennifer startled Danny out of the deep recesses of his thoughts.

He coughed once to dislodge a piece of doughnut, then gave the girl a hasty appraisal. She was now more sensibly attired in dark blue snow pants and jacket, a pair of substantial appearing galoshes and that same kooky-colored head scarf.

"'Bye, Aunt Hilda," the girl called as Danny opened the door.

"Goot bye, jungen," the old lady replied. "Haff a nize time playink in der schnow."

Danny, still munching his doughnut, settled for a parting wave.

The pair of them stared steadily at Mrs. McClatchy's as they tramped along the opposite side of the street, as if hoping they might glean some more information from a long, hard look at the place.

"Between Randolph running away and that man disappearing, the police certainly have their hands full, don't they?" Jennifer commented, hoping to induce a little conversation out of her companion.

"Yeah," was all she got in reply, as Danny was content to use his mouth solely for the purpose of masticating the last remnants of his chocolate doughnut.

As they reached the corner, they looked back toward McClatchy's in time to see three figures emerge from the boarding house and enter the police car. Danny recognized the uniformed figure of Hornville's police chief, Pat Lathrop. The other two men, dressed in civilian garb, hats and topcoats, he could not recall ever having seen before.

"Do you recognize them?" Jennifer asked.

"Only the chief."

"I wonder who the other two are."

"Outa town detectives, I bet," Danny speculated.

"How would you know?"

"Because we ain't got any in-town detectives here, is why," Danny replied, smiling smugly to himself as his devious answer seemed to perplex the girl for the moment.

"But how do you know they're detectives at all?" Jennifer finally asked again, eyeing the boy critically.

"Well, they sure don't look like TV repairmen, do they?" he answered as the two of them watched the police car drive off in the opposite direction.

"No they don't, smarty," Jennifer sounded a trifle annoyed as they resumed their walk down Packard Avenue. "But that doesn't make them detectives, either."

"Don't it bother ya that when that guy disappeared, the only people the cops come to see was yer Aunt an' Uncle?"

"It did seem curious. I never saw the man come into the shop, but I thought perhaps my Aunt and Uncle might know him."

"I'm guessin' they didn't 'ticlarly know 'm. Only about him."

"Meaning what?" the puzzled girl asked.

"Well... when didja come to Hornville? I'm guessin' just before school started, yes?"

"Yes, but..."

"Well, so did he."

"How do you know?"

"Never mind, I know. He come here when you come here, an' our cops seem awful excited 'bout his disappearing an' you let on back in the dime store the cops knew somethin' 'bout yer family..."

The girl looked at him dumbly, her hand to her mouth, as though struck by some sudden revelation. Lost in thought, the pair marched on in silence toward the Wausupee River and Homer Peckley's house.

CHAPTER 21

Pow Wow at Peckley's Boatyard

Jennifer and Danny found Homer in the boathouse back of the Peckley residence, the hub of that small private enterprise known locally as Peckley's Boatyard. Homer was lackadaisically applying a paint brush to a long rowboat resting upside down on a pair of sawhorses. The double doors of the boathouse stood wide open, catching the noon sun.

Surprise showed in Homer's face as he sighted Jennifer, and he greeted his visitors with something less than total enthusiasm. He eyed the girl suspiciously.

"Jennifer has come up with some pretty intrustin' stuff," Danny said, feeling it necessary to explain the girl's presence.

Homer was chomping on an apple, the fourth of nearly a dozen clustered on a handy bench, judging by the visible remains.

"Have a apple," Homer indicated the fruit with a wave of his dripping brush.

It was the lunch hour, and they were hungry, so the visitors accepted their host's generous offer. Jennifer ate her apple like a lady, no doubt because she was a young lady. Danny ate his like a gentleman because his still sore mouth afforded him no alternative.

"I 'spose youse guys got called 'bout Butchie, like I did, "Homer said.

Jennifer indicated that she had; Danny said he hadn't been home, but felt sure he'd hear about a call when he returned.

"Yuh know he prob'ly run off 'cuz a-what youse guys done tuh him," Homer advised them unnecessarily, and they nodded in reply. "If he don't show up healt'y purty soon, I'd hate bein' youse guys when ol' lady Hecker starts in astin' questions on Monday," the redhead continued, and his visitors nodded again, glumly. "Could be when she hears he's missin', she might start astin' *before* Monday."

Danny hadn't considered that possibility. It almost killed his appetite for the apple he had in hand. But not quite.

"He just *has* to turn up all right," Jennifer said with the fervency of a prayer, "For everybody's sake."

Homer resumed application of the brush to the rowboat, layering on a fresh coat of the craft's existing color, a shade known among the local boat people as Peckley green. Then he paused again and looked directly at his friend. "Yuh know what got you'n Butchie tanglin' inna first place, don'tcha?" lectured Homer, casting a subduing glance at the girl. Jennifer lowered her eyes and continued to nibble at her apple as she studied the cracks in the boathouse floor.

"Lay off, Homer," Danny growled, his glance at his friend at once angry and beseeching. "I got her into this with that phony story 'bout yer Uncle Herman an' the car stealer..."

A look of alarm spread over Homer's face, and he glanced apprehensively from the unseeing girl back to his friend.

"Oh, she don't know everythin' yet," Danny dismissed Homer's unspoken concern with a wave of his hand. "But she's already guessed that that part ain't true, an' besides, she knows a few things we don't know," he added. "You know," he suddenly decided, "long as we're all here, maybe we should kick this business aroun' together, an' just maybe it'll make some sense."

"Kick what biz'niss 'roun'?" Homer asked warily, wondering what possessed his usually tight-lipped buddy. He was still leery of the girl.

"Believe it or not, Homer," Danny began to explain to his friend, "we got another disappearin' act on our hands, an' prob'ly the guy what's disappeart is in trouble, but maybe we can do somethin' if we think on it. Butchie we can pretty well guess what's happened to him, but Lord knows where he's holed up. He'll just hafta show up when he's good an' ready," Danny added hopefully.

A new disappearance was startling news to Homer, and it was all the excuse he needed to abandon his paint brush and sit down beside his collection of apples, the better to pay attention to his friend.

Danny related to Homer Jennifer's story concerning Mrs. McClatchy's missing boarder, and their observation of Police Chief Lathrop and companions while en route to Homer's place. He also alluded vaguely to some problem involving Jennifer's family and the authorities prior to her arrival in Hornville.

Homer sat listening, his jaws working spasmodically, hardly able to eat his fifth apple. Awestruck, he looked at Jennifer, who was still studying the boathouse floor, and wondered what interest the law could possibly have in such a little slip of a girl.

"Jeeminy Moses!" the redhead exclaimed. "Whatcher sayin' is dat dis guy disappeart, which is what we wanted; but duh cops is mighty curious, which maybe ain't good, 'cuz maybe duh guy din't wanna disappear, which maybe is bad, 'speshly fer him, 'cuz maybe he's a cop, which don't make no sense, 'cuz maybe he's in cahoots wit' Jennifer's Aunt 'n Uncle, which even more don't make no sense, 'cuz maybe duh law's after Jennifer, which hasta be plumb crazy! I don' geddit," Homer shook his perplexed head.

"Aw, ya stoop! I didn't say the cops was after Jennifer. I just said maybe they was keepin' a eye on her."

"Why?"

Jennifer looked up at Homer, staring at her, saw that he was expecting an answer. "It's very possible. I just never thought about it," was all she had to say before resuming her study of the boathouse floor.

"It really don't matter," Danny waved a hand at Homer to shush any further questions on that topic. "Point is, if this guy is a cop, why'd he disappear, an' why don't the other cops seem to know?"

"But he ain't no cop," Homer declared emphatically. "Yuh heard Sharkey say dat guy wuz Doggie Blodgett's friend."

Jennifer looked up, curious about the new names introduced into the discussion.

"I heard Sharkey say he *thought* the guy was Doggie's friend. He coulda been wrong, ya know."

"He din't act like no cop," Homer defended his position.

"He didn't act like a car thief, either," the girl interjected, reminding the boys of her presence.

Homer ignored the implied criticism. "If he's a cop, den who kilt Mr. Goozman? Cops don't stab crooks an' make it look like car accidents."

"That's a good question, Homer," Danny put in. "An' if he's a cop, why'd he disappear?"

"Yuh awready ast dat," Homer reminded him. "An' I ain't got no answer. It makes more sense he's a crook, so I say good riddance tuh bad garbage, an' let's ferget 'm."

"But what if he ain't no crook? Why are the Millers more worried now he's gone than when he was around? An' the police chief hisself is lookin' fer 'm, which is more'n they'd do if some guy just skipped out on his rent."

Homer shrugged wearily. His brain was suffering great strain trying to comprehend the problem. "Maybe he jis' slipped on a sidewalk somewheres, bashed his head an' got snowed on," he tried. "Duh snow plows'll turn him up."

Danny eyed his friend narrowly. "Not very likely," he replied sarcastically. "I'm 'bout convinced he's a cop, and didn't mean to disappear."

"Meanin' What? He wuz kid-snatched, er sumptin'?" Now Homer's voice was sarcastic. "Fine cop he'd be, let hisself get kid-snatched."

"It's possible," Danny argued. "Didn't you say there was this Illinois car parked by Sharkey's place?"

"Yeah, an' I went past dere dis mornin'. Still dere, same place, like it ain't moved. It's all snowed on, but I kin tell it's duh same car. If duh owner kid-snatched yer guy, he sure din't go very far. I t'ink yer nuts."

Danny pondered Homer's negative remarks and ignored the insult. "Ya know, that's a point; the way it snowed Wednesday night, nobody could get very far. Even if somebody started outa town, they'd had ta come back. It's a long ways to anywheres else, 'speshly if yer kidnappin' somebody."

"Well, if yer t'inkin' Sharkey has got a new friend an' dey has kid-snatched dis guy what's disappeart an' has 'm at Sharkey's place now, dere's a easy way tuh find out, an' leave us outa it free an' clear. Let's try wunna dem a-non-eemus phone calls to duh cops."

"No. No good."

"Why ain't it?" Homer challenged.

"'Cause what if the cops go there, an' the guy ain't there? They 'pologize to Sharkey, an' go away.

But, Sharkey figures, who's the only one in this town can tip the cops he's a big crook?"

"You."

"Right! An' I don" like that," Danny shivered. "So he don't know my name, he'll still be lookin' fer me harder'n ever. No, before we turn 'm in, we gotta make sure he's caught red-handed."

"Maybe dis guy ain't dere. Maybe he's in duh river awready, like Doggie wuz," Homer opined.

"Maybe. Maybe not. I gotta find out."

"Why make trouble?" Homer pleaded. "If we don't make none, maybe we won't get none."

"It'd be hard enough to do nuthin' if the guy was a crook," Danny countered. "If the guy turns out to be a cop, an' we coulda saved 'm, we'd hate ourselves ferever."

"What a stew," Homer shook his puzzled head, and then looked at his friend. "So whaddaya gonna do?" he asked.

"Let's just kinda mosey up towards the Snug Harbor an' see if that car's still there. But not get too close, though. It gets dark early now, an' if that car ain't dug out an' gone by dinnertime, maybe after dinner you'n me can do a little snoopin'."

Homer looked at Danny a trifle incredulously, then sighed and shrugged in resignation. "Yuh know," he said, "fer a guy who sez he don't like trouble, yuh sure could fool a guy sumptimes." He stood up and pocketed the rest of his apples. "Okay, let's go."

Jennifer had listened to the boys' conversation with great and growing interest, fairly bursting with questions at every added detail she had gleaned, but prudent enough to keep quiet lest she discourage the boys from talking freely. But now she could contain herself no longer.

"Who is this Sharkey Bates?" she asked excitedly, tagging after the boys as they emerged from the boathouse. "I know who Mr. Guzman is; he's the dead man Homer found. And isn't this Blodgett the man whose body they found in the river on the first day of school?"

The two boys looked at each other, then at the girl.

"Jennifer, yer gonna hafta keep mum about anythin' you hear us say," Danny admonished her. "Otherwise we could get into a real pecka trouble."

"I can imagine!" the girl exclaimed, pop-eyed. "You boys aren't talking about car thieves, you're talking about murderers! How'd you two ever get mixed up in anything like that?"

The two boys exchanged looks again. Homer was obviously wary of taking the girl too much into their confidence. But Danny had clearly reached a decision.

"Homer, I ain't quite figgered it out yet, but somehow Jennifer is tied up in this thing. It's only fair we should take her in with us, an' maybe she can help us. She's helped plenty already."

"I dunno. She ain't tol' us every tin' she knows," Homer grumbled, eyeing the girl.

Jennifer looked away from Homer's sharp gaze. "I can't," she said. "I'm not supposed to say anything to anybody. All I feel free to say is that I've never connected what I know to anybody or anything that's happened around here, except now perhaps with that man at Mrs. McClatchy's boarding house."

"Well, him I conneck wit' everytin' what's happint aroun' here," expounded Homer. "We wouldn' be in dis mess if we hadn'a seed 'm in duh first place. Why even Butchie would be home yet, 'steada took off."

Danny had to think about that last statement of Homer's, but when he mentally sorted out the events leading up to the butcher boy's departure, he concluded that Homer was right.

"I'm sorry you don't feel you can trust me, Homer," Jennifer said quietly, seemingly near tears. "Perhaps I should just go home."

The girl's doleful look made Homer feel like a cad, even though he didn't know what a cad was. He looked at Danny and received no encouragement from that lad's impassive face.

"Okay," Homer grumbled. "If Danny don't care, I don't care. His neck's in duh noose furder den mine is. We'll letcha in on jis' dis one t'ing, since yer in on it anyhow. But I sure don't see how yuh figger in it," he grumbled on, shaking his red head.

Jennifer smiled so sweetly at Homer it almost made him sick.

"C'mon, let's go see if that car's still there," Danny put the trio back into motion.

The little group idled its way up Front Street toward the Snug Harbor tavern. By asking astute questions as they moved along, Jennifer managed to learn the salient facts about the boys' involvement in the murky events plaguing Hornville. That is, when Danny and Homer weren't occupied with crowning each other with the chunks of packed snow left by the snow plow.

Eventually they drew in sight of the Snug Harbor, the long building stretching out over the water on its broad pier. Somebody operating a small Jeep-mounted plow was busily clearing the front parking lot where several cars were still marooned, while a few other men dug around the cars themselves.

Well out on the pier and parked close to the tavern, away from the activity and out of sight of the public entrance, a solitary sedan stood nearly buried in a drift of white snow.

CHAPTER 22

Snug Harbor Hooligans

The boys met again at Homer's after dark, and this time stumped up Front Street with alacrity altogether unlike their dawdling traipse along the same route earlier that afternoon.

The plan was simple. Homer was to go into the Snug Harbor and inquire after Sharkey Bates, pretending to seek a small favor for his father. This would accomplish two things: ascertain that Sharkey was still around, and if so, fix his approximate location in the building. Then Danny and Homer would plan their next move.

As they moved along, Danny recounted the grilling he had received at the dinner table regarding the phone call seeking information about the missing Butchie Brockman. He had been obliged to return the call to the Hornville police station, only to tell them in truth that he, too, knew nothing of the present whereabouts of the missing boy. As yet, apparently nobody but the principals involved made any connection between Danny's fight with Butchie and the latter's subsequent disappearance.

Butchie's flight had been aired on the radio, and even rated a blurb in the evening edition of the Milwaukee daily. Before dinner, Danny had read that paper carefully for any mention of Mrs. McClatchy's missing boarder, but found none.

The weekly edition of the Hornville Bugle had also arrived that evening, late, and Homer's heroics as a bean counter and body finder had been relegated to the lower reaches of the front page by a photo and bulletin describing the missing Randolph Brockman, and the posting of a five hundred dollar reward by his parents for information leading to the boy's return.

"Boy, dat's What we oughta be doin' 'steada worryin' 'bout dat cop, er crook, er whatever he is. We oughta be findin' Butchie fer five hunnert bucks." Homer was a pragmatic soul.

"Who knows where Butchie is? This guy we at least have a hunch."

"An' What if he ain't dere?"

Danny hated to consider the possibility. "I don't know. Then we might have to go tell the cops, an' face all kindsa music. But I sure don't want to."

"Butchie looks like a better bet tuh me," argued Homer. "Much more safer, an' much more profitubble."

"But where is he? My Pop says they've had guys trampin' all over every place on snowshoes, an' ain't found hide nor hair. He says they're even thinkin' 'bout draggin' the river," Danny shivered. "Yuh don't think he'd do anythin' crazy like that, do ya?"

"Naw," Homer scoffed, "Too cold."

The crisp, black sky was spattered with stars, and an uncertain north wind tossed up curlicues of powdered snow which dusted Front Street as they twisted across it. Traffic was light; only twice during their mile-long trek were the boys forced to share the plowed lanes of Front Street with passing cars.

They reached a point opposite the Snug Harbor. Danny stood shivering in the shadows of a darkened warehouse while Homer ambled slowly across the partially plowed parking lot toward the neon-lit corner doorway of the tavern. Plainly, his lack of speed as he approached the place indicated Homer still had some misgivings about his mission. But after skirting several parked cars, the reluctant redhead at last reached the door, and then, pausing briefly as if to steel himself, opened it and entered the tavern. Danny heard a few notes of tinkly music before the heavy door swung shut.

Silently stamping his chilled feet in the muffling snow, Danny wondered if Homer would ever emerge from the Snug Harbor again. It seemed as though his friend had been inside the place forever, even though actually only a few minutes had elapsed.

A car moved slowly down Front Street, its tire chains rattling as the car crunched through the crusted snow. The vehicle turned into the Snug Harbor's parking lot and rolled to a halt close to the tavern's entrance. Several people emerged from the car, their laughter carrying easily through the crisp night air; a typical group of Friday night revelers.

Danny watched as the cluster of people moved toward the tavern door before filing inside. Then he smiled to himself, relieved, as he saw a shorter figure pop out the door and weave through the group. It was Homer, all right, and he jogged across the long parking lot as easily as his oversized galoshes would allow.

The redhead slowed to a walk as he crossed the street toward Danny, the vapors of his breath plainly visible in the street lamp light. Then he paused to look all around before rejoining his friend in the shadows of the warehouse.

"Sharkey's dere," Homer announced flatly, a hint of excitement in his voice.

"Didja see 'm?"

"No, but I sure heerd 'm! He's got dis guy Al dere what tends bar sometimes, an' I sez I wanna see Mr. Bates, an' he sez go 'way Sharkey's busy, an' I sez I gotta see 'm my ol' man sent me, so Al he picks up dis phone an' rings a buzzer an' I hears dis voice right t'rough duh phone say "Yeah?" It's Sharkey, he sounds so sore dis Al he pert-near drops duh phone."

Homer paused to wipe his nose on his sleeve, then started again. "Well, dis Al sez Boss, Josh Peckley's kid is here… he wants tuh see yuh, Sharkey sez what fer, dis Al sez what fer. I sez my ol' man wants Mr. Bates should donate a door prize for duh Boatyard Operators Christmas Ball, dis Al sez Josh wants tuh bum a bottle a' booze fer some wingding, Sharkey I c'n hear roar like a bull sez tell dat ugly son of a moochin' minnow peddler he should go soak his pointy head inna bait bucket don't bodder me no more I'm busy, and dis Al he put-near drops duh phone again he sez sorry, Sonny, duh Boss sez no, t'anks."

The redhead was nearly breathless from his lengthy soliloquy, but he wasn't through yet. "But dat ain't duh best part," he panted.

"No? What else?"

"Well," Homer continued, "while dis Al's got duh phone, I kin hear from Sharkey's end a coupla udder guys loud, like dey wuz arguin', only I can't make out what dey're sayin'."

"So! Sharkey's got some mad friends! That's good!"

Homer was perplexed. "So what's so good about it?" he asked.

"So let's go hear what they're fightin' about," Danny enthused, rubbing his chill-stiffened hands together. "An' quick, before they stop fightin'."

"Yuh gone cuckoo? Yuh fergot awready las' time he *shot* atcha? Let's go make a a-non-eemuss call tuh duh cops, tell 'em tuh go find out what duh argumint's all about."

Danny was studying the side of the Snug Harbor that he could see. Far down the length of the building, well out on the pier, yellow light slanted out of a pair of windows onto the snow. "You've been in there," Danny questioned his chum. "How's it laid out?"

"No a-non-eemuss phone call?"

"Not just yet. Let's find out a coupla more things first."

Homer shrugged resignedly. "Okay," he sighed, looking toward the Snug Harbor. "Backa duh tavern part dere's dis big warehouse part, where Sharkey's got his likker an' boat gear an' all kinds a junk stashed. Backa dat's duh house part, where he lives, and 'way at duh end is dat office wit' duh trap door where yuh met 'm duh first time. Yuh plannin' tuh meet 'm again?"

Danny quivered. "Not if I can help it. This time we'll be more careful."

"How?"

"Look here – this side a' the pier is all snowed under yet. Everybody's usin' the other side, past the front door. See them lighted windows way down? That's prob'ly the house part, an' where he 'n them guys are right now. Walkin' out on that snow'll be like walkin' on feathers. We should be able to get real close."

Homer studied the lit windows and pondered the plan. "Wit' all dis snow, an' dem lights out front, it ain't so dark, yuh know. Somebody'll spot us gettin' over dere."

"So let's go down the street a ways, an' come up below the river bank to the pier. That way somebody's gotta come across to where it ain't plowed to see us, and that ain't likely."

Homer studied the layout again. "Okay, fearless leader," he said finally. "Let's go."

Ten minutes later the boys were struggling up the steep, snow-slicked incline of the river bank approaching the unplowed side of the pier. They reached the pier level, and found themselves only steps away from the still-marooned car which Homer had earlier pointed out as the vehicle with the Illinois license plates.

Danny led the way out onto the pier, his galoshes sinking deeply into the spread of unbroken snow. Occasionally the capricious wind would bring to their ears faint snatches of music from the tavern's juke box. Once they were startled by a flash of headlights on the snow behind them; they waited until whoever had arrived in the car, parked out of their sight, and was heard to enter the tavern.

Again they resumed their cautious advance along the dark side of the building, passing a tall set of double doors hung on an overhead rail.

"Duh warehouse part," Homer whispered. "Dey even back trucks out dis far."

Now they were approaching the first of the lighted windows. The bottom halves were curtained and thin shades were drawn down to mid-window. This would make it difficult to see in, but almost impossible to see out, a satisfactory compromise as far as Danny was concerned.

They had come to listen, not to see, and the listening was getting good. Danny crouched as he passed the window, stationing himself at the far side and giving Homer access to the near side. Both boys leaned cautiously against the building and slid an ear toward the gaps left by the ill-fitting storm window frames. The first voice the boys heard clearly was an unfamiliar one:

"Don't hit 'm again, Sharkey. You've had 'm knocked cockeyed for mosta two days now."

"Aw, he's been fakin' it, the louse!" Sharkey's familiar, rasping tone.

"Not alla time," came another strange voice, soft yet sinister. "Yuh hit 'm again, yer liable tuh kill 'm."

"That's the idea, ain't it?" Sharkey again.

"When we're satisfied this is the mug what bumped Max, *we'll* settle his hash," came the first voice again. "That's our orders. We don't need ya to do our work fer us."

Sharkey again: "I'm tellin' ya, Lefty, he's the clown! Doggie Blodgett's pal."

The first voice again, apparently the man addressed as Lefty, and sounding irritated: "Yeah, yeah, for two days you been tellin' us, and I'm sicka listenin' to ya. Just once I want to hear him admit it. Why, we can't even figger out who this joker is. Nuthin' on 'm but a rod."

"Well, that's somethin'," Sharkey's voice again. "And his clothes got Chicago labels."

"Like I said before," replied Lefty. "Lotsa people buy clothes in Chicago. Whaddya think, Clyde?"

"We can't bump this bird until we label him," said the soft, sinister voice. "And we can't risk takin' 'm back to Chicago until we're sure we can get outa here. What's up with that, Sharkey?"

"Radio says mosta the highways is plowed clear, but more snow over the week-end. And now the local cops think maybe that butcher's kid was snatched, so they set up roadblocks. Checkin' all the traffic outa this area."

Lefty swore a magnificent oath. "Whyn't that punk kid stay home, eat turkey like everybody else? We could be rollin' outa this burg! One more blizzard, we could be hung up here for a week, with cops creepin' all over the place. I don't like it!"

"Take it easy, Lefty," soothed the menacing voice of Clyde. "I'm gonna try somethin' different with our unco-operatin' friend here. Sharkey, douse 'm with some more water."

The boys heard a shuffle of feet, the sound of a tap running, more footsteps, then a splashing sound followed by a low, indistinct moan.

"He's comin' to again. Let me at him," said Clyde.

There was the sound of light slapping. "Hey, buddy, are ya hurt? Let me help ya, pal." It was the same disturbing voice of Clyde, but sounding almost sweet and very persuasive.

"Help… help me…" Cracked, feeble, tortured words. The boys felt compelled to bolt for aid at the sound of them, and at the same time were held spellbound by the drama inside.

"Sure, pal, sure," came Clyde's unctuous words. "Just tell me what happened to Max Guzman."

"Guzman…" The tortured voice sounded again, struggling, incoherent. "Guzman…" The syllables came as though uttered semi-consciously. "… that… no good… got… he deserved."

"See, I toldja!" It was Sharkey, and his voice was jubilant. Danny could have sworn he heard the old crook jump up and down.

"Aw, shaddap!" snarled Lefty. "He didn't say he bumped Max."

There came a vicious, thumping sound, and the tortured voice gave a sharp cry trailing off into a soft moan.

"No, and he ain't likely to," came the sinister voice of Clyde, no longer sweet. "But what he said is good enough for me, 'cause we gotta get outa this hick town. See," he continued triumphantly, "like the wise old owl said, honey catches more bugs than a belt in the chops."

"That sure was slick, Clyde," Sharkey gloated. "He thought you was helpin' 'm. Now let's get ridda the bum."

"I dunno," Lefty grumbled uncertainly.

"Sharkey's satisfied," Clyde's evil tone became absolutely icy. "And now I'm satisfied. Let me hear how satisfied you are, Lefty."

"I'm very satisfied," Lefty was suddenly most agreeable. "What'll we do? Deep-six him in the river outside?"

"Not off my pier you don't!" protested Sharkey. "You guys messed it up last time when you got too lazy to take Doggie outa town an' dumped 'm off the Central Avenue Bridge. I don't want anybody spottin' this guy around here. I don't even want 'm bobbin' up in the spring!"

"Cool it, Sharkey," Clyde warned. "Lefty an' me has dropped twelve jobs in the Chicago River – none of 'em been found yet. Can we help it you got rivers here people can see through?"

"Yeah," chimed in Lefty. "Besides, it didn't look so clear in the dark. It looked nice an' soupy."

"Well, with all this snow, the river's runnin' deeper and muddier," Sharkey tried to soothe the wounded feelings of his cohorts. "But we gotta get this guy well away from here before we dump 'm, and where he ain't likely to be found."

"How about we dig out the car, stick 'm in the trunk?" suggested Lefty.

"We ain't haulin' anythin' even three feet in that car," Clyde vetoed the suggestion firmly. "Until that lost brat's found, the cops are likely to swoop down on anythin' what looks outa place."

"Yer right, Clyde," agreed Lefty. "We can't afford to get stopped, even if we ain't haulin' no body. Maybe we oughta dump the car, too, an' let Sharkey here drive us to Milwaukee. The cops ain't likely to stop yer pick-up truck, are they, Sharkey?"

"No," replied the proprietor of Snug Harbor. "But if you ain't haulin' a stiff, why dump yer car just so maybe ya won't get stopped?"

"'Cause it ain't our car," Clyde's tone was sarcastic. "Ya think we're so dumb we use our own car to do a job with?"

"Jumpin' Jehosephat!" The eavesdropping boys could plainly hear the tremor in Sharkey's voice. "A stolen car with outa state plates, sittin' on my pier?"

"Relax, you old woman," cut in the cold voice of Clyde. "You got a boat?"

Clyde's thinking was immediately apparent to Sharkey, as well as to the uninvited listeners.

"Yeah," Sharkey replied. "But not big enough to hold a car…"

"Help… me," groaned the tortured voice again, and continued to moan deliriously. The boys tensed as they heard footsteps within, then sickening thumping sounds. Impulsively, Homer pressed his face against the window to see what he could see.

"Back off!" Danny hissed, and Homer resumed his silent stance against the building.

"Whaddaya keep bangin' that guy for, Sharkey?" asked Clyde. "He's gonna be dead soon enough."

"He makes too much noise," the tavern keeper growled. "All that yowlin's gonna stir up some of my customers. Hey, where ya goin', Lefty?"

"Back in a minute," came Lefty's casual reply, and the boys heard a door close quietly.

"There's gotta be a bigger tub around here somewheres," Clyde resumed the business discussion. "We need it bad, and we need it tonight, so that we can ditch the hot car and this bum together out in the lake. Then you gotta drive Lefty and me outa here first thing in the mornin', before that new storm hits."

"Mmmmm," Sharkey mused. "I think I can get a boat. The car'll hafta sit on the rear deck, but we can cover it with a tarp. But diggin' that car out'll be a real job. And how do we get it on the boat?"

"I seen that winch you got on the enda yer pier here. Get a long rope, you can use that winch to yank that car right outa the snow, an' then set her on the boat. Reminds me of a job we done once in Cleveland."

"I dunno," protested Sharkey. "That winch is a lightweight, for loadin' campin' gear, light cargo, stuff like that. It'll slide that car over the snow, all right, but lowerin' it onto a boat, all that weight is liable to jerk it loose right off the pier…"

Danny and Homer, shivering silently as they concentrated on hearing the plot being formulated within the building, suddenly froze with fright. One of the double doors servicing the warehouse portion of the building slid partially open and a man stepped out into the deep snow of the pier, framed in the dim light slanting through the open doorway. He had a gun in his left hand. He pointed the gun right at them.

"Well, I'll be," the man exclaimed. "Yer either a couple a' midgets, or a couple a' kids. Ya wanna listen so bad, c'mon inside, where it's warmer."

The boys had never seen the man before, but they recognized the voice. Lefty. He stood between them and the shore. The deep snow made running impossible. Danny's heart plummeted to his galoshes and Homer nearly fainted.

The boys looked at each other, completely devoid of ideas. Then meekly submitting to the insistent invitation of Lefty's beckoning gun, they marched slowly toward the open doorway. Upon reaching it,

Danny made a lame attempt at talking himself and Homer free.

"Gee, Mister, we didn't mean no harm," he tried, feigning wide-eyed innocence. "We was just playin' hide an' seek."

Lefty was a lean, bony type, youngish and dapper, with a rat-like face and teeth to match. Now he flashed those tobacco-stained teeth at Danny, his lips curled in hard amusement.

"Yer footprints sez you went straight to the window, which is a odd place to hide," he leered. "But if you can convince the boys inside, I'll take yuz up front and buy yuz each a root beer."

Reluctantly, Homer led the way into the dimly lit interior of the building, stamping his feet to shake the snow loose from his galoshes. Danny and Lefty followed suit, except that in Lefty's case the snow had caked his socks and trousers well above his street shoes.

"Blasted stuff!" the gunman swore quietly as he stamped and brushed most of the snow off him. Then he closed the tall sliding door.

Pointing with his pistol, Lefty guided the boys on a zigzag course through the warehouse area, around stacks of furniture, boating gear, beer and liquor cases, and assorted barrels, boxes and loose material. A naked bulb gleamed over a closed door. The boys stopped in front of it.

"Go on in," Lefty ordered, and with a trembling hand, Homer turned the knob and swung the door inward. The door opened into a large, well-lit kitchen. Prodded from behind by Lefty's gun, the boys shuffled into the room.

Sprawled on the floor was a big man, his ankles and wrists securely taped together, his face bruised and bleeding, his clothes torn and disheveled. He appeared to be unconscious.

Seated at the kitchen table was a stocky, dark man with bright beady eyes staring out from beneath the brim of his hat. He looked puzzled and annoyed.

Standing on the far side of the room was Sharkey Bates, huge, bulky and graying. He stared at the boys, pop-eyed and flabbergasted.

"Look what I found listenin' outside the window," Lefty chuckled evilly. "Mini-fuzz!"

"You!" Sharkey gasped, his eyes riveted on Danny's face. "We've met before, ain't we, Sonny?"

Danny stared back, petrified. He barely managed a nod. Sharkey strode forward, grasped Danny's jacket front in his huge paw, and snatched the boy right off the floor. Now they were nose to nose, and Danny was treated to an admixture of fury-filled eyes, bad breath and bristly whiskers.

"What's yer name?" Sharkey roared.

"D-D-Danny," the boy answered as quickly as he could.

"Yer whole name!" Sharkey demanded, and even as Danny tried to control his chattering teeth to answer, the huge man swatted him across the side of the head with the back of his free hand, knocking the boy right out of his own grasp and sending him spinning across the room. His senses reeling, Danny found himself propped against the still form of the unconscious man heaped on the floor. He decided to lie still.

"What's his name?" he heard Sharkey's snarl again.

"D-Danny Johnson," Homer squeaked, and despite the terror that gripped him, Danny still had to marvel at his friend's attempt to cover for him.

"You don't know these brats?" came the malevolent voice of the man seated at the table. It was Clyde.

"This ugly one I know," Sharkey replied, pointing at Homer. "That other one I seen snoopin' around here before," he added, not bothering to go into detail. "How'd you come by 'em, Lefty?"

"I thought I seen somethin' through the window," answered the gunman. "So I figgered I should take a look-see."

"Good boy, Lefty," hissed Clyde. "Sharkey, how come we got kids playin' Peepin' Tom on us?"

"That's what I'd like to know," the big tavern keeper growled. "What you brats up to, little Peckley?"

"We, uh," Homer's voice cracked, and he began again. "We wuz jist lookin' fer my ol' man."

"Scurvy liar!" Sharkey bellowed. "Not an hour ago, my bartender Al said you was up front, tryin' tuh mooch a free bottle fer some rum-dum party!"

Again his huge paw lashed out, slapping Homer head over heels into a corner. The boy sat there blinking and dazed, holding his head, his eyes refusing to focus.

"Boy, you sure ain't a very friendly bar keep, the way you like to hit people," Lefty chirped. "Youse guys think maybe the cops sent these kids to nose around here?"

"No," Clyde answered decisively. "The cops don't use kids. They was probably just tryin' to steal the booze Sharkey wouldn't give 'em free. Whatever it was, it don't matter. The point is, can we afford to let 'em go?"

"____ no!" Sharkey swore. "They seen and heard enough t' blow the lid off everythin'! They gotta take the same trip as Blodgett's buddy here."

Danny had heard more than enough. Jumping up, he bolted for the kitchen door. But galoshes aren't track shoes, and Lefty had merely to stick out his foot to send the boy sprawling.

Then Homer dashed toward the window, fully intending to dive right through it, but Sharkey snatched him right off the floor by the shoulder of his jacket and laughed derisively as the boy's legs churned uselessly in the air.

"Bring that other punk here, Lefty," the huge innkeeper commanded as he toted Homer across the room. Sharkey stopped upon reaching a door, opened it to reveal a partially filled clothes closet. He tossed Homer into one corner of it, causing the boy to bounce off the wall before he hit the floor.

"He's all yers, Sharkey," Lefty presented the big man with Danny, holding the boy's arm twisted behind him. Sharkey grabbed Danny's jacket collar and propelled him into the closet, where the boy encountered a tangle of foul-smelling fishing togs before having his fall broken by a pair of wading boots.

The door slammed shut, and in the instant darkness that followed, the boys could hear a key turn in the lock. Homer sat in stunned silence, but Danny's ear was against the door immediately after the lock snapped shut.

Clyde resumed the conversation in the kitchen. "How long it gonna take ya to get that boat, Sharkey?"

"Not long. I'll have her at the end of the pier within an hour. I'll give two short blasts on the horn, ya' can come out 'n help me tie her up."

"Okay. Two short toots. Meantime, we'll take good care a' the passengers," Lefty snickered.

Danny heard a door slam, signaling the departure of Sharkey Bates, then the sound of a kitchen chair scraping on the linoleum floor.

"Siddown, Lefty. We'll play some more gin rummy," came Clyde's cold monotone.

"Ya sure ya wanna, Clyde? Awready ya owe me a hunnert eighty-four bucks."

"I always pay ya what I owe ya, don't I? But if I ever catch ya cheatin', so help me, I'll peel ya like an orange."

"You know me, Clyde. Honest as the day is long."

"Days is short, this time a' year. Just shuddup an' deal."

CHAPTER 23

Kid-Snatched!

The two quick, throaty blasts heralding the return of Sharkey Bates with a boat were plainly audible to Danny and Homer as they sat disconsolately on the floor of Sharkey's kitchen closet. It was stuffy in that small, dark room and the clothes hanging there reeked of fish and stale tobacco. Both boys had unzipped their jackets to cool off.

"It sure didn't take him long to get back," Danny whispered. "What time ya think it is?"

Homer had been sniffling quietly in his corner, but now he wiped his nose on his sleeve and tried to regain his composure. "Prob'ly ain't nine a'clock yet," he said. "Too soon yet fer anybody tuh miss us."

Through the thick door the boys heard Clyde order Lefty to go help moor the boat, and it seemed no time at all before Lefty and Sharkey were back in the kitchen.

"How's our big friend?" they heard Sharkey ask.

"Ain't stirred. Not a peep outa him since you left," Clyde answered.

"Maybe he's dead already?" speculated the huge innkeeper. There seemed to be a hopeful note in his voice.

"Naw, I don't think so," Clyde replied. "But he's gonna be soon enough. You got some rope to pull that car out?"

"Yeah, I'll get it. There's some cord in that drawer there fer lacin' up the kids."

Terror mounted in the boys as they listened breathlessly to the activity beyond the closet door. First came the ominous sound of approaching footsteps, then the metallic click of the key working the lock. The door swung open, and the sudden influx of light caused the boys to blink as they were greeted by Lefty's malevolent leer.

"Good news, gang," he smirked. "We're goin' for a boat ride."

Grabbing Danny by the arm, he yanked the boy out of the closet as he slammed the door in Homer's face. Danny struggled briefly against the clutch of Lefty's hand, but the contest ended quickly and predictably as Lefty pinioned the boy on the floor, his knee pressing cruelly on Danny's back.

With practiced hands, Lefty bound the boy's wrists and legs together with light, strong drapery cord, and finished the job with a wide swatch of adhesive tape sealing Danny's mouth. Then Lefty opened the door to retrieve Homer.

The sight of Danny trussed up and helpless on the floor prompted Homer to cry out and kick frantically, but a sharp blow on head sent his senses reeling. His body went limp as a rag doll, and Lefty had no further trouble duplicating the tying and taping job he had performed on Danny.

Sharkey came back into the room, snow clinging to his boots, pink and puffing from his exertions in the cold night air.

"I got the car pulled out, clear down to the store room door," he announced. "That winch is pullin' it over the snow slick as Santy Claus' sled!"

"Fine," Clyde hissed, a satisfied smirk creasing his dark face. "You take the big lug there, stick 'm in the front seat. Lefty an' I'll toss these liddle punks in the back."

The boys could only struggle feebly and uselessly now as they watched Sharkey lead the way, dragging the big man by his bound ankles through the warehouse and out the partially opened double doors into the deep snow blanketing the pier. The boys themselves made the trip as a couple of bags of laundry might, Homer slung casually over Lefty's shoulder and Danny tucked up under Clyde's arm.

The car doors were standing open. Sharkey, handling his sizeable burden with apparent ease, tossed the bound man into the front seat and slammed the door. Then Homer and Danny found themselves bounced onto the back seat and the door shut on them.

Struggling to arrange themselves more comfortably, they listened to the muffled sounds of their antagonists at work outside. The whine of the winch's electric motor was promptly followed by the lurch of the car, jerked into smooth motion across the deep snow. A shadowy figure walked alongside the moving car; it appeared to be Lefty.

No lights were used to conduct the operation at the pier's end, the semi-darkness of a wintry night affording sufficient illumination for the business at hand. The towing motion gave way to a tilting and lifting as the gap between winch and car closed. The winch boom was not tall enough to lift the car free of the pier, and the boys could feel a lateral motion as the boom swung out over the water, dragging the car and its unwilling occupants over the edge of the pier.

Aided by the snow, the rear end of the car suddenly slipped free, and the big car dangled straight up and down in mid-air like a hooked fish, spinning slowly around at the end of its cable. The boys tumbled toward the rear window, and Danny glanced up apprehensively, fully expecting to see the big man come sliding over the top of the front seat and crash down on them. Instead he caught a glimpse of the man's knee hooked behind the steering wheel, holding him securely in place.

Outside, the straining boards of the pier popped and groaned, and Sharkey swore.

"Why don't you guys steal little cars?" he moaned. "That big clunker's gonna tear out my winch!"

"Just shuddup an' lower away," came Clyde's voice from below.

The brief downward motion ended as the car's rear bumper contacted the boat deck, followed by scraping sounds as the car was lowered onto its wheels and maneuvered into place on the deck.

"Nice job, Sharkey," Clyde was heard again. "Now let's get this tub underway."

Again the boys struggled to seat themselves upright, Danny making it just in time to see the bulky form of Sharkey come scurrying down the pier ladder, with the slender silhouette of Lefty following after.

The boys did not get an opportunity to see much. They could see the outline of a cabin topped by a wheelhouse forward, and that the rear deck holding the car was barely big enough for the job.

Then they watched as the figures of Clyde and Lefty advanced toward them, unfolding a shapeless mass as they came, each working along one side of the car. The shapeless mass turned out to be a large tarpaulin which soon draped the car completely, blacking out the car's interior.

The boys huddled together in the utter darkness, shivering more from trepidation than the penetrating cold. A salty tear or two escaped their eyes, but the tape binding their mouths would not even let them whimper. The gloom prevailing under the tarpaulin was no deeper than the despair pervading their hearts.

They listened as the footsteps of Lefty and Clyde faded forward, heard the cabin door slam shut, felt the throb of powerful engines come to life beneath them, felt the motion of the boat gliding out onto the deepened waters of the Wausupee.

"You boys all right back there?" came the low, even words out of the blackness right in front of Danny and Homer, nearly startling them right off the car seat. "Just keep your heads; we're not dead yet."

CHAPTER 24

Trapped on the Wausupee

"There's one thing to be said for this cold air," the voice in the blackness continued. "It sure does clear a guy's head."

Homer and Danny listened almost unbelievingly to the strange but not unpleasant voice. They had both considered the man in the front seat to be too far gone to be any kind of a factor in their apparently extremely limited futures. But now he was stirring, very much alive, and even offering them words of encouragement! They listened to the man struggling in the darkness, apparently trying to sit up.

"Ooooooh," the man groaned, his pain obvious. "I ache all over. I thought that big, fat Shark-bait or whatever his name is would kill me about ten different times. I owe him a few."

"Mmmmmm," Danny tried to talk, working his mouth against the tape. He tried to rub it off on the shoulder of Homer's jacket, but made no progress at all.

"I know you can't talk," the man replied. "I saw them tape your mouths. Listen, I can get on my knees on the seat here and lean toward you. You lean my way and I'll use my teeth to peel the tape off your faces. Then maybe we can figure something out."

Danny and Homer leaned forward toward the sound of the man stirring around in front of them. Suddenly Danny felt the man's breath on his face. Their heads bumped slightly in the blackness.

"Take it easy, sonny," the man cautioned. Danny felt the man's whiskered cheek against his, then his teeth catching at the corner of the tape and biting down on it. Danny jerked his head away, peeling the tape off his mouth as he did so. His face burned.

"Ptui!" spat the man, ridding himself of the tape. "Let me peel it off, boys," he admonished, "or you'll yank out what's left of my teeth."

"You next, Homer," Danny gasped, working his sore face. He could hear the peeling process being repeated in the dark next to him.

"Ow, dat stuff sticks," were Homer's first words since Lefty had clouted him in the head.

"Ptui," went the man again. "That's better. Now let's find out a few things. First, how did you kids ever get into this mess?"

"It's yer fault, Mister.," blurted Homer. "If yuh hadn't hung aroun' town after yer buddy Blodgett turned up dead, we wouldn' be here now."

"*My* buddy Blodgett?" the man echoed. "You sound exactly like the hoods running this tub we're on. Where'd you get that idea?"

"Yuh wuz at his funeral, wuzn'tcha? And takin' movie pitchurs."

"How did you learn that?"

"We knows more aboutcha den yuh t'ink. An' Sharkey sez yer Doggie Blodgett's pal."

"Hah!" the man exclaimed disgustedly. "Everybody seems to know something about me, while I don't know anything about anybody. If I ever get out of this mess alive, I think I owe it to the taxpayers to turn in my badge."

"Are you a cop, Mister?" Danny asked.

"Of sorts," the man answered. "You called the other boy Homer. What's your name?"

"Danny," was all that Danny would admit to. "What's yours?"

"Schultz. Just call me Eddie Schultz. I can't tell you two apart in this coal mine, but I think I recognized one of you as the kid who used to follow me home from the restaurant for awhile. Right?"

Danny gulped.

"Wuzn't me," Homer replied, still suspicious. "But if yer a cop, yuh sure don't act like one. Always creepin' 'roun' Packard Av'noo…"

"Believe it or not, fella, I had a job to do there."

"Like What? Robbin' duh bakery?"

The man laughed. "Not exactly," he said, and then added, "but it wasn't stuffing pumpkins down chimneys, either."

Silence.

"This is beginning to make a little sense," the man called Schultz continued. "Two kids hiding behind the bakery Halloween night. The next day I see one return to retrieve some forgotten laundry, and pretty soon that one starts shadowing me. Would that be you, Danny?"

"Maybe," Danny mumbled. One thing for sure, Danny thought, this guy could figure like a cop.

"I read the local paper," the man went on. "I'll bet those guys looking for you that night were some of the members of that club with the stuffed chimney. And I'll also bet that the times I've seen the two of you pussy-footing around the neighborhood, you were the other kid, Homer."

Again silence filled the blackness of the canvas-draped car. Then Danny spoke up.

"If you're a cop, Mister Schultz, why are Sharkey an' his friends after you? Have you been 'vestigatin' them?"

"Not a bit, and that's one of the confusing aspects of this thing," the man replied. "I've never even heard of those mugs up front before, and when they grabbed me coming back from the restaurant the other night, I was absolutely flabbergasted! That Sharkey character keeps insisting I'm the late Doggie Blodgett's sidekick, and that I killed Max Guzman.

"More than that – it's like he's trying to sell the idea to those other hoods. Pretty quick I figured that it was some kind of a mix-up, and that if they found out I was a cop, I'd be dead in a hurry. So I played dumb, hoping the local law would come looking for me."

"I seen Chief Lathrop over at Mrs. McClatchy's," Danny volunteered, by now convinced that the man was being truthful. "Also some strange guys who looked like detectives. Are you a detective?"

"I'm a federal agent," the man answered. "But outside of a little picture-taking at Blodgett's funeral, just to see if anybody interesting might be in attendance, Blodgett and Guzman and these other bums are not my case. I just happened to be handy to do the photography for the Blodgett thing, but I'm beginning to get the idea that that little detour from my primary assignment might be at the root of my troubles with you boys and that crew up forward."

Homer was still suspicious. "When Sharkey wuz kickin' yuh on duh floor, yuh said sumptin' not so good 'bout Mr. Goozman…"

"Sonny, I don't know how long I was on that floor, and half the time I didn't know where my brains were. Max Guzman was as crooked as they come, and my only regret where he's concerned is that some other hood got to him before the law did.

"Believe me, I was as surprised as anybody when I heard he had been murdered right under my nose, so to speak, just as Blodgett was, but nobody working with me on my particular case has made any connection between the two murders and the assignment I'm working on."

"Just what are ya workin' on, Mr. Schultz?" Danny asked, inwardly debating with himself as to whether or not he should inject Jennifer Markham's name into the conversation.

"Never mind about that right now," the man replied. "But now that we're acquainted after a fashion, what are we going to do about our immediate problem? Perhaps you also heard what our hosts have planned for us?"

"We heerd too much too good," Homer answered ruefully. "Purty soon we'll come tuh duh rapids. After dat, it ain't hardly a mile out intuh duh lake. Dat's where dey'll dump us."

"Darn, I was hoping for more time!" the man exclaimed. "The way this boat's moving, that probably doesn't give us more than ten minutes."

The boys could hear the man straining at his bonds. Finally he grunted and gave up.

"I'm not getting anywhere like this," he said. "Maybe we could roll down one of these windows and break it to create a cutting edge."

"I got a jackknife in muh pockit," Homer informed his fellow prisoners.

"Good Lord, son, why didn't you say so?"

"Nobody ast."

"Homer, you nitwit!" Danny scolded his chum. "Get it out, quick!"

"I can't. I can't get muh hand in muh pockit. You geddit out, Danny."

The boys squirmed toward each other in the blackness, Danny probing awkwardly with his bound hands under Homer's jacket and into the pocket of his jeans. In short order Danny managed to fish out the knife.

"I got it," Danny announced. "But I can't open it."

"Jis' hold it still an' let me feel of it," Homer told him. "I'll open duh right blade."

Again the boys groped together in the darkness, their bound hands, stiff with cold, working clumsily to open the knife. The boat beneath them lurched heavily, rocking them to one side. Danny felt the knife slipping from his grasp.

"We're in duh rapids," Homer said. "Wait'll we get t' the rough."

"The knife! I dropped the knife!"

"For pity's sake, don't lose it!" implored the man.

Both boys frantically swept the rear seat cushion with their tied hands, the impenetrable darkness seeming to magnify their problem enormously. Danny's fingers brushed the cold, smooth handle.

"Here it is!" he cried, trying to grasp it. The knife was threatening to slide behind the seat cushion, and the more Danny probed for it, the farther it slid.

"Don't bump me, Homer; it's goin' behind the seat."

"Easy, Danny," advised the redhead.

"Careful, boy, don't panic," counseled the man.

Danny sat still until the boat stopped pitching. The rapids safely negotiated, he again began to probe for the knife, wedging his hands between the seat cushions. Every contact he made with the knife caused it to slip away.

In desperation, he spread the fingers of one hand scissors fashion and advanced them to a point he thought would reach the knife. Then slowly he closed his fingers. He felt his frigid fingertips grasp the very end of the knife.

"Please come," he prayed aloud, and carefully withdrew his bound hands. The knife came along. "Whew!"

"Hold it good," Homer instructed, "an' let me at it."

Once more the clumsy groping in the darkness, Homer's fingers feeling for a familiar blade. Finding it, he used his fingernails to grasp its notched back and unfold it from the handle, held steady by Danny's pressing fingertips. Homer worked the blade out until it was completely open.

"Okay, pal," Homer spoke again. "Jis' hold her still an' let me do my own cuttin' so's my hands is still on when I'm done."

Danny grasped the handle firmly in his fist now, holding it in place as Homer sawed his bonds on a blade heretofore used principally for trimming willow branches, gutting fish and halving apples. The drapery cord parted quickly and fell away, and Homer paused briefly to rub some circulation into his wrists and hands. Taking the knife from Danny, he quickly cut his legs free, then carefully cut the cord binding his friend.

"How's it going, boys?" the man up front asked anxiously.

"Fine," Danny answered, rubbing his wrists. "We're all done."

"Then please hurry and cut me loose," the man pleaded. "We haven't got much time."

"Cut 'm loose, Homer."

"What if he ain't no cop?"

"My boy, what do I have to do to convince you? Recite the departmental oath?" the man implored. "Have some faith in the judgment of your friend."

"Yuh sure he's a cop, Danny?"

"Pretty sure, from what I been able to figure out."

"My Uncle Herman's on duh State Highway Patrol, yuh know; dis guy don't remind me none a' Uncle Herman."

"There's diff'runt kinds 'a cops, Homer, like detectives, an' I think Mr. Schultz here is some kinda detective, so cut 'm loose."

"Homer," the man tried again, "We're going to have some mighty rough customers to deal with in just a few minutes, and we need each other if we're to have any chance of coming out of this alive."

"He's right, Homer. Hurry up," Danny added anxiously.

"Well-l-l" the reluctant redhead finally agreed. "Okay." He felt for the man in the darkness, located his muscular shoulder and slid his hand down the shirt-sleeved arm to the man's wrists, bound securely behind him. He recoiled at the warm, sticky feel of blood.

"Hurry, boy," the man urged. "Time's a-wasting."

The big man was much more tightly bound, with tape as well as cord, but Homer deftly sliced through the accumulation to free his wrists.

"Thank God," the man sighed, moaning as he worked his stiff arms and rubbed his sore wrists. "Two days of this . . . here, Homer, let me have that knife."

Again groping for each other in the inky blackness, Homer transferred the knife to the man's hand. The boy quivered slightly at the strength apparent in the man's grip. Then he sat back with Danny as they listened to their new ally cut his ankles free. Beneath them, they could feel the boat begin to pitch and rock.

"Dem's duh waves," Homer said. "We're startin' out intuh duh lake."

"Listen, boys," the man instructed them. "Don't open the car doors. Just roll down a window, and try to slide out and under the car without disturbing the canvas too much. Make as little noise as possible."

"What are you gonna do?" Danny asked, already rolling down a window.

"I'm going out a window, too, but I'll stay under the canvas instead of getting under the car. Then we'll wait for them to make the next move. I'll keep your knife, Homer. I may need it."

Silently, the trio eased themselves out of the car and onto the deck of the boat. Danny and Homer rolled under the car, shivering as much from apprehension as from the chilling sting of the lake wind. The man crouched down next to the car, knife in hand, the canvas draped over him. Silently they waited.

CHAPTER 25

Brave Boys and Bullets

The trio had not long to wait. It seemed that they had hardly settled themselves when the rumbling engines below deck slowed to idle, doing little more than holding the bobbing craft steady on the choppy waters of Lake Michigan. The night wind flapped the tarpaulin draping the car, disguising the seizure of shivers shaking the trembling boys and their tense ally.

Forward, a door opened and closed again. Two pairs of footsteps were heard.

"I'll handle the winch, Lefty," Sharkey's voice boomed over the whistle of the wind. "You hook the cable under the front bumper an' peel the tarp off. Then I'll swing the front end over the rail to where she's just balancin'; after that we can clear the winch an' tip 'er into the drink."

"Aye, aye, Skipper," Lefty replied jovially, fumbling with the tarp. "The fish eat good tonight."

Lefty lifted the lead edge of the tarpaulin and threw it back on the hood of the car. The night was darker out on the lake, with no snow to heighten the dim light of the waning moon, and no lights were visible anywhere on the boat. Still the boys could make out Lefty's feet as he stood at the front of the car, and his hands as he worked to secure the winch's hook under the front bumper.

"Take up the slack there, Sharkey," Lefty called. The winch's motor whirred and the front end of the car rose abruptly, taking the tires nearly a foot off the deck. Danny raised his head, peering out of the gloom beneath the car. He could see the bulky form of Sharkey Bates perched at the controls of the winch, silhouetted against the night sky.

"Let's get on with it," shouted Sharkey. "Peel off that tarp."

"Don't rush me, Sharkey," came Lefty's loud reply as he struggled with the draped canvas. "This thing's heavy."

Breathless, Danny and Homer could sense the crouching man next to them, knife in hand, tensing for the attack as Lefty threw the heavy tarpaulin back further on the car's hood. Then, circling to the side of the car, away from the concealed man, Lefty proceeded to push the canvas up over the car's windshield. Suddenly he paused.

"Whatsa matter?" the impatient Sharkey snarled.

"I can't see anybody in the car. It's so dark…"

At that instant the man called Schultz vaulted over the hood of the car, the buckling sheet metal resounding under the impact of his body. All the boys could see was a tangle of legs on the narrow strip of deck between the car and the rail, and then only very briefly, for the struggle ended almost as soon as it began. A single shot rang out, a sickening "thunk" was heard, a splash, and then only a single pair of legs was visible at the rail. The boys lay paralyzed with fear.

"He's loose!" Sharkey shouted, terrified, scurrying towards the cabin.

"Halt!" barked the man standing next to the car. It wasn't Lefty's voice, and Danny and Homer heaved a collective sigh of relief.

Sharkey, however, paid the voice no heed, bolting through the tiny cabin doorway and slamming the door shut behind him. The man moved forward in pursuit, but ducked behind the winch as a rear window of the wheelhouse above was smashed. A volley of pistol shots poured through the broken window, ricocheting off the metal mast and housing of the winch. A single shot was fired in return.

"Blast! He's got Lefty's gun!" Clyde roared.

Sharkey used the butt of his hunting rifle to punch out the glass in one of the cabin windows and promptly pumped two shots in the direction of the winch. Hardly twenty feet separated the duelists, yet apparently none of the shots had struck the man crouching at the base of the winch mast, hunched against the gear box housing.

Another shot by Sharkey, this one careening off the winch's anchor plate and thumping into the bottom of the partially raised car, shaking loose a fine shower of scale rust and dirt on the boys huddling in the dark beneath it. The straying slug made Homer and Danny acutely aware of their exposed position.

"Let's get behind duh car," Homer urged.

"Not the way those bullets skip around," Danny whispered. "Let's go over the side and crawl in through a porthole or somethin'."

"Yuh ninny!" Homer chided him. "Dis tub ain't got no portholes. Yuh t'ink dis is duh Muskegon ferry? Heck, dis is jis' Erv Taschner's ol' fishin' trawler. I reckanize it now."

"So where can we hide?"

"Well, maybe dere," Homer pointed in the dark.

"Where?"

"Dat t'ing stickin' up in fronta us. Dat's a hatch cover. We slide it off an' duck outa dis war. Den we pray our guy wins."

The boys took advantage of a lull in the action to crawl toward the hatch. Danny could see that their new ally, still snuggling against the winch, was watching them.

"What are you boys up to?" the man whispered, casting a wary eye toward the darkened windows forward.

"We're goin' downstairs to get outa the way," Danny whispered, even as he and Homer reached the hatch cover and began to lift it off.

"Good idea," the man replied softly. "And if you find anything useful down there, like a jacket or overcoat, let me know. Right now I'm more likely to freeze to death than get shot."

"Want my jacket?" Danny offered, delaying with the hatch cover.

"I'm afraid you're not quite my size, boy."

Homer finally pushed the hatch cover away. A dull shaft of light diffused in the night air, indicating some source of illumination below. Homer popped into the open hatch like a gopher into his hole.

"It's the kids! They're goin' below," Danny heard Sharkey exclaim as he slid in after Homer, grasping the lip of the hatch with one hand to keep from dropping on his head.

A single shot tore into the wooden hatch lip the instant his body had cleared it, so unnerving Danny that he released his grip prematurely and fell into a heap below. The boys heard another single shot fired in return, followed by a fusillade of shots and a torrent of curses from the direction of the cabin.

"I'm okay, fellas," came the strong voice of their ally. "How about you guys?"

"We're okay too, I guess," Danny called back, gathering himself up from the plank floor to which he had fallen.

A small bulb screwed into a wall socket over the door leading aft illuminated the scene below deck, a crowded but orderly array of reeled smelt nets, marine gear, lockers and a tool crib. A single passageway led forward into what appeared to be a small galley.

The passageway was secured by a steel door in a steel bulkhead, with an arrangement that permitted locking from either side. Homer was already closing it in anticipation of visitors from up front. None too soon. Almost immediately they heard a rush of footsteps in the galley, and a resounding bang on the steel door as if kicked in frustration.

"I shoulda wrung yer fool necks when I had the chance!" Sharkey's voice came through loud and clear.

"Aw, go soak yer fat head," Homer jeered, making sure that the door was securely locked. He jumped back as Sharkey gave the door another sharp kick, but it held firm, much to the relief of both boys. After a moment's silence the big barkeep could be heard to leave, muttering dire threats.

"Is there any way he can get around us?" Danny asked, with full faith in his friend's superior knowledge of boats.

"Not unless dere's some way a' crawlin' all duh way back t'rough duh bilge, an' I don't t'ink dat fat slob could make it nohow," Homer replied confidently. "'Course, if dey wipe out our friend up dere, we're trapped like rats."

"Let's see how he's doin'," Danny said, starting up the short, straight ladder suspended from the hatch overhead. He stopped on the second step up, taking care not to expose his head to a shot from the wheelhouse. "Mr. Schultz," he called. "How ya doin'?"

"I'm freezing, that's what I'm doing. Did you find anything down there for me to wear?"

"I fergot to look," Danny said sheepishly, dropping to the floor and scurrying toward the lockers. The very first one he opened contained a neat stack of foul weather gear, and he promptly selected a short, lined black rubber rain coat which looked large enough to fit the sizeable Mr. Schultz. Wrapping it into a tight bundle, he again mounted the ladder.

"Mr. Schultz," he called out.

"Yes?"

"Here it comes," Danny alerted him, arching the bundled coat basketball fashion in the direction of the mast.

"Perfect throw, sonny!" the man praised him.

"Jist don't stick yer neck out, Mr. Schultz," Homer warned him from his position at the bottom of the ladder.

"Don't worry," the man replied cheerily, then after a moment added, "Man, this coat sure keeps out the wind." They could hear him snap the metal clasps on the garment. "That makes twice tonight you guys have saved my life."

"Whatcha gonna do tuh save ours?" Homer asked.

They could hear the man chuckle in the darkness outside. "Time's on our side, boys," he said. "These hoods can't land this boat anywhere until they've disposed of us, and they know they're going to have to risk getting their heads shot off in order to do that.

"I figure you boys have been missed by now, and come morning there should be plenty of people out looking for you. Trouble is, sunup must be a good seven or eight hours off, and those thugs up front know exactly how many bullets I have left in this gun. And the sky is clouding."

Sure enough. Through the open hatch, the boys could see the first of a fleet of great ragged black patches sailing swiftly over a sea of stars.

Danny turned and spoke quietly to his friend. "Now do you believe he's a cop?" he asked.

"Purty dumb one if yuh ast me," Homer retorted in a low tone. "Sharkey an' dat udder crook, dey kin also hear everytin' he sez, an' he's sayin' 'way too much."

"I haven't told them anything they haven't already figured out for themselves," the man said, obviously having overheard Homer's remark, and causing the redhead to blush. "The point is, we can afford to wait, and they can't. So the next move is up to them."

"Maybe, an' maybe it ain't," Danny replied, inspired by the sound of the boat's idling engines.

"Meaning what, young man?"

"Meanin' the motor is right here in the backa the boat. Maybe Homer'n me can go pull a wire or somethin', an' those guys won't be able to take us anywheres."

"Splendid idea!" the man exclaimed. "That'll take control of this boat right out of the hands of those pirates."

"You brats let them engines alone!" Sharkey's voice boomed out of the darkness. "This lake can get nasty in a hurry an' with no power to hold 'er into the weather, this tub'll capsize!"

"We'll take that chance, boys," the man on deck overruled Sharkey. "Go unplug the engines."

"Great idea, Danny!" Homer enthused, leading the way back toward the engine room. "Why didn't I t'ink a' dat?"

He opened the small door under the tiny light bulb, revealing a short, narrow stairway leading down to another door. Immediately the sound of the idling engines intensified, and they suddenly became louder still as somebody up in the wheelhouse opened the throttle wide, surging the boat into motion.

"Where'd ya suppose they think they're goin'?" Danny shouted above the roar of the engines as he and Homer clutched the rail and worked their way down the rocking passageway.

"I dunno, but dey ain't gonna go very far, dat's fer sure," Homer shouted back. The redhead flicked a light switch and pushed open a door marked Engine Room.

The roar in that tiny but well-lit chamber was almost deafening. Two gleaming diesel engines vibrated in wells divided by a catwalk, nestled under the stern hold used for storing the fish catch.

Homer's apprenticeship in his father's boatyard was not wasted. Expertly, he eyed the machinery, then turned the petcocks governing the fuel supply to each engine. The engines sputtered and died almost immediately. A crashing silence filled the room, and the lights dimmed as the generator quit spinning and the boat's batteries took over.

"Homer, yer a genius," Danny complimented his friend.

"It was yer idea, pal," Homer returned the compliment. "Now we kin bob like a cork 'til somebody spots us."

Quickly the boys made their way back to the open hatch, and Danny hopped to the second rung of the ladder.

"Mr. Schultz," he called. "Can ya see anythin'?"

"Not much," the man replied. "The sky's clouding up fast, the wind's picked up, and the lake's getting rougher. You think we're in for a storm?"

"My Dad said we're 'sposed to get another blizzard over the weekend," Danny replied.

"But tuhday's still Friday," Homer protested.

"Prob'ly in about one hour, it'll be Saturday," Danny enlightened him, then called out toward the open hatch again. "Can ya see how close we are to shore, Mr. Schultz?"

"I can't see the shoreline, but I thought I saw auto headlights once or twice. Is there a road along the shore?"

"Lake Road," Homer said aloud, but more to himself than to anyone else. "But we must be purty far out, if he ain't even sure he seed 'em."

"If I remember my astronomy correctly from my boy scout days," the man continued, "it appeared by the north star that our crew was steaming due south for about two minutes before you unplugged them. But now all the clouds have pretty well put an end to any further star-gazing."

Without warning, another barrage of gunfire suddenly rained on the area of the winch, the ricocheting slugs pinging off the metal housing in all directions. One bullet whistled through the open hatch, prompting Danny to let loose of the ladder and drop onto Homer. Both boys sprawled on the planking.

"Fer cryin' out loud!" Homer protested, rubbing his bruised posterior. "Yer liable tuh kill me 'fore Sharkey does!"

Danny ignored his sputtering friend and leapt to his feet, again mounting the ladder, this time stopping on the first rung. The firing above ceased as suddenly as it had begun.

"Mr. Schultz," Danny called out. "Are ya okay?"

"For the moment," the man replied. "But between the cabin and the wheelhouse, they're trying to get a wider angle on me, and my safety zone here is getting pretty narrow."

"Can ya thinka anythin' me an' Homer can do?"

"I was coming to that. That Sharkey and his friend must be feeling pretty desperate, and as time passes they'll get more so. I think they're setting me up for a rush by one of them during one of these barrages while the other one keeps me ducking bullets. So if you hear any movement on deck, holler loud! You'll be able to hear anything like that better down below where you are than I could up here."

"Yes sir! We'll be all ears," Danny promised.

"All one of 'm hasta do is take off his shoes, we won't hear nuttin'," Homer commented quietly.

"Let's hope they ain't as smart as you are," Danny replied. "Or I know! I betcha Mr. Schultz just said that fer them to hear, so's they'll try what you said an' he'll suck one of 'em out into the open."

"An' maybe he ain't t'oughta it, neider. I still t'ink he ain't so smart."

"Maybe we oughta warn him about it."

"But if we do, we're tellin' dem udder guys, too, an' maybe *dey* ain't t'ought a it."

"But what if *they* have, an' he ain't?"

"Yeah, but What if *he* has, an' *dey* ain't?" Homer's tone clearly revealed his perplexity, and he shook his head, dizzy from the mental effort. "Maybe we oughta jis' shuddup an' lissen," he suggested.

"Yeah."

For a moment silence reigned, with the only sounds being those of the choppy waters slapping the hull of the bobbing boat, and the rising wind. Looking up, the boys could not see a single one of the many stars which had brightened the sky earlier that evening.

Instead, a scattering of snowflakes were seen darting swiftly across the open hatch, each catching for an instant the dim light from within the hold. Apparently the notorious capriciousness of Midwestern weather was about to demonstrate itself once more.

Unexpectedly, the boat rolled heavily to starboard and a crest of spray broke over the port side. The automobile on deck, its front end suspended by the winch cable, skidded and thumped against the rail.

"That's what you get, you wise guy," Sharkey's harsh voice boomed through the darkness. "There's a real blow brewin', and you've killed the engines. Comes a big comber, we'll be keel up like a June bug."

"Isn't that what you had in mind for us in the first place?" the man on deck taunted him.

"Let's get sensible, an' we'll all live," Sharkey snarled back. "Let's make a deal."

"What kind of deal?" came the skeptical response.

The boys listened to the conversation intently, their hopes rising.

"Let's start up the engines again, I'll run this tub ashore, you give me an' Clyde an hour's head start. How about it?"

"I've got a better proposition," the man replied. "You and your friend surrender to my custody, we steam right back to Hornville, the boys and I have hotcakes and sausages at Tiny's Waffle Shop, you guys have bread and water at the county jail."

"Buddy, you ain't very funny," Sharkey sneered.

"You don't do much for my sense of humor, either," the man retorted.

"Buddy, you don't know this lake like I do," Sharkey's voice was almost pleading. "We're in real trouble."

The bobbing boat suddenly lurched again, as if to bear him testimony. The partially suspended car skidded violently to portside, its rear fender crunching against the rail.

"I'll guess we'll just have to ride her out, Skipper," the man replied cheerily, and Danny wondered how long it might be before the increasing pitch and roll of the boat would dislodge the man from behind his protective cover and give his antagonists a clear shot at him.

"Why don't he take Sharkey's deal?" Homer whispered vehemently. "Dat ain't no smart cop up dere; dat's a dumb comedian!"

"Maybe he don't trust Sharkey," Danny defended. "Sounds fishy, he would trust us to give 'em a hour's head start."

"So what could Sharkey do?"

"I dunno."

Any further speculation was cancelled by another fierce fusillade, the bullets pinging musically off the winch, and the boys instinctively retreated from the open hatch, even though it wasn't in the direct line of fire.

Anxiously they listened for any rush of footsteps which would indicate a direct assault on the position of their embattled ally. Instead, the staccato of gunfire was interrupted by a sharp splitting noise, then a tremendous roar accompanied by a brilliant burst of orange color which briefly seemed to fill the hold with a sunset glow.

"Wh-what happint?" Homer gasped, standing wide-eyed and petrified.

Danny dashed toward the ladder and raced up the rungs. Heedless of any danger, he popped his head above the level of the hatch lip to see what he could see.

A spectacle at once eerie and terrifying greeted his eyes. Aft, the suspended car was a mass of flames, a pool of liquid fire spreading out from it. Forward, all the rear windows of the cabin and the wheelhouse had been blown in; the empty black rectangles stared back at Danny like so many unseeing eyes. Several flecks of fire sizzled on the wooden superstructure and elsewhere on the deck, some snuffing out almost immediately, others seeming to burn with increasing intensity. Over the entire deck a fiery glow arched into the black night, streaked by a wind-whipped scattering of fat snowflakes.

The boys' newfound friend laid sprawled flat on his back, apparently unconscious, one hand nearly reaching the hatch. His singed hair was smoking, and a small splotch of flame danced merrily on his raincoat, threatening to broil his chest.

Unhesitatingly, Danny hoisted himself to the deck and with his galoshes wiped out the flame on the man's chest. The acrid stench of the burning rubber raincoat pinched his nostrils, and he could feel the softened sticky rubber coating adhere to his footgear.

The boat pitched forward now, and the fire spreading from the blazing car trickled liquidly toward Danny. Homer's head popped into view above the hatch lip.

"Grab his arm, Homer!" Danny commanded, doubling the unconscious man's legs up over his body and shoving his shoulder into the man's hip pockets. But Homer grabbed an oncoming foot instead, and yanked.

Together the boys flipped the large, limp form through the open hatch, again forcing Homer into the unsought role of fall breaker. He tried his unwilling best, but the tumbling two hundred pounds of deadweight overwhelmed him, and the pair of them went crashing to the floor, Homer first.

Danny's own effort had left him on his hands and knees at the edge of the hatch as the unconscious man had fallen away from him. He glanced toward the oncoming tide of fire which ebbed and flowed with the uncertain motion of the boat on the troubled lake, and his eye fell on the gun, evidently the one the man had taken away from Lefty.

He swung around on his knees to retrieve the weapon just as a shot sounded behind him. The sharp tug at his jacket gave way to a seared feeling along his ribs.

More surprised than anything else, the boy automatically followed through with his motion, picking up the gun as he continued to spin around. The second shot missed him completely. Unthinking, he pointed the weapon toward the form visible in one of the blank windows of the wheelhouse and squeezed the trigger. The revolver's recoil almost tore it from his hand, but the jolt seemed to restore Danny's wits.

Still clutching the weapon, he slid swiftly into the open hatchway, making a grab for the ladder with his free hand as he went. He missed the ladder, but not Homer. That poor lad had not quite recovered from the last disaster which had felled him when he spotted Danny tumbling through the opening overhead. He tried to get out of the way, but failed completely.

"Cut dat out!" the prostrate redhead protested. "I can't take no more."

"But they're shootin' at me!" Danny hastened to explain. "I think they shot me."

"Dey did?" Homer asked, suddenly anxious and solicitous as he scrambled to his feet. "Where'd dey getcha, pal?"

Danny laid down the revolver as he got up on his knees, unzipped his jacket and pulled up his shirt and undershirt, exposing his meatless rib cage to the dim light of the compartment's lone bulb. An angry red mark about four inches long angled across his ribs, but the oozing blood was already coagulating.

"I t'ink yer gonna live, pal," Homer announced, examining the wound critically. "Den again, maybe not," he added, turning his attention towards the fiery glow visible through the open hatchway. The snowflakes spiraling into view reflected red. "What happint up dere?"

"I think somebody shot a hole in the car's gas tank," Danny speculated. "The car's all afire, an' so's the backa the boat, an' there's burnin' gas sloppin' all over it."

Homer glanced anxiously around. "I don't see no fire 'stingusher," he said. ""Should I sing out duh hatch, see maybe Sharkey's got one he kin borra' us?"

"Don't be silly," Danny scoffed. "Ya'd prob'ly getcher head shot off."

"What's silly?" Homer argued. "Dis boat burns up, dem guys is cooked gooses, too. We eider gotta put dat fire out, er get offa dis boat. An' purty quick, too," the redhead added, the crackle of flames becoming increasingly audible.

"I think if them guys had a fire 'stinguisher, they'd be tryin' to use it by now," Danny surmised. "That's if they're done combin' the glass outa their hair. That 'splosion really blowed the windows in on 'em. Just look what it's done to Mr. Schultz."

The boys turned their attention to the unconscious man, sprawled grotesquely on the plank floor. A low moan escaped his lips, and he showed signs of stirring.

"Maybe we bring him aroun', he might have some bright idears fer a change," Homer suggested hopefully.

"I think maybe ya had the right idea when ya said we better get off the boat," Danny replied, cradling the man's singed head. "Whyn'tcha holler at Sharkey we'll make the boat motor right so's he can run us all ashore? Long as we got this gun, we can watch out he don't try to trick us."

"We gotta do sumptin' quick, dat's fer sure," Homer mumbled anxiously as he dutifully mounted the ladder and turned his face upward toward the open hatchway.

The incoming snow was thicker now, drifting out of nowhere into the heightening red halo of firelight. No snowflakes fell on Homer, however; those which might have were reduced to a fine rain by the time they passed through the heat wafting across the deck in advance of the flames. "Oh, Mr. Bates," Homer called out politely, taking care not to expose his head to the opposition. He received no reply.

"Mr. Bates," Homer sang out again, cocking his head to listen, but hearing only the steady crackle of flames above the intermittent whines of the wind. Below, Danny sat with the revolver gripped in both hands, the man's head still cradled in his lap, fearfully guarding against any surprise assault.

"Hey, yuh, Mr. Bates!" Homer shouted, venturing another step up the ladder. Again no reply.

The bobbing boat lurched heavily, the prow dipping into a trough formed suddenly in the churning waters. The last of the flowing gasoline sloshed past the open hatch, blazing as it went. Only the raised lip kept the liquid fire from cascading down on the occupants of the compartment below. Homer retreated from the flames, suddenly aware that breathing had become a problem.

"We gotta git," he gasped. "Else we'll be cooked like spuds under a campin' fire."

The big man moaned again, stirred, and Danny began to shake him. "Hey, Mr. Schultz," he urged. "Wake up. Please wake up." He gently slapped the man's bruised face several times, and at last was rewarded by a fluttering of eyelids. The man's eyes darted about wildly as consciousness returned, and he sat up with a start.

"Oooh," he groaned, holding his head. "What happened?"

"The car blew up," Danny answered him simply. "An' the boat's on fire."

The man looked up and saw the dancing flames threatening to encircle the open hatch. "Is there any way of putting it out?" he asked.

"We ain't got no fire 'stingusher, an' if dem bums up front has got one, dey sure ain't usin' it," Homer put in. "Why, dey won't even *talk* wit' us."

The big man struggled to his feet, grasping the hatch ladder for support, and peered out at the flames consuming the car and the boat's rear deck. Then he ducked down to get a breath of air.

"No fire extinguisher is going to quell that little bonfire," he said, trying to keep his voice calm. "But a boat this size should be equipped with an inflatable raft, or possibly even a life boat. Have you looked around?"

A look of uneasy recollection spread over Homer's freckled face. "Hey, dat's right! Ol' man Taschner had a rowboat hung up at duh bow a' dis tub, on a hand winch yet. Yuh t'ink maybe dem bums took a powder on us?" An anxious Danny couldn't wait to find out. He thrust the revolver into the man's hand, and with a recklessness born of near panic, he dashed to the heavy door leading to the galley, unlocked it and yanked it open.

No one there.

He rushed through the galley and up the short flight of stairs in the passage leading to the cabin, unlighted except for the glare of flames flooding through the glassless windows to stern.

Empty silence.

Hurrying to the windows forward, he found that the fire's dancing illumination gave him all the light he needed to see the small hand winch standing naked in the falling snow, its slack cable dangling in the choppy black waters of Lake Michigan.

CHAPTER 26

Captain Homer at the Helm

The other two reluctant passengers aboard Erv Taschner's doomed fishing boat were only steps behind Danny. They joined him at the cabin's front windows, which were still largely intact.

"So that's what they did," the big man said ruefully. "Took off in the lifeboat and left us to burn. Well, from the looks of that lake, I'm not sure they're any better off than we are."

"Sharkey ain't no ama-choor on duh water," Homer grudgingly gave credit where credit was due. "He'll prob'ly make it okay."

"Homer, are ya sure there ain't no other raft or rowboat aboard?" Danny asked his friend.

"I don't t'ink so. Only some life jackets in dem seats dere," Homer replied, pointing to several lockers lining the cabin wall.

"We'd soon freeze to death in that water," said the big man. "Possibly we can make a raft out of something before that fire burns us out or splits the hull and sinks us."

"Me, I got a better idear," Homer said determinedly. "I ain't no ama-choor on duh water, neider. Danny, yuh remember What I done tuh dem fuel lines in duh engine room?"

"Yeah. You turned them little handles sideways."

"Put 'em back duh way dey wuz," Homer instructed him. "I'm goin' topside an' crank dis tub up. Maybe we kin beach 'er before we gotta choose 'tween fryin' er' freezin'."

The big man looked at Homer in surprised admiration. "You mean you can operate this vessel, young man?" he asked.

"His dad's got the third biggest boat yard in Hornville," Danny called out proudly, his words trailing behind him as he dashed toward the galley en route to the engine room, spurred by new hope.

"Sekunt biggest," Homer corrected his friend as he mounted the ladder to the wheelhouse. The big man pocketed his weapon and came up right behind him. It took Danny less than a minute to reopen the fuel line petcocks and rejoin his companions in the wheelhouse.

The presumed heir to Peckley's Boatyard studied the maze of controls, switches and dials studding the panels surrounding the pilot wheel, only to have his contemplations interrupted by a huge wave which rolled the boat sharply to starboard and sent the three of them tumbling into one another.

The ship righted itself as the crest of the wave broke over it, the flying spray drenching patches of decking soon sizzling again with new flames, and the advancing edge of the fire continued to creep toward the cabin.

Homer took his post again and began to manipulate the controls as his companions anxiously watched. He pressed a thick button, and from the bowels of the vessel came a grinding sound, then a tremble, uncertain sputtering, and finally the rumbling throb of powerful twin diesels.

"Yea!" Danny cheered.

"Well done, Skipper!" the big man clapped Homer on the back. The skinny redhead grinned nonchalantly as he engaged the propellers and took command of the wheel. He flicked a battery of switches and illuminated every light on the boat not yet affected by the fire. The snowflakes falling about them dazzled brightly in return.

"Now tuh beach dis tub," Homer said as he spun the wheel, causing the boat to lean hard to starboard. "I'll head 'er straight fer shore, an' youse guys pray dat it ain't very far."

"How d'ya know which way is shore?" asked Danny, trying to stare a hole into the swirling mass of the mounting blizzard as the chugging craft began to pick up speed.

"Maybe I can't read ol' lady Hecker's books so good, but a compass I kin read," Homer replied confidently, tapping the large glass-covered dial in front of him. "We head due west." He eyed the panel again, pulled a lever, and broad wiper blades began to sweep the clinging snow from the glass.

"Heck, I'm not even sure which way is up," said the weary man, plopping onto a wooden bench and resting his head against the wheel-house wall. "Every bit of me aches, I stink like burnt tires, and my chest feels like it's on fire…"

"It was," Danny informed him. "I betcha got some dandy blisters underneath that raincoat."

"Is that how it got like this?" the man rubbed his hand over the hardened burned spot.

"Danny putcha out wit' his boot," Homer told him. "I seed him do it. Dat's when he got shot."

"They shot you, boy?" the man eyed Danny with genuine concern.

"Just barely," Danny replied, suddenly made aware of his seared sore ribs.

"Dey jis' scratched duh side a' his belly," Homer went on to explain. "Rub a liddle spit on it, pal," he advised his friend. "Dat'll fix it inna jiffy."

"It's okay now," Danny politely declined the redhead's medical advice. Nor did he want to admit how much the wound really pained him.

Again the man leaned his head back wearily and closed his eyes. "They were shooting at you, and you kids still got me down into that hold," he wondered aloud. "I'm losing track of how many different times and ways you kids have saved my hide."

"Well, it ain't saved yet, Mr. Schultz," commented Danny as he observed the approaching flames flare to new heights. "The fire's reached the backa the cabin, and it's goin' up pretty good."

The flames were licking over the edge of the cabin roof, not six feet from the shattered rear windows of the wheelhouse. Further astern, a black island of charred deck lay ringed by the flames consuming the heavy hardwood rail, and the once-shiny car had been reduced to a twisted mass of smoldering metal except for the dirty yellow flames still licking away at the remains of the tires.

The well-seasoned timber forming the cabin made perfect fuel for the crackling blaze, spreading steadily forward. The sight and sound of it was all too apparent to the trio in the wheelhouse, and the heat soon would be.

Danny and the man watched the intensifying flames with growing anxiety. But their attention swiftly shifted to the rear deck where the steel corpse of the car suddenly broke through the weakened timbers into the hold below, and the heavy winch, leaning grotesquely as its fire-rotted support gave out, came crashing after. A cascade of sparks tumbled skyward, mixing eerily with the falling snow. Soon bright flames were leaping through the gaping hole, feeding on a fresh supply of fuel.

"That's right over the motors, ain't it, Homer?" Danny asked.

"Yeah," replied the redhead.

"Where are the fuel tanks on this boat, sonny?" the man asked him.

"Back dere some'rs," came Homer's laconic answer as he continued to concentrate on the compass, keeping the needle at right angles to the course he steered.

The man turned his attention back to Danny, who stood as if hypnotized by the approaching flames.

"Son," he said, "Let's see, you're Danny, is that right?"

"Yeah," Danny answered, turning his head toward the man.

"I should get to know your names," the man continued. "Our skipper there answers to the classic title of Homer, is that correct?"

Danny nodded affirmatively, albeit with a question on his face. Classic was one word he had never thought of in connection with his happy-go-lucky buddy. Matter of fact, he wasn't sure what it meant, but it sounded impressive.

"Danny," the man went on, "Would you mind fetching some life preservers from those seat boxes downstairs before the fire takes over down there? I'm not anxious to take to the water, but pretty soon we may have no other choice."

Danny nodded dutifully, and made his way down the narrow stairwell to the cabin, where he crunched across the shattered glass to the row of lockers lining the walls. Keeping one eye on the flames curling around the posts of the pane-less windows, he threw back the lid of the first locker. It was full of books, games and puzzles.

Not much use for those right now, he smiled to himself. The contents of the next locker were much more to his liking. He helped himself to three bright orange, alpaca-stuffed life jackets of the half-dozen or so neatly stacked therein, and made his way back up to the wheelhouse.

"Good boy, Danny," the man praised him. "Here, let's get these on." The man took two away from Danny, set one aside and proceeded to don the other.

Danny examined the one remaining to him, struggled into it and then managed to make an arrangement of sorts with the loops and straps on the front of the strange garment. It seemed far too large for him, and he felt a little like the top half of some oversized pumpkin.

"Here, Homer," the man said. "Let me hold that wheel steady while you put this on." He held out the third life jacket.

"Ain't gonna need it," Homer announced matter-of-factly, his eyes riveted to the compass dial.

"Why not?" The man couldn't hide a quiver of excitement in his voice. "Are we that close to shore already?"

"I don't see nuthin'," Danny said as he peered into the thickening veil of incoming snow, patiently slogged aside by the steady sweep of the long wiper blades.

"'Course not, yuh ninny," Homer chastised his land-lubber friend. "Feel! Feel dat?" The churning boat seemed to elevate gently, then just as gently settle down.

"Dem's groun' swells," Homer explained, the excitement mounting in his voice. "Dat means duh water ain't so deep no more. Purty soon dey'll shape up intuh breakers; dat shore ain't gonna be more'n maybe a hunnert yards off."

Danny looked back at the fire. It was eating through the cabin roof now. More of the rear deck had caved in, and the aft section of the boat took on the appearance of a giant charcoal pit. Pungent smoke curled up the stairwell from the cabin below. Still the engines rumbled on, and the motion of the boat became a steady rocking as it rode the incoming surf. Soon even the swirling snow could not completely hide the crests of the breakers sliding along the prow.

"I see the waves!" Danny clapped his chapped hands joyously. "Homer, ol' buddy, I think we're gonna make it!"

"Jis' pray we don't get hung up on no rock before we get tuh duh beach," Homer cautioned him. "As it is, we're prob'ly gonna hafta do some wadin' tuh get ashore."

"Oh, I'm prayin', I'm prayin'," Danny clasped his hands and closed his eyes. "Lord, give us a break," he voiced his feelings earnestly.

"I've had so many these last couple of hours," the man broke in, "I'm afraid to…" His words were cut short by a shuddering thud which threw him and Danny against the wheelhouse wall. Homer clung desperately to the wheel. The boat seemed to hang up and teeter precariously for an instant, then plunged back into the racing surf and continued on.

"Boy, I betcha dat tore a hole in 'er belly," the struggling redhead exclaimed. "Youse guys better brace yerselfs. No tellin' what we'll bang into next."

Spoken like a prophet, and none too soon. Homer's two companions had just settled themselves against the forward wall of the wheelhouse when a series of thumps and bumps from below culminated in a jarring, splintering crash, the bow of the boat pitching sharply upward. Homer nearly catapulted through the wheelhouse window but hung on grimly, and finally found himself flung to the floor.

"Are you all right, Homer?" asked the man who was also sprawled out on the floor, alongside of Danny.

By way of reply, Homer scrambled to his feet and over to the wheelhouse door.

"All ashore what's goin' ashore," he announced, sliding back the door and leading the way forward onto the boat's tiny bridge. Danny was right behind him, and the big man brought up the rear, stepping cautiously.

Hastily they made their way down the ladder to the foredeck, the ladder being as much horizontal as vertical now, the crazy tilt of the grounded vessel leaving none of its surfaces on their usual planes.

There was no visible beach. The prow of the ship had hung up in a huge jumble of surf-lashed rocks, black in the flickering lights of the ship; ice-coated and snow-crowned, they mounted out of sight into the flake-filled sky. Every incoming breaker first jammed the broken boat further into the stony clutch of boulders, then threatened to sweep it back into the angry lake.

The trio slipped and clawed their way up the inclined deck, struggling against a slick mixture of fallen snow and frozen spray. Danny chanced upon a cable leading back from the prow, slick and stiff as an icicle, but would it aid him in reaching the blunted bow? He went first, inching his way, hand over fist. He reached back to give Homer a hand, and then together they aided the struggling man. Gasping for breath, the three of them paused to recover, clutching the forward rigging of the vessel.

Another breaker struck the stern of the boat, grinding its prow further into the unyielding rocks right at their elbows before tilting the boat away again. The engines quit, the flickering electric lights dimmed and died, leaving only the dancing flames to light the wild scene.

"We've got to get up on these rocks before this boat decides to go back to sea," the man shouted over the noise of fire, surf and wind. "Be careful not to slip down between the boat and the rock. The next wave will smash you flat."

The boys nodded, and the agile Homer mounted the rigging. Waiting for the shuddering ship to still briefly, he swung out onto a flat outcropping of rock, struggling to maintain his footing in the foot-deep snow topping it, while below Danny and the big man waited, poised to catch the boy if he should fall. But the lithe redhead tipped himself forward and settled safely on all fours in the snow.

"You next," the man said, motioning upwards with his thumb.

"You next," Danny told him. "It'll be easier with Homer pullin' and me pushin'."

Together they climbed the rigging. Mr. Schultz grasped Homer's outstretched hand, let go of the rigging and swung against the rock, getting his arm over it. Danny swung out and with his shoulder shoved mightily under the man's feet; with Homer tugging and hauling above, the federal agent was soon perched safely on the rock. Then he stretched out on it and extended a strong arm toward Danny.

"Just give me your hand, Danny boy," he shouted.

Danny reached for it just as the burning boat lurched wildly when another breaker slammed it from astern. Frantically, Danny hugged the rigging as he saw himself snatched away from the outstretched hand. The wave dashed well up on the rocks, soaking the already half-frozen boy with icy spray. The dying vessel settled back, the frozen rigging crackling under the strain. Danny watched the man's big hand coming back into reach.

"Easy duz it, pal," Homer shouted encouragingly.

The boat shuddered, and Danny stretched to reach the beckoning hand. He lunged for it, grabbed at it, felt it closing on his wrist, felt it miss!

He dropped to the sloping foredeck and shot down its slick surface like a ricocheting hockey puck, slamming into the forward wall of the now blazing cabin. His senses reeling, saved from more serious injury by the bulk of his life jacket, he scrambled to his feet and instinctively began clawing his way back up the foredeck. Then he paused, shaking his head to clear it, and this time deliberately sought out the friendly frozen cable. Finding it, he once again quickly gained the rigging at the prow.

Still another breaker wracked the doomed fishing boat, and Danny clung to the rigging until the wild pitching subsided, all the time praying that the boat would not yet backslide into the deep. Once again he mounted the rigging; once again he reached for the outstretched hand.

"Careful this time, boy," the man shouted. "Don't let go of the ropes this time until I've got you."

An explosion rumbled and rocked through the bowels of the gutted vessel, spewing thick, oily tongues of dirty flame through the crumbling decks amid ship. Danny felt the frozen rigging begin to collapse in his grasp as the tall mast supporting it began to teeter.

"Jump, Danny, jump!" Homer shouted, and Danny leaped at the arm straining towards him, feeling the rigging collapse underfoot like a net of wet spaghetti. Wildly he clutched at the sleeve of the man's raincoat, felt the big hand clamp around his forearm. Even through his jacket, it felt like a vise. It felt wonderful.

CHAPTER 27

Serendipitous Refuge

From the top of the bank, the trio could look almost straight down through the drifting snow into the blazing bowels of the gutted vessel, over fifty feet below. The wheelhouse was a fiery torch, and flames were breaking out of the forward hatch.

Another explosion had tilted the boat further, and every incoming breaker cast a quantity of spray into the broad, blazing bowl of the hull to be turned instantly into hissing vapors by the leaping flames. The whole effect reminded Danny of some massive mishap on an immense kitchen stove. Eventually the lake would have to win, but for the time being the blaze burned merrily on, intent on consuming itself.

"There were times there when I wouldn't have bet two cents on our chances," the man said quietly, now having only the sound of an uncertain wind to contend with.

"Yeah," Homer agreed. "T'ings sure din't look so good dere a couple t'ree times, dat's fer sure."

Danny, well-soaked and feeling half-frozen, could only think agreement. His chattering teeth signaled his urgent desire to depart the scene and seek some place of refuge.

"I agree, Danny," the man seemed to read his thoughts. "My feet feel as though they're about to fall off, too. Let's find ourselves a road, a house, a car, something. But let's be careful not to lose each other in the dark." He led the way as they hiked single file through the deep-shadowed dim whiteness of the snowy night. Danny followed, and Homer brought up the rear.

The man followed the edge of the bank, looking for some sign of a trail through the thick, snow-laden growth. For a long moment the mass of brush and trees gave Danny the feeling that it might go on endlessly, but almost immediately the wall of vegetation came to an abrupt ending, giving way to a small clearing. The trio stopped, and together stared disbelieving. Probably not a hundred yards away, dim but distinct through the filter of snow, a soft light shined, framed as though by a window.

"What luck! What utter luck!" the man exclaimed. "Come on, boys," he motioned to them as he started walking rapidly toward the light. "I think our troubles are just about over." The boys followed after, making such speed as the deepening snow and their water-logged galoshes would permit.

It was a house, all right, and the man had already mounted the broad, snow-drifted porch and was knocking on the door as the boys approached. The soft light came from a tall, old fashioned kerosene lamp, set on a table directly in front of a lightly curtained window. Also visible through the window was a huge stone fireplace framing a cheery blaze.

The trio stood shivering for about half a minute, awaiting a response to the knocking. But none seemed to be forthcoming, so the big man applied his freezing knuckles to the door again, loudly.

"Ouch, that smarts," he said, rubbing his stinging digits.

"Wh-who's there?" came a small quavering voice from within. And yet, Danny thought, it was somehow strangely familiar.

"We're friendly types," the big man boomed, trying to sound friendly. "But we're lost in this storm, and we'd like to warm up a bit, and perhaps use your telephone if we may…"

Several seconds elapsed, and then the rattling of the door chain was heard. The door opened slowly, and the first thing seen was a kerosene lantern, held aloft and shining out at them.

"You guys!" said the face beneath the lantern, sounding surprised. "Whaddaya doin' out here?"

The surprise was mutual, at least on the part of Danny and Homer.

"Butchie Brockman!" Homer exclaimed, and that was all he could manage.

"You fellas know each other?" the big man asked happily, still rubbing his stiffened hands together. "Wonderful! Why don't you ask young Mr. Brockman if he'd let us into his home for awhile?"

"Well, it ain't my place, but c'mon in anyhow," Butchie said, swinging the door wide. "Y'all look miserable."

Butchie's assessment was a gross understatement. Soaked, shot, singed and, in the case of the man, at least, unshaven, the appearance of the trio trooping toward the warmth of the fireplace left much to be desired. Homer and Danny faced the fire. The big man stood with his back to it, looking around.

"You say this isn't your place," he addressed Butchie. "Where are your folks?"

"Home, I guess," the Butcher Boy answered uneasily.

"Well then, who's here with you?"

"Just you guys, I guess," Butchie replied. "How'd you guys get out here?" he repeated his previous question.

"That's quite a story," the man answered. "But as long as we're alone, peel off all those wet clothes, boys, every stitch. Are there any clothes here we can borrow?"

"Just lotsa men's clothes, in the closets an' the dressers," Butchie replied.

"Those will have to do then," said the man, kicking off the sodden shoes and working on the clasps of his fire-scarred rain coat. "Sure hope some of 'em are my size. Is there a phone here, young man?"

An ironic laugh burst forth from Butchie's lips. "Boy, you gotta be kiddin', Mister," he said.

"Well, I see some electric fixtures here, evidently not working," the man observed. "This storm has probably knocked down a few power lines..."

Butchie looked at him quizzically. "Wouldn't matter here much," he said. "They got a motor out back fer makin' the lights work, but I couldn't make it start. I found these kerosene dealies in a shed, an' a big can a' juice to fill 'em."

"You have to generate your own power here?" the man exclaimed wonderingly. "Boy, you are isolated! What are you doing here all by yourself?"

Homer, about half-peeled, answered him. "Last day a' school he runned away, dat's what, an' rafts a' people been lookin' fer 'm fer two days. Yuh been here since yuh lit out?" he asked Butchie.

"Yeah, just about," Butchie answered, somewhat subdued. "I wanted to go home Thanksgivin' Day, but the storm Wednesday night blew away the boat."

"Boat?" the man all but shouted. "For Pete's sake, where are we?"

"Don'tcha know?" the runaway asked, obviously puzzled. "Duck Island. That's why I been wonderin' how youse guys got out here."

"Oh, boy, that means we still need rescuing," the man said, shaking his head and smiling wryly. "Well, if you'll fetch us some dry clothes – Butchie? Is that what I heard the boys call you? – we'll bring each other up to date and make some plans."

The obliging butcher boy disappeared with the lantern and soon returned carrying an assortment of clothes which he dumped on a sofa, then disappeared again to return laden once more, this time heavy on the socks, shirts and underwear.

The bullet crease on Danny's ribs had apparently bled some due to his later exertions, and stripped down he made a gory spectacle. But a wet wash cloth soon reduced the wound to its proper perspective, and the man treated and bandaged it, using the contents of a first aid kit discovered in the bathroom. The man also found some ointment to spread on his own reddened, blistered chest, and then allowed Butchie to treat and bandage his bloodied wrists.

Only Homer had escaped apparently unscathed, and clad only in his endless freckles, he was the first to rummage through the pile of clothing, seeking the makings of a new outfit. But the clothes were all man-sized, and Homer finally settled for a pair of oversized hunter's socks and a long flannel night shirt which drooped from his shoulders, hid his hands and nearly touched the floor. He solved at least part of the problem by rolling up the sleeves. Then using a coil of cord he found in the kitchen, he strung a line across the big living room from one door to another door to yet another door and back to the point of origin, anchored at the topmost hinges. Over these he hung in haphazard fashion the assortment of wet clothing.

His and Danny's galoshes were set upside down to drain, and the wet shoes of all three new arrivals were arranged on the hearth near the fire.

Meanwhile the helpful Butchie, obviously pleased to have any kind of human companionship after nearly three days of self-imposed exile, was busily preparing pans of canned soup and cocoa on a wood-burning stove in the kitchen. Keeping one eye on his culinary efforts, he spread an assortment of crockery and eating utensils on a table in the corner of the living room, and from somewhere dug up a box of stale crackers, a jar of peanut butter and a box of prunes.

The two wounded members of the party had their turn at the assortment of clothes, with Danny faring no better than Homer did. He settled for a pair of red woolen socks, the top half of a pair of pajamas, and a man's fingertip length robe which, on him, extended well below his knees.

The only adult in the group easily came out the best. From the two-piece long-handled underwear through plaid wool shirt, hunting breeches and fur-lined slippers, every item fit him as though it were his own. "I don't know who owns this place, but it sure was nice of him to stock my sizes," he smiled, thoroughly pleased.

"Belongs to some rich bugger from Indiana," Butchie explained. "Jus' comes up here fer summer vacation, or to hunt geese an' ducks. Wintertime he keeps his boat at Peterson's boatyard. My dad sells 'm meat every summer, an' a couple a times he let me come out here with Mr. Peterson to deliver it."

"My ol' man should have clients like dis," Homer remarked enviously as he looked about the well-appointed place.

"Any other residents on the island?" the man asked Butchie.

"Nope. This is the only house. There's a couple a' sheds, an' a boathouse on the beach, but no boat. Pretty small island, y'know; maybe half a city block."

"No, I didn't know," the man replied. "But how far are we from the mainland? And from Hornville? It can't be too far."

"Only a mile er so from the shore," Butchie told him. "An' maybe five from Hornville."

"Most every Janiary, the lake freezes over from here tuh the shore," Homer interjected helpfully.

"Well, we're not about to wait six weeks to see if it does this winter," the man smiled. "As soon as the weather breaks, we're going to build ourselves a fire out there they'll be able to see clear down in Milwaukee."

"Think anybody saw our boat burning?" Danny asked quietly. Thus far he and Butchie had hardly exchanged a glance, much less words.

"I doubt it," the man answered him. "That snow storm out there makes for mighty short visibility."

"Who's boat was it?" Butchie asked. "How'd it catch fire? And what were ya doin' out in it anyway? Lookin' fer me?" The butcher boy was full of questions.

"Nah," Homer scoffed. "Me an' Danny figgered yuh'd turn up when yuh wanted."

Then in his own unique, inimitable style, Homer enlightened Butchie with a narration of the past evening's events, from being caught and trussed up at the Snug Harbor through the gun battle on the burning trawler, the flight of Sharkey and Clyde, and their narrow escape on the rocky shore of Duck Island. Surprisingly, Homer accomplished his singular oration without embellishment; but then, none was needed.

During Homer's vivid discourse, the amazed Butchie grew increasingly stupefied and goggle-eyed. He had been curious about the man's and Danny's injuries, but now that he knew the nature of them, he was simply awed.

"Geez, an' I thought I had troubles, jus' 'cause I was gettin' lonesome," mused the boy, stacking new logs on the fire while the newcomers sat down to hot soup and cocoa. Then he came over to join the famished diners, pouring a cup of cocoa out of the pan.

"Is that right, Butchie? You're a runaway?" the man asked between spoonfuls of soup.

"Yeah, but I'da been home the next day if the boat I borrowed hadn't blowed away," he explained.

"You sure picked a lousy day for it, young man, what with the holiday, the blizzard and all."

Butchie hung his head, somewhat at a loss for words in the presence of Danny and Homer.

"Aw, poor Butchie he got a liddle sore jis' cuz Danny here laced 'm up n' stuffed 'm in duh closet at school," the redhead put in, unable to resist the opportunity to tease the chagrined butcher boy.

"Danny and his girl friend, you mean!" Butchie shot back, his temper quickly aroused.

"Jennifer is *not* my girl friend," Danny spoke grimly through a mouthful of noodle soup.

"You sure hang around her a lot," Butchie sneered.

"At least I don't try to smooch 'er in the bushes," Danny retorted, and he enjoyed watching the fuming Butchie turn color. His body was too sore, and he had been through too much in the last few hours to have any further fear of the consequences of arousing Butchie Brockman.

"Hey, hold on, fellas!" the big man tried a firm but friendly voice as he rapped his spoon on the table for order. "I thought I sensed a little coolness between you guys. Now what the reasons may be I don't know, and it's really none of my business. But I get the feeling that you've never been good friends."

"Boy, yuh kin say dat again," Homer chimed in.

"Well, I'm not about to get involved in any long-standing feuds," the man continued, smiling as he laid a hand on each of the two glowering antagonists.

"But as the only citizen of legal age present, I vote for a truce to extend at least until all of us return safely to Hornville. In the meantime, let's try to get along for the good of all of us. No more harsh words, men."

Danny was just as happy to return to his noodle soup, and Butchie resumed sipping his cocoa. The fear and loneliness of his exile had abated somewhat, and he was again yearning for revenge.

"The girl you mentioned," the man spoke again, breaking the surcharged silence, "That wouldn't happen to be Jennifer Markham, would it?"

"Yeah, dat's duh one," Homer was the only boy who cared to reply. "Yuh knows her?"

"A little. Possibly you attend the same school?"

"Yeah, she's in all our class. Not a bad kid, fer a girl."

The man chuckled but said no more and the supper continued in silence. What the meal lacked in variety it compensated for in quantity, and everybody had his fill. The warmth and nourishment did much to restore body and spirit.

The man concluded his meal with a tremendous stretch and yawn. "Boys," he said, "I think I can safely say that we've all experienced one of the longest and hardest days of our lives. I know I have," he shuddered, "and I hope I never experience the likes of it again.

What we all badly need is a little shut-eye, and in the morning we can tackle our problems anew. Butchie, what's this place got to offer in the way of sleeping accommodations?"

Butchie picked up the lantern and led the way to the one and only bedroom, revealing a double set of bunk beds arrayed against opposite walls. But compared to the living room with its glowing fireplace, the bedroom seemed like a refrigerator, so the bunks were promptly stripped of mattress rolls, pillows and blankets to be reassembled camp style in front of the great stone fireplace, newly primed with thick logs.

The lantern and oil lamp were extinguished, leaving only the firelight to probe the darkened corners of the room. Outside, the steady sifting of snow began to diminish and the wind softened its wail. Peace reigned within and about the snow-wrapped cabin, marked only by the deep breathing of the marooned foursome, and Homer's occasional raucous snore.

CHAPTER 28

Showdown with Sharkey

The rudely prodding foot in Danny's sore ribs roused the boy from nightmare terrors of flaming ships to angry thoughts of an irritating Butchie Brockman, but when he finally managed to pry apart his sleep-sealed eyelids, he was dismayed to discover that reality more closely resembled his nightmare.

As his eyes came into focus, the bad dream hulking over him took on the shape and coloring of the feared and detested Sharkey Bates, and the sharp jolts inflicted by his booted toe convinced Danny that the substance was there as well.

Frightened, the boy sat up, trying to collect his wits. The light from the dying embers of the fire had been superseded by the brightly glowing kerosene lamp, turned up high. Through the frost-laced windows filtered the first evidences of a gray dawn.

"On yer feet, boy," Sharkey rasped. "Get over on the couch with the rest a' them."

Still trying to comprehend, Danny, somewhat hampered by his outsized pajama top, abandoned the warmth of his makeshift bed and stumbled over to the couch where sat the other three occupants of the cabin.

The blinking night-shirted Homer was still coming to; Butchie sat gape-jawed, goggle-eyed and terrified; the man was angry and tense. Danny squeezed in on the end next to Homer, who was returning swiftly to reality now and shuddering at the realization of it.

In back of the snow-flecked, rifle-toting Sharkey stood Clyde, his coat and hat encrusted with icy snow, awkwardly stacking fresh kindling on the fire with one hand while he clutched his pistol in the other.

"Man, I gotta have heat," the shivering Clyde hissed, "or I'm gonna die!"

The gunman turned to face the four prisoners huddled together on the sofa. A heavily bloodstained handkerchief wrapped around his head and extended below his fedora, covering his ear, and several bloody streaks marked his dark, scowling face. Sharkey's broad face, too, and also his huge hands, showed several fresh cuts and scratches. A long, thin shard of glass thrusting through the peak of Sharkey's yachting cap gave the answer. The cabin and wheelhouse windows, shattered by the exploding gasoline tank, had evidently made quite an impression of the pair.

"We'll be all right now, Clyde," the big barkeep assured his companion. "But first we gotta figure out how to get ridda this collection." Then turning his attention to the man on the couch he snarled, "Whatcha do with Lefty's gun?"

"It's still on the boat, I guess," the man replied evenly.

"Don't lie!"

"Search me." The man raised his arms.

Danny mentally sifted through his recollections of the previous hectic evening. The last time he had seen the gun was in the boat cabin. Mr. Schultz had slipped it into his raincoat pocket. The raincoat was now draped with all the other damp clothing over Homer's makeshift wash line. Danny stole a furtive glance toward the raincoat, hanging where the line anchored on the bedroom door hinge. One corner of the coat sagged.

The man's offer to be searched seemed to stymie Sharkey for the moment, and the man continued talking. "How did you bums manage to make it here?" he snapped. "I figured the lake had finished you for sure."

"Take more'n a little fuss 'n foam to sink this old water dog," Sharkey chortled, thumping his barrel chest. "Truth is, closest call we had was when ya put-near run us down with that blasted fire-boat. But then ya made a nice beacon fer us when ya piled up on the island."

"You knew the island was here, I suppose."

"Didn't realize it was Duck Island 'til we started rowin' around it, lookin' fer a place to land," Sharkey continued obligingly, the melting snow starting to drip from the bill of his mariner's cap onto his pea coat. "Then when we come on the boat house, we decided to hole up there until the storm quit an' then see who managed to get off the boat safe. Sorry to see ya all made it."

"Who's the extra punk?" Clyde put in from his place by the rekindled fire. "There's one more there'n we started out with."

"I know you, don't I, boy?" Sharkey eyed Butchie quizzically. "Ain't you the butcher's kid what run away the other day, got everybody lookin' for 'm?"

"That's right, Mr. Bates," Butchie nodded vigorously. "Remember sometimes I help deliver steaks to your tavern with my dad? I just wanna go home now; I don't know anythin' 'bout what's goin' on. Honest." He raised his hand as if giving a pledge.

The Snug Harbor's proprietor chuckled grimly, his yellowed teeth glistening in his blood-streaked, livid face, flushed near maroon by the hours in the cold. "Sorry, boy, but you just happened to pick the wrong time to run away, an' the wrong place to hide."

"So what're we gonna do?" Clyde cut in. "Pretty soon its daylight already, the whole county's gonna be lookin' fer them kids; they're even gonna be lookin' for you out on the lake since you borrowed that boat."

"Yer right; time's awastin'," Sharkey agreed. "They'll probably be flyin' out over the lake and this island in a coupla hours, an' they'll spot the boat fer sure. It'll take some tall story tellin' to explain what happened to the boat, but I won't have a chance if there's any trace of this bunch on the island. We're gonna hafta dump them an' all their stuff in the lake. And we gotta keep this place clean. No blood, no nuthin'."

Danny shuddered as he heard the fate of himself and his companions being discussed as casually as if a picnic were being planned.

"What about me?" Clyde asked. "I can't have no fuzz rescuin' me. They'll ask too many questions, like what am I doin' 'way out here in Little Siberia? And what am I doin' with you?"

"Right again," Sharkey agreed. "There can't be no connection between me an' this bunch, and there can't be no connection between me an' you. So after we dump these guys, I'm gonna hafta set ya ashore with the lifeboat, then I gotta row back out here an' let myself be rescued."

"It won't work," Danny chimed in matter-of-factly from his place on the couch, stalling for time.

"Why not?" Clyde hissed.

"Footprints," the boy explained brightly. "The snow's quit now, and there's two sets already – yours an' yours," the boy pointed at Clyde and Sharkey. "And if ya march us out there, there's gonna be a lot more. How ya gonna 'splain that?"

Clyde swore. "The punk kid's right," he growled. "Are we gonna hafta carry 'em outa here dead?"

"Shooting's much too messy to clean up, to say nothing of the bullet holes," the man on the couch put in. "How're you going to do us in? Put bags over our heads?"

"Maybe we'll just strangle all 'a ya, smart guy," Sharkey snarled.

"Why not start with me?" the man beckoned the big barkeep, smiling grimly. Sharkey spat at him in reply.

"Find some rope, Clyde," he called to his cohort. "We'll tie 'em an' tote 'em to the boat. It's only two trips apiece, and we'll walk Indian fashion, use the same footprints. I'll walk yer other prints out there one time, make believe they're mine, comin' an' goin'."

Clyde didn't have far to look for rope. He began stripping the clothes off Homer's wash line, starting with the length extending from the kitchen door to the front door.

The group on the couch sat watching him, quiet and tense, their fears having given way to a faint glimmer of hope borne of the brief reprieve granted to them; it seemed they had been all through this before. Except for Butchie. He blubbered.

"I just wanna go home, Mr. Bates," he wailed. "I don't know nuthin' – I won't say nuthin' to nobody. Please."

"Get a move on there, Clyde, it's getting light outside," Sharkey impatiently urged his confederate, ignoring the butcher boy's tearful plea. Homer didn't, despite his own qualms. He glared at Butchie, the disgust and contempt he felt as prominent on his face as his freckles.

But Danny and the man at the far end of the couch paid the lugubrious lad no heed, for each was keeping the corner of his eye on busy Clyde, who was proceeding rapidly along the wash line toward the raincoat with its sagging pocket.

Down came several socks and assorted underwear, then a shirt. The raincoat was next.

"I'll get a knife for ya from the kitchen, Mister," Danny blurted. He couldn't think of anything else to say.

"Haw!" Clyde roared, and Sharkey guffawed gleefully.

"Next he'll be tryin' to join up with us," the big barkeep cackled, hardly able to contain himself.

"Sorry, kid. We ain't got no boy scout division," the reptile-eyed Clyde leered at the cowering Danny, who shrank back into the couch.

But the ruse had worked. Clyde was now clearing the last drooping strand of laundry. The loaded raincoat had sunk to the floor unnoticed, right in front of the open bedroom doorway.

The length of cord finally cleared of clothing, Clyde loosed it from the several hinges, letting it fall to the floor. Pocketing his pistol, he disappeared into the kitchen and returned almost immediately, brandishing a long knife. He cut several short lengths of cord off the nearest end.

"We'll start with Blodgett's buddy there," Clyde flourished the carving knife to indicate the man.

The man sighed. "Are we going to start with that again?" he complained. "Beats me how you ever came to connect me with a small-time punk like that."

"Shuddup an' quit stallin'!" Sharkey interrupted loudly, his eyes glittering. "Just get over there and lay down on yer belly," he snarled at the man, jerking his rifle in Clyde's direction.

Danny, studying Sharkey's flashing, angry eyes, thought he also detected fear. His thoughts raced back to the conversation between Sharkey, Clyde, and the late and unlamented Lefty; the conversation he and Homer had eavesdropped on only hours before, and he sensed another opportunity.

"Mr. Schultz here din't kill Mr. Guzman." Danny addressed himself to Clyde. "Mr. Schultz couldn't do a thing like that; he's a cop."

"Shut yer dirty trap er I'll blast ya right now, ya lyin' whelp!" Sharkey raged, jabbing his rifle right at the end of Danny's nose.

His tongue suddenly paralyzed, the boy slouched back into the sofa, fervently wishing the cushions would split asunder and swallow him. Homer leaned away, as if afraid of any ricochet; Butchie was trying to hide behind the man in question, who sat tense and poised on the very edge of the couch.

A charged silence filled the room after Sharkey's outburst. Clyde stood by the kitchen door, knife in one hand, rope in the other, his dark jaw slack, his beady eyes darting, questioning.

"What?" his eyes locked on the man at the end of the couch. "You supposed to be a cop?"

"A treasury agent, to be specific," the man answered.

"Baloney!" Sharkey scoffed. "They're just stallin', Clyde, and we can't afford the time. Let's get on with it."

Clyde ignored the directive and continued to question the man. "If yer a cop, whyn'tcha say so when we was workin' ya over at Sharkey's place?"

"I quickly got the idea that if you found out I was a cop, I'd be dead in a minute, but as long as you thought I was somebody else, I had a chance," the man explained. "I stalled hoping the local law would find me, since I missed my regular evening contact with Chief Lathrop. Instead, nobody shows up but a couple of junior G-men," he winked at Homer and Danny. "You tried, fellas," he told them gratefully.

Clyde shifted his searching gaze to Sharkey, standing uncertainly in front of the couch. "If this guy's a cop, then who bumped off my friend Max Guzman?" he demanded.

"Don't let 'm make fools of us, Clyde," Sharkey replied, backing away from the couch and facing his cohort. "You know we shook 'm down good, didn't find nuthin' on 'm said he was a cop."

"*You* laid 'm cold, *you* rifled 'm after Lefty 'n me snatched 'm and brought 'm to yer place," Clyde corrected. "*You* didn't come up with nuthin' that said he was anybody at all!"

"I'm tellin' ya," Sharkey insisted, regaining some of his composure. "He's from Blodgett's old mob, he done in Max."

"Maybe," Clyde answered, his hands still clutching the rope and the knife. "We'll see." His riveting gaze switched back to the man on the couch. "What's a funny money man doin' in a jerkwater burg like Hornville?" he asked.

"I was on an assignment," came the careful reply. "But believe me, it had nothing to do with Blodgett or Guzman or you or this big fat clown here," the man indicated Sharkey.

"You lie!" Sharkey snarled at the man, his knuckles whitening as he gripped his rifle.

"Steady, Sharkey," Clyde's voice was a low hiss. The rope slipped silently from his hand. "Just one more question." Once more he fixed his eyes on the man. "Answer me this, buddy; who's the biggest phony dough passer in Chicago?"

"That would probably be Tito Guckenberg," the man answered confidently.

"How 'bout that, Sharkey?" Clyde's deadly gaze switched again to the big barkeep, the hissing voice low and menacing. "Only guy likely to know that would hafta be a syndicate man or a T-man, and I know this bum ain't no syndicate man."

The knife dribbled from Clyde's fingers as his hand flashed towards his bulging coat pocket. But Sharkey was faster; the rifle clenched in his huge fists barked twice sharply in quick succession. A gurgling gasp escaped Clyde's mouth. He staggered back against the kitchen doorway and crumpled to the floor.

The shots were as a signal to two of the occupants of the couch. Simultaneously, the man dove for Sharkey as Danny bolted for the raincoat and the bedroom door, voluminous pajama top flying.

The alert Sharkey was not caught unawares. Even as the man's flying tackle bore him crashing to the floor he swung his rifle butt viciously against his assailant's skull. The man slid limply to one side, unconscious.

"Stop, you brat!" Sharkey bellowed at the fleeing Danny, who snatched up the fallen raincoat and, with his feet flailing and red stockings drooping, skid skater-fashion on the polished floor right through the bedroom doorway.

Struggling to regain his footing, Sharkey snapped off a quick shot toward the flying pajama. The slug drilled through the slamming door, swung shut by Danny as he zipped by, and ricocheted harmlessly through the window beyond.

Sprawled on the bedroom floor, the boy pawed wildly at the bulky mass of raincoat, the long pajama sleeves hampering his hands. Snatching the sleeves back to his elbows, he again clawed at the heavy rubber folds in desperate search for a pocket, the pocket with the weapon. He heard the heavy tread of Sharkey thunder across the living room floor; his frantic fingers found a slit in the garment, slid through to close on the cold steel handle of the revolver.

Sharkey's foot crashed against the closed door, sending it slamming back against the bedroom wall as Danny yanked the weapon free of the raincoat.

"Run, Danny, run!" Homer screamed, aiming a flying tackle at Sharkey's leg. It was like tackling a tree trunk, but it caused the rifle to jerk upward as Sharkey fired.

On his knees, clutching the revolver in both his small hands, Danny closed his eyes to the monstrous figure towering over him and squeezed the trigger again and again and again. Two loud reports rang in the room, followed by a series of metallic clicks as the hammer fell repeatedly on spent chambers.

CHAPTER 29

Rewards... and Repercussions

Sunday morning breakfast at the Hornville Community Hospital was pretty much the same as the rest of the week; oatmeal, fruit juice and milk or coffee.

Partakers of the limited fare this particular Sabbath morning included the occupants of one entire three-bed ward; a big man nursing a hairline skull fracture, a blistered chest and numerous cuts and bruises; a thin boy, tired and pale, suffering from an assortment of abuses acquired over the past several days, including a bullet crease across the ribs; and a restless redhead, apparently suffering from nothing but indignation.

"Observashun!" Homer huffed. "What dey gotta look at me for? Yuh t'ink I wuz a mental case er sumptin'!"

He slid out of bed and began to pace the floor, the backless hospital gown revealing the generous spread of freckles on his southern exposure.

"How's your head this mornin', Mr. Schultz?" Danny asked, observing the third member of the group dig into his cereal with obvious relish.

"Pretty good, thank you," the man replied, casting a smiling glance toward the pacing Homer. "I see where one of us is about ready to fly this coop. How're you feeling yourself, Danny?"

"Okay, I guess; a little tired. I hope they let us go home today."

"Oh, I'm sure they will, or tomorrow at the latest. As for me, I'm probably stuck here for a few days. We middle-aged types don't heal as fast as you kids do."

"How about Mr. Bates?"

"Oh, he's going to live; I talked to Chief Lathrop by phone this morning. You gave that Sharkey quite a belly ache, but he's a pretty tough old pirate. They've already moved him to the state prison hospital."

The man smiled grimly. "Yep, the old boy thought he was dying, and his conscience bothered him so he had to tell how he killed Max Guzman to keep Max from tellin' the syndicate that some snoopy kid had found him out. Afraid the mob would eliminate him as a weak link, no longer useful but knowing too much. Then he tried to make Guzman's death look like an accident, but when Max's body was found so quickly and the true cause of death revealed, Bates tried to make me the fall guy."

"Even so, I'm glad I didn't kill 'm," Danny said, slumping back on his pillow. "But I'm more glad fer me than fer him."

"Wish't yuh had," the pacing Homer grumbled. "He wuz gonna do in alla us. Too bad he din't at least cream dat yella' rat-fink, Butchie."

"I think I know what Danny means," the man addressed Homer somberly. "It was not a pleasant exchange I made with Lefty on the boat – your knife for his gun. But I had no other choice."

Homer flinched as the grim meaning of the man's words sank in; he asked for no further details.

"Well, I guess I'm glad Butchie didn't come to no harm," Danny put in, "but again, more fer my sake than fer his."

"You boys shouldn't be too hard on Butchie," the man counseled them. "Remember that he underwent quite a strain, stranded for two days, alone in that storm. And it's hard telling how people will react when suddenly confronted by great danger. Given another opportunity, he might prove to be a real friend in need."

"Haw!" Homer scoffed. "Dat guy ain't got no friends. Jist a big fist an' a big mout'."

"Perhaps that's his trouble," the man replied. "But considering what the three of you have just endured together, can't there be a little less mutual animosity? I can't imagine either of you two being afraid of him."

"Boy, that's for sure," Danny replied.

"*You* said it, pal!" Homer thumped his skinny chest, a regular redheaded Tarzan. "After tanglin' wit' dem crooks, we don't scare so easy no more."

"Get back in that bed, young man!" a strong female voice spoke sharply, and Homer vaulted under his sheets, more to hide his embarrassment than anything else. A matronly, graying nursed popped through the open doorway, directing a friendly frown at the erring Homer.

"Here's the Sunday funnies," she said, plopping heavy editions of the Milwaukee Journal on each of their beds. "But I suppose you'll be more interested in reading about yourselves."

Turning to leave, she paused long enough to wave a reproving finger at Homer. "You stay in that sack, Sonny, until doctor says you can get up," she warned the redhead before departing.

"Wow! She's worse'n ol' lady Hecker," Homer shuddered. "Must be her mudder."

"How about that headline?" spoke the man, holding up his copy of the newspaper. "Youths Solve Gangland Slayings, Rescue Kidnapped T-Man" read the bold, black double line dominating the page. "Also Locate Stranded Runaway," the man read the subheadline aloud. "Sounds like you boys did everything but pay the national debt."

"Maybe you kin do dat wit' yer share a' duh ree-ward fer findin' dat skunk Butchie, Mr. Schultz," Homer chuckled.

"No, that reward properly belongs to you and Danny," the man said. "I deserve no part of it. Fact is I'll be forever indebted to you for saving my life."

"That's good yuh don't want none a' Mr. Brockman's money," Homer replied. "Five hunnert bucks I kin divide by two, but by t'ree it don't come out so good."

"Didja tell Mr. Brockman ya didn't deserve the bike ya won?" Danny asked his friend.

"Yeah, jis' like yuh said," Homer nodded vigorously. "When he wuz here las' night, I tells 'm quiet-like I had inside info on how many beans in duh bottle, he should give duh prize tuh somebody else; he sez I don't care my Randolph counted duh beans fer ya, ya saved his life, so keep duh bike, he sez, an' Danny's gonna get one, too, and duh people what won duh contest legit is gonna get dere prizes anyhow. Watcha gonna do wit' a nut like dat, Danny?" Homer shrugged. "He wuz happy like a clam he got his knuckle-headed brat back."

"That's just great," Danny said, not really meaning it. But it looked as though his Darling Little Brother was about to inherit a used bicycle, several sizes too large for a first-grader.

"How can you guys sit there and yak like a couple of old ladies when you've got your photos on the front page?" the man chided them gently. "You'd think you were used to being famous."

Danny had in fact been studying the large photo, and hating it. The picture, captioned "Hornville's Heroes," showed Homer and Danny debarking from the helicopter on the parking lot adjoining the local police station. They had come in on the second flight, along with Butchie.

Homer had dressed again in his own clothes, and was shown smiling and waving at the photographer jauntily, but Danny hadn't felt good for much after his showdown with Sharkey, and had been content to lie down and leave things in other hands until it came his turn to leave. Consequently, the photo showed him sitting morosely on a stretcher, the tent-like pajama top drooping from him. He wished now he'd at least mustered the energy to dress before leaving Duck Island.

The first Saturday morning flight from the island had returned the more seriously injured treasury agent and Sharkey, and an inside page full of photos showed each of them being removed by stretcher from the helicopter, plus several other photos of the principals in the drama, and the local lawmen and citizenry involved in the previous morning's hectic search and rescue operations.

Another photo showed an aerial view of snow-drifted Duck Island, with the cabin, the boathouse on the beach, and the wrecked hulk of Erv Taschner's fishing boat plainly seen. It was a black streamer of smoke arising from the still smoldering remains of the gutted vessel which had attracted the spotter plane at the break of Saturday's dawn. The helicopter had been guided in by Homer waving a bright pennant – the other half of Danny's impromptu costume, a colorful pajama bottom.

Mug shots of the late Doggie Blodgett and Max Guzman completed the page, together with a photo of the canvas-wrapped remains of Clyde, returned by launch from the island together with the unhappy Mr. Taschner's life boat. There was no photo of Lefty, nothing of him having been found to photograph as yet.

"Hey, Mr. Schultz," Homer looked up from his perusal of the picture page. "Under yer pitchur here it sez treasury agent Arnold O'Brian. How come dey don't know who yuh are?"

"I've been waiting for one of you boys to pick that up," the man laughed sheepishly. "Our divisional office goofed putting out that name for me. I was just getting used to Eddie Schultz."

"Yuh mean neider one is you?"

"That's right. I get a new code name for each assignment. And you boys might as well know that while Sharkey and his friends had me, my job here concluded. I'll be leaving town as soon as I can get out of this bed."

"So whatcha been up to?" Homer persisted. "Somebody been spreadin' monopoly money aroun' here?"

The big man laughed, but quit with the pain of it. "Not exactly," he said looking at Danny, who lay with his eyes closed. "I think Danny has guessed that my assignment involved the Markham kids.

"Their father is an investigating attorney for our department in Cleveland, and he's been gathering the goods on some pretty rough customers. His family was threatened – in fact, they almost got Timmy once – so we hid them out here with the Millers, who are distant relatives. Timmy isn't old enough to know or say much, but Jennifer knew what the score was, and so she had strict instructions to keep mum, to prevent any kind of leak.

"But warrants were issued in Cleveland Friday," the man continued, "and most of the arrests have already been made. So the Markham kids are free to go home now, although I understand that the Miller's have asked if the children might remain for the rest of the school year."

Danny was pleased to hear that Jennifer's troubles included nothing that was embarrassing or derogatory, and he sort of hoped that the Millers might have their way, although he didn't say so. Instead he asked, "So all that creepin' aroun' you were doin', you was just guardin' Jennifer 'n her little brother?"

"That's right. I thought it would be an easy though tedious job, a small town being tough for any suspicious-looking stranger to hide in, but I forgot that that definition also included me. I suspect that's what brought me to your attention, and also Sharkey's when the department took advantage of my convenient location to film the crowd at Blodgett's funeral.

"Blodgett was a suspected small-time counterfeit-money passer, and you never know what leads an old, familiar face in a crowd like that might hatch. Unfortunately for me, Sharkey apparently never had a police record. Not even so much as a traffic ticket."

"He's got a dandy now," Homer opined.

"Yes, and at his age, I doubt if he'll ever be free to bother anybody again."

"Cleveland," Homer pondered the name. "Ain't dat duh capital a' Ohio, Danny?"

"Nah, ya ninny," Danny corrected his best friend. "Cincinnati."

The man coughed apologetically. "Well, I always thought Columbus was, but then geography isn't my strong suit," he said.

"Don't feel bad 'bout it," Homer hastened to reassure the man. "Yuh don't hafta be no jogerphy perfesser fer yer job, do yuh?"

"Well, of course, the more you know the better. But other things are more important in my work. Take Danny there. He's got the instincts to be a good cop. And heaven knows this country needs 'em."

Danny looked at the powerfully built man lying opposite him. "I'll never be big like you," he said, making comparisons depreciatory to his own slender frame.

"Size isn't everything," the big man reminded him. "Mine didn't do me much good with Sharkey, but you sure cut him down to size. You never quit, and that's what counts.

"Sometimes in this law enforcement business you get the feeling that just about everything and everybody is against you, then something happens to remind you how absolutely vital your work is, and you keep plugging away. Law enforcement is not the career for a quitter, Danny, and you're not a quitter. And by golly, that goes for you, too, Homer," he smiled at the redhead.

"Quitter?" Homer echoed. "Heck, I ain't even a joiner. I like playin' cops n' robbers fer fun, but after yestidday, I'd sure hate workin' at it. I t'ink I'll stick wit' my ol' man in duh boat business. Boats is more fun, and easier, too."

"And some day, young man, I'll bet you have the biggest boatyard on the Wausupee."

"Maybe duh biggest in duh whole county," Homer said with conviction. "Whatever yuh do, Mister, yuh gotta t'ink big," he advised the man.

Danny had now opened his paper and was studying the picture page.

"Ya sure look a lot better this mornin' than ya did comin' off that whirly-bird yesterday, Mr. Schultz, or whatever yer name is," Danny commented.

The man smiled. "Schultz will do. I'm just glad I had a chance to phone my wife early this morning and reassure her before she saw or read anything like that. Of course, she knew I had been missing for two days."

"So yuh got a fambly aroun' here somewheres, huh?" Homer queried shrewdly, playing detective.

The man nodded. "Yes, but I'll not say where. Matter of fact, we're expecting more family, and if it's a boy, I won't know if I should name it Danny or Homer."

"Chee!" Homer enthused, flattered. "A nee-phew! I ain't never been a uncle," he said.

The man chuckled again, but guardedly this time, so as not to jar his tender head. "Well, whether or not you get to be an uncle, I promise that on my next assignment that I'll use the code name Homer Peckley. It's a natural," he said, not bothering to explain his meaning.

"Great!" Homer bubbled, flattered to bursting. "An' it's a easy speller, too. By da t'ird grade I knowed it by heart awready! Now take poor Danny dere," the energetic Homer bounced out of bed again and pointed a teasing finger at his reclining friend. "His name comes in sec-shuns."

Danny defended his family surname simply by lowering his eyelids. That was all the energy he cared to muster at the moment.

"Well, Daniel Van Kuyper is a rather ponderous handle for so young a lad to tote around," the man agreed, a twinkle in his eyes, and Danny was secretly glad he had never told anyone his middle name, Alexander. "But I know that Mrs. Markham was certainly impressed by it. She talks to her kids regularly by phone, and it seems Jennifer told her about some gallant young man named Van Kuyper who took quite a bit of abuse defending her honor. I understand Mrs. Markham's looking forward to meeting this young man."

"Great," Danny mumbled from behind his closed eyelids, with absolutely no enthusiasm whatsoever.

"She tellyphones reg'lar alla way from Cleveland, O-hio?" Homer asked disbelievingly. "Whyn't she come wit' her kids, save all dat phone bill?"

"Mr. Markham wanted her to, but she felt it her duty to stay with her husband while he was under pressure," the man explained. "You fellas might as well learn now that when a woman makes up her mind, nobody's going to change it for her but herself."

A grim truth, Danny thought, thinking of the iron-willed women in his life. Men were much more reasonable to deal with, more logical.

"Yuh better had watch dat Jenny," Homer teased again, trying to draw some reaction from his friend. "She'll prob'ly grow up tuh be stubborn like her mudder."

"*You* watch 'er," Danny retorted lamely, the best he could manage, for in fact he harbored a faint hope that Jennifer might just possibly be free of the vagaries seemingly manifest throughout all woman-kind.

"Now, let's not be knocking Jennifer; she's a pretty good little gal," the man defended her. "I understand she was pestering Mrs. Miller Friday evening to go meet you fellas somewhere, and then when the police called all your classmates in the middle of the night trying to locate you, she told them about your suspicions and plans regarding Sharkey, even though she knew this could mean serious trouble for her. So when the police couldn't locate Sharkey either, and then found he'd borrowed a boat, boy, did everybody get excited."

Danny shuddered at the revelation of Jennifer's intentions to force her company on them Friday evening. What if they had let her come along, and she, too, had fallen into the hands of Sharkey and the imported killers? He shook his head sadly. Evidently Jennifer was as kooky as the rest of her gender.

Homer sat perched on the edge of his bed, chin in hand, thoughtfully pondering what he had just heard. "Hey, Danny," the redhead asked his shut-eyed friend. "Yuh t'ink she meant tuh horn in on us by duh Snug Harbor Friday night?"

"Sounds like it," was Danny's quiet reply.

"What a dope!" Homer expostulated. "Don't she know girls is 'sposed tuh stay home wit' dere mudders bakin' cookies?"

"My, such old-fashioned ideas for such a young lad," the man chided the freckle-face gently. "Well, she's probably doing just that today. I heard that the Millers are donating some goodies for the assembly and party to be held in your honor at school tomorrow. Chief Lathrop's going to be there, and the mayor, and the Brockman's are going to thank you publicly and give you boys that reward, besides supplying all the cold cuts..."

Danny raised a droopy eyelid and fixed the treasury agent with a gimlet eye. "Boy, you sure seem to know a lot we don't know," he said.

The man smiled and patted his bedside telephone. "While you dunderheads have been sleeping like newborns, I've been in touch with the outside," he replied. "Maybe you guys are still on Thanksgiving vacation, but I've had a little catching up to do on my work."

"A assembly in our honor!" Homer fairly jiggled with delight. "Wit' food yet!" He patted his stomach. "An' a ree-ward!" He rubbed his hands together in joyful anticipation. "Holy Toledo, What a blast dat's gonna be! Ain't it great, Danny?"

"Mmmm," Danny mumbled.

"Aw, yer still worried ol' lady Hecker's gonna nail yuh fer lacin' up Butchie an' stuffin' 'm in duh closet. I tell yuh don't worry 'bout it, ol' buddy," Homer tried to reassure him. "By now it's all fergot."

Yes, there was that little incident. And beyond that, innumerable questions from his parents, and endless lectures. And no doubt a sharp curtailment and much closer supervision of his extracurricular activities, for awhile at least. But there was no getting away from it; he'd have to face the music sometime. And it boded to be a regular concert.

"I talked to Jennifer briefly this morning, Danny," the man's voice intruded into the boy's woeful musings. "She said she was preparing a special surprise to present to you at the assembly tomorrow."

Danny turned his head, let his eyelids fall open. Through the wide window, beyond the rooftops of Hornville, he could see the inviting slopes of Hickory Hill sparkling in the morning sun, its thick thatching of snow-encrusted woods making the whole of it resemble a gigantic cauliflower. It looked simply grand, ideal for chasing rabbits. And if there was to be any opportunity in the near future to play hooky, it would have to be soon, before the clamps on his activities were screwed down tight.

He turned his head to look at Homer, his Number One Pal, faithful and true, wondering if his old friend would be of like mind.

"I wonder if dey is gonna give us any medals?" Homer mused aloud.

Sadly, Danny let his eyes close. Like minds? Apparently not.

The End

Biography

Fred Wrazel was born and raised in Cudahy, Wisconsin, a blue-collar suburb of Milwaukee, on the western shore of Lake Michigan. Fred quit high school in order to join the Army and thus qualify for the G.I. Bill. He is a graduate of Marquette University, class of '53.

In 1949 he married Janet Helding, of Racine. In 1954, they packed all their worldly goods into a two-wheel trailer, hitched it to their '48 DeSoto Club Coupe, and headed West with their three kids on a baby mattress in the back seat. (This was LBSB, i.e., Long Before Seat Belts.)

After a brief stay in Idaho, they settled in the San Francisco Bay area. In 1962 the family moved to Fresno, California, where Fred and Janet still reside in their own home, and remain active in business and the community.

Edwards Brothers Malloy
Oxnard, CA USA
February 12, 2016